THE CHANTEUSE
FROM CAPE TOWN

THE CHANTEUSE FROM CAPE TOWN

JOHN CONSTABLE

Published by Ink!
2022 Text @ John Constable
2022 Cover design by Jacqueline Abromeit

A CIP catalogue for this book is available from the British Library.

Paperback ISBN is 9781399935159

Typeset in Garamond Classic 11.25/14 by Hewer Text UK Ltd, Edinburgh
Printed and bound in Great Britain by Clays Ltd, Elcograf S.p.A.

ink! By The Author School
Kent, England, United Kingdom
Email: inkpublishingservices@gmail.com
Website: www.inkpublishingservices.co.uk
Socials: @services_ink

This one is for Hester, my darling wife, without whom, for so many reasons, this book would never have been written.

CHAPTER ONE

Leaving the God's Time Car Wash, I made the steep descent down Russell Road with the warm waters of the Indian Ocean spread before me. Where the road forked, I took the exit for Summerstrand and drove past the Campanile following a route as soulless as an LA freeway. The traffic though was done with its rush hour frenzy and so I made good progress past the apartment blocks overlooking the waterfront. They had names like Sea Spray and Ocean View, and architecture with not nearly as much creative flair.

I was on my way to a meeting with chartered accountant, Eugene du Toit. He wanted to see me urgently but not at his firm's plush offices in a converted bungalow off the Cape Road. Rather he requested a *tête-à-tête*, as he put it, at an apartment he leased close to the Boardwalk.

Yet as I drew near my destination, my cell phone sang out. I fumbled it to an ear and heard a voice tell me the venue for my appointment had been changed because of a re-scheduled meeting in Cape Town. This made no sense as I was no more than ten minutes from Port Elizabeth's airport. But, like that guy who sang about having no particular place to go, I got directions and pointed the Mustang's nose northwards.

I drove inland beyond the town of Uitenhage and into farming country where I picked up a dust trail that wound up by a copse of wild fig. From there, a sign marked a track leading to a gate topped with razor wire and cameras. At my approach, the gate opened revealing a corridor with electrified fencing. At its end was another gate and it too slid aside noiselessly.

1

On the far side was a large house constructed in the Cape Dutch style. The façade was brilliant white, and the windows barred, as was the glass in the heavy front door. I stopped the car in the shade of a carob tree and killed the engine.

In the hot still air, I closed my eyes and focused on my breathing to ease the churning in my stomach and the pounding of my heart. There was no reason for these symptoms. It was simply what my shrink calls anxiety. It was a feeling of insecurity, of being unsafe, and it could be as debilitating as living with one leg.

This time though I wasn't discomforted for long as a couple of Alsatians provided distraction by hurtling towards the car. Startled, I looked up and saw a tall thin man by the open front door. He was wearing sand-coloured chinos and a light blue shirt, open at the neck. Stirring himself to acknowledge me was evidently too much effort as he did no more than bark an order at the dogs and gaze at me, much as one might view some strange specimen of wildlife that had unexpectedly fetched up on his doorstep. It reminded me of the looks I got when I took up golf. Some of those old Dutchmen thought I should be pulling their golf trolleys, not striding the fairways with them and airing my views about the harsh reality of white monopoly capital.

When the dogs retreated at last, I climbed out of the Mustang and approached. Close to, I lifted my shades and flashed a smile in greeting. In response, the man offered a hand with long bony fingers. 'Eugene du Toit,' he said, bloodless lips forming the words with care.

I took his cold claw. 'Solomon Nemo. But you can call me Sol.'

'Come with me, *Mr.* Nemo.' Abruptly, du Toit turned on his heel, leaving me to shut the door.

I followed the accountant's spare figure through the house. From the kitchen area, I heard low voices and a radio playing Afrikaans pop; not my bag at all.

We went as far as a huge living room where a collection of mounted heads on one wall looked down upon a collection of stinkwood furniture. I couldn't decide which garnered the greater dislike.

My host led me through double doors to a stoep which had a view over a well-tended garden. At the boundary, two lines of tall electric fence topped with razor wire ran parallel to each other. This level of security piqued my curiosity.

Du Toit offered me a cane chair at a circular table decorated with a mosaic of blue and white tiles roughened with age and wear. Awaiting use was a silver tray laden with china, an ornate coffee pot, and a jug of iced lemonade and crystal glasses. Nearby were a propped tablet and two smart phones. An open pilot's case loaded with files stood on an adjacent chair.

'If you want refreshment, help yourself,' my host said carelessly as he sat down. At his back was a brick-built *braai* or BBQ with a stack of wood to one side and a line of empty whisky bottles on a shelf above. I doubted any were other than single malts. 'I trust you weren't incommoded by my summons,' du Toit added.

I was suddenly irritated by his arrogance. 'I'm trying not to feel pissed if that's what you mean.' Abruptly, I settled myself into a chair opposite him. I grabbed the lemonade and poured a glass as my mouth was parched.

Du Toit gazed at me with piercing eyes. He was long in the trunk and so he sat taller than me. 'What I wish to tell you, Mr. Nemo, surpasses secrecy,' he began, looking down his thin nose. 'Nothing I tell you today is to be repeated at any time, anywhere, under any circumstances. Do I make myself clear?'

I would have ventured some wisecrack but didn't get the chance as one of the phones vibrated. Du Toit started and then picked up. 'Ja?' he said.

What followed meant little to me. There was some stuff about commercial mortgages, a lot more on the valuation of goodwill, and a textbook's length of blah about different debt instruments. In response, du Toit wrote in a leather-bound notebook using a Montblanc fountain pen.

Me, I tuned out.

Sipping my lemonade, I looked beyond the electric fences where rough pasture fell away into a valley. In the distance I discerned the glint of water on a reservoir and a gaggle of farm buildings at one side.

Friend Eugene finished at last and laid the phone and notebook aside. He seemed perplexed by something and his prominent forehead, accentuated by a receding hairline, was furrowed with worry lines. In my experience, this is often the effect money has on people. How much or how little you have isn't relevant in the worry stakes if you're built that way.

'Time's money,' I said, trying to be helpful.

That snapped du Toit out of it. 'We were talking about the need for secrecy,' he said. 'I'd started explaining . . .'

I cut in. 'Message received first time round.'

My host looked at me pointedly. 'I'm acting for Mr. Franco Zarakolu,' he said.

It was my turn to be perplexed. 'You work for Frank?'

'Work for isn't the expression I'd use. He's been a client for about 18 months. We provide accounting and legal services.'

'Frank had an accountant in Jeffreys for 20 years or more,' I said. 'I don't recall him ever having much use for lawyers.'

If my host was annoyed at my sideswipe, it didn't show. Instead, he carefully lifted the propped tablet and turned it to face me. 'Tell me what you see,' he said.

Fact was I could see less than Jonah inside the whale. The sun was the main culprit, but the screen was also smeared. I turned my chair round and put the tablet onto my lap. I made out a woman holding a newspaper in front of her chest. Closer examination confirmed the paper was *Die Burger.* Its political affiliations have changed since apartheid, but I seldom read it. 'What am I looking at?'

'Don't you recognize her?' asked du Toit.

I scrutinized the screen more closely. The picture quality wasn't great but nevertheless something started to squirm in my gut. 'Is that Mira?' I said at last, looking up.

Du Toit nodded. 'That's Frank's wife with today's edition of the paper.'

A void seemed to open in the pit of my stomach. Whatever my thoughts about Mira, I knew Frank was besotted with her. 'How long's this been going on?' I asked.

'Six days. I receive an email with that picture every morning. I check each day's headline changes with *Die Burger's* website to verify authenticity.'

'Proof of life,' I volunteered. 'But photos can be doctored. Have you had the images checked?'

'I'm not a cretin, Mr. Nemo', said du Toit, reaching for the coffee pot for the first time. 'Each and every one has been checked. Their authenticity isn't in question.'

I watched him pour black coffee into a fancy bone china cup with a gold rim and add sugar. I doubted it would sweeten him any.

'Have you any idea who has her?'

It's said there's many a slip between cup and lip. Du Toit slipped for his raised coffee cup never reached his lips. 'How should I know?' he said. 'Really, how would I?'

'How much do they want?'

'50 million.'

A year or two before, I'd have reacted differently. Probably whistled out loud, gasped audibly, or dropped my jaw a metre or two. But now? I was the guy who'd blown a couple of million bucks changing cars five times in seven months. From personal experience, I knew you can get complacent about large piles of cash. 'I don't think Frank has that sort of money,' I said.

Du Toit smiled. Actually, it wasn't a smile but a smirk. 'That's for me to know and you to wonder about,' he said. 'But I'm sanguine as regards the current position. All the money will be raised within the next few days.'

I absorbed this dumbly until it struck home that the shock of Mira's kidnap had addled my brain. 'Where's Frank?' I said. 'Hell, why isn't he here?'

Then I got another jolt.

'Frank had a heart attack,' said du Toit.

'W-When?'

'Two days ago. He's in the ICU at St. George's.'

'I-I didn't know that. I was working a case in Windhoek and got back late.'

Du Toit shrugged his shoulders and consulted his watch.

I waited for him to say something more and, when he didn't, I asked impatiently, 'You mind telling me how he is?'

'I believe he's comfortable. But Frank's health isn't the issue. I have his power of attorney and his instructions are unconditional. He wants Mira back whatever the cost.'

'Are the police involved?

'What do you think, Mr. Nemo?'

I'd worked for the SA Police Service for almost seven years until they kicked me out for speaking my mind once too often. The experience had left me with some regrets but more anger. 'I'll take that as a no. What's Frank's view?'

'His view isn't really an issue either. I told Frank if he involved SAPS, I couldn't act for him. I wouldn't trust those *kaffirs* to find my dog in its kennel.'

This sort of bullshit is still heard from certain quarters of the old guard. But these days they don't parade it. It's the sort of stuff saved for the country clubs and the hunting expeditions and the house parties.

'I guess you got me here to do more than shoot the breeze,' I said. 'You want to tell me where I fit into all this?'

'Left to me, you don't,' said du Toit flatly. 'You're simply a complication I can do without. But Frank wants you at the exchange. He needs you to bring Mira back to him personally. He told me you can handle yourself if there's trouble.'

I couldn't recall being described in that way before. True, I was registered with the security industry people covering my investigations work but that didn't mean much. Thinking about it, I suppose it was about my ability to land a few punches in a fistfight, shoot a variety of guns with a measure of accuracy, and wield a knife without self-harming.

But what he was describing was something else. Kidnappers don't hail from the ranks of the Salvation Army or get asked to judge fancy dog competitions. With what was at stake here, these mothers were likely to be as amenable as a nest of Cape cobras.

Against that, I couldn't walk away. There was a debt I owed Frank. The fact it had been outstanding for more years than I liked to acknowledge made my duty all the plainer.

'How's the exchange to be made?' I asked.

'ETF.'

'Electronic transfer of funds?' My surprise was acute. 'How does that work?' For the first time, Du Toit looked puzzled, so I spelt it out for him. 'A funds transfer is done in the blink of an eye. But getting Mira from the place of exchange to a place of safety, for example a police station, takes time. Make a single transfer and she could be snatched back within seconds.'

'So the payments need to be staged?'

I nodded. 'You catch on fast. Of course, the details will have to be negotiated and you'll need my help with that. That means we'll have to work together. How do you think you'll cope?'

Du Toit didn't answer at once because he was distracted by the buzz of an aircraft engine. I followed his gaze and saw a monoplane emerge from the left and pass across my line of sight. There was a flash of sunlight on its wings before it was hidden by a fold in the ground as it descended to the distant valley floor.

'Be assured I'll cope fine,' said du Toit with another of his unattractive smiles. 'But that's for later. I must go. The plane's my ride to Cape Town. The trip should sort out the last of the fund-raise.' With that, he closed the tablet and transferred it and his notebook to the pilot's case.

Abruptly, he stood up, pocketed one phone and responded to a call on the other. 'Yes Karl, I heard it,' he said. 'Get the car up here at once and tell the pilot it's wheels up in ten minutes. I don't want my time wasted.'

I hadn't moved so du Toit lowered his eyes to mine. 'I'll be in touch,' he said.

I got up and he extended his claw again. 'I'm sure you can find your way back to the front door.'

'I'll try and give it my best shot.'

Turning away and walking back through the house, I heard du Toit's voice call out, 'He's on his way through.'

As I approached my car, there was a line of garages I'd not noticed on my arrival. To one side a big man sat in a chair with the Alsatians at his feet. He was wearing a bush hat and a holstered pistol. He looked chilled but his eyes were watchful. As I climbed into the Mustang, he touched a hand lightly to his hat brim and smiled but I don't believe the gesture was to do with any feeling of fellowship.

CHAPTER TWO

For several days after that, du Toit did the brain work while I got to do the legwork.

We kept in touch during the period, but I can't say that communication with him fostered rapport. I think du Toit was so used to snapping his fingers and having everyone race to do his bidding that he found teamwork impossible. Me, I never was a team player in the first place and an aversion to authority was second nature.

I put up with it because it fulfilled Frank's wishes. But I had grave misgivings about shutting the police out and was forthright in telling him so. It wasn't the first time the subject had been broached when I remarked, a day after he was discharged from hospital, 'Look Frank, this isn't the way to do this. SAPS have the experience and expertise to handle the situation. They also have the resources. If they need to, they can deploy the Task Force. I don't know what . . .'

But Frank's impatient hand, rising from the blanket covering him, silenced me. He was propped up in bed at home and his strained countenance had little more colour in it than the pillows supporting him. 'Leave it as it is Sol,' he said, his voice cracking with emotion. 'I'm trusting du Toit to handle the financial side and I'm trusting you to safeguard my interests on the ground.'

'Safeguard your interests! I'm one guy against . . . against I don't know what.'

'But you've made a plan for the exchange, Sol. And I happen to think it's pretty good. Also, don't forget du Toit's now sold the arrangement to the other side.'

That was where the discussion ended, despite my further entreaties. As Frank and I were like father and son, it wasn't my place to force my opinions down his throat, particularly as he was ill and vulnerable.

Two days later, I found myself abandoning a rented car at the Walmer Park Shopping Centre. When I got out and closed the door, the cell the kidnappers had given me chirruped. Once again, I listened to a voice, rough as a rock-strewn path. 'Look for a fat mother in a Toyota *bakkie*,' it said. 'You ride with him. You copy?'

I tried but by then the phone was dead.

The Centre was crowded with morning shoppers. I stood irresolute. Suddenly, a small boy in rompers detached himself from his mother and made a beeline for me. I bent down and caught him before he veered into the path of the circling traffic. Gently, I pushed him back the way he'd come. Looking up from loading shopping into a white Ford Ranger, his mother mouthed a thank you and flashed me a well-flossed smile. I guess it's one reason they call us the Rainbow Nation. Just one happy, smiling band of brothers and sisters striding out with arms linked towards the mother country's pot of gold.

'Nemo?' called a voice behind my back.

I turned to where a *bakkie* had pulled up. The car was a Toyota pick-up and had seen better years. I wasn't sure as regards the driver. He was about 130kg of palpitating flesh, his chin a blur of grey stubble and his forehead beaded with moisture.

'I'm Nemo,' I said.

The driver shoved open the passenger door. 'Get in,' he ordered. I climbed aboard and closed up. 'Put the cell in the cubby-hole.'

I did as he asked dumping it among a collection of used score cards, decorated in the red, white, and blue of the Boer Republics.

It was then I became aware of a miasma. It was stale sweat and almost overpowering. But there was an overlay of something else.

Brandy fumes. Whether from Klipdrift or Richelieu I couldn't tell.

'Mind if I open a window?' I asked.

As a grunt was the man's response, I took the initiative and grabbed the winder. It stuck after half a turn. Given the car's condition, this came as little surprise. The interior looked like it last had some TLC around the time of 9/11.

The Toyota rolled out of Walmer, turned right onto William Moffett, and made for the coast.

'Aren't you supposed to ask me, "Where to?"' I ventured sarcastically after a few minutes.

From bloodshot eyes, the driver gave me a look as kindly as a firestorm.

I lapsed into silence. When we reached the ocean, the *bakkie* headed towards the port at Coega, thought better of it half way along the road to Bluewater Bay, and then raced back to the City. After that, we crisscrossed Port Elizabeth driving in and out of the industrial area and adjacent suburbs. We must have passed the Stadium, built for the World Cup, at least half a dozen times.

'I reckon we're not being followed,' I said at last, by now thoroughly nauseated by the smell in the cabin and the Toyota's clapped-out suspension.

Another grunt was the rejoinder but, with a glance at his watch, the driver reached a decision. Abruptly, he turned in a street lined with warehouses and put his foot down.

A short time later, we picked up the N2 heading out of the City and drove towards Baywest. After that, we left the highway and took a winding road towards the sea. Where road became rutted track, I spotted a family of baboons grooming each other beneath a coral tree.

At last, we drew to a halt.

'Bounce,' said the driver without preamble as he pulled up the handbrake. When I didn't move, he reached across, making my stomach turn in the process, and flung the passenger door wide.

'Bounce,' he repeated furiously jerking a thumb in the direction I was meant to go.

Gasping for air, I got out and almost retched. By then, the *bakkie* had turned and blasted away in a biting cloud of dust.

I looked at my watch. It was almost noon. I heard a chopper high in the sky and started to walk downhill towards the sea and the rendezvous. Nervous anticipation made me increase my pace.

Next, I broke into a trot and after that began to run. I didn't know why. There was plenty of time for the exchange. In any event, they'd wait for me. I was the key to unlocking 50 million bucks.

But still I ran, my bright green T shirt, with the black smiley face, stuck fast to my torso. I cursed my long pants put on for reasons of concealment. Frisking, when I transferred to the rental, deprived me of the Tomcat in the ankle holster. But they missed the switchblade taped to my thigh. A nasty weapon for a nasty world but I wasn't about to turn the other cheek if it came to a fight. That required faith stronger than mine.

The air was still and very hot. My bare arms, the colour of *caffe macchiato* became slick with sweat. So too was the long black hair at the nape of my neck, now reduced to sodden rat tails. On either side of the track, scrub and thorn bushes pressed in on me.

I covered nearly a half kilometre before scenting the tang of the ocean. Then, rounding a corner, I saw dunes and sprinted for them. As the ground rose, I made a determined effort to power up through the loose sand. By the time I reached the top, my legs were jelly.

Laid out below, I saw the sea pounding the shoreline, the misted air filled with the crashing of the breakers.

I ran across the beach and stopped when one wave, bolder than the rest, covered my shoes. Out to sea, I saw the chopper flying the agreed parallels with the coast. Vainly, I looked round for some sign of life.

But, at the ocean's edge, the sea mist impairing my vision was suddenly torn apart. It revealed a couple of large SUVs parked shoulder to shoulder some distance off. As I watched, one detached itself and sped towards me over the wet sand. It pulled up too close for comfort. There were two guys aboard wearing reflective shades. Each had a bandanna concealing his face.

The passenger jumped down and removed his sunglasses. He stared at me aggressively. For the first time, I felt fear. Every instinct was telling me to run. His eyes were wild and the handgun in his belt shouted its own warning. Without ceremony, he thrust a satellite phone at me. 'Make the first call,' he said.

I confronted him, stone-faced. 'N-Not until I see Mira.'

'She's in the other car.'

I peered in the direction of the second SUV. There were figures in the cab and one of them could have been a woman. 'Get her to show herself,' I said.

Impatiently, the kidnapper turned away from me. He raised an arm and circled the air as though throwing a lasso.

The response was immediate. One door of the vehicle opened. A tall man got out and a woman fell after him. She fell because she was handcuffed to his right wrist.

Dishevelled, black hair awry, and sagging with fatigue, either from exhaustion or drugs, I barely recognized Mira.

'OK motherfucker, make the call.'

I took the phone and punched in du Toit's number. He picked up immediately. 'Ja,' he said with something like excitement in his voice.

I spoke the agreed code words. 'Case White.'

'Case White confirmed. Await my status update.'

I waited. The kidnapper in front of me was as hyped as a bush squirrel on speed. The other one stayed in the driver's seat and vented his stress by blipping the throttle.

'Status good,' said du Toit a moment later. 'I repeat status good.'

I cut the connection. 'It's been transferred,' I said to the kidnapper. 'You'd best confirm receipt.'

It was a three-stage process. The first payment of 10 million was complete. The second required my walking half the distance between the parked vehicles. Mira would do likewise from her side, so we met together and alone in the middle. After that, I'd phone du Toit again and a further 20 million bucks would vanish into cyberspace. The balancing payment was to be made when the chopper landed on the beach having spotted my T shirt with the smiley face. It would take off with the two of us aboard once the last transaction had been processed.

It was as safe a plan for Mira as I could devise.

It wasn't perfect, but nothing is.

It wasn't risk-free, but nothing is.

And because it was neither perfect nor risk-free, it fell apart.

In front of me, the kidnapper convulsed and his white shirt blossomed red. It was like watching a time-elapse film of some grotesque bloom bursting into flower. In an instant the guy staggered towards me. But he didn't cause the intense pain and burning sensation in my chest. Nor did he cause me to be driven backwards. As I fell, the SUV accelerated the other way. Then I was down, the sun lancing my eyes. Before I blacked out, the last thing to reach my ears was the crash of the breaking waves.

CHAPTER THREE

The angle at impact of a bullet determines its retained energy if it ricochets. At an angle of 10 degrees, it preserves about three-quarters of its power.

The shot fired from the dunes hit the kidnapper and ricocheted into my chest fracturing a rib and puncturing a lung. Subsequent fragmentation of the bullet caused other wounds.

My memories of that time are disjointed and confused. I recall the heat of the midday sun beating down on my face after I fell, the excruciating pain in my chest, and my fight to get enough air. People came and went with no obvious purpose. Occasionally they stood over me and shielded my face from the sun, but this relief seemed accidental. Eventually, somebody dropped to their knees and lifted my hand to take my pulse. He started asking questions, but his words were ripped away in a maelstrom of noise and whipped-up sand. I turned my face away and began to cough uncontrollably. I don't remember stopping and must have passed out.

When I came to, I was in a helicopter lying flat out across four seats at the rear. In front of me the pilot kept up a running commentary through a headset and next to him sat a uniformed SAPS officer. He had a face longer than a longcase clock and it wore an expression of what I could only describe as solicitous hopelessness.

We landed at the Livingstone Hospital helipad in Korsten. From there, I was transferred by ambulance to a private hospital near Cape Road. They gave me a thorough examination and prepped me for emergency surgery, X-rays having shown a lung puncture.

I had SAPS protection for four days after that. Whether they thought I was in danger or that I was a danger was something that never became clear. Either way, somebody sat outside my room round the clock. On occasion, a face would poke round the door and take a look at me. Often, the face smiled as though to encourage my recovery and I would smile back and try to look brave.

Later, I was operated on again to remove fragments of metal left in my body from the bullet's disintegration. This set my recovery back and left me wondering how long I was going to be stuck inside a room with only insipid framed prints to distract me. In truth though, I found even breathing exhausting.

This time was painful for other reasons as well. I suspect that was down to all the meds. This cocktail precipitated frequent drifting in and out of the shadow world of my childhood over 30 years before. My recollections concerned my mother who died when I was six. I dreamed I heard her voice and felt her soft brown arms enclosing me. The heady scent of the gardenia she sprayed over her long and lustrous hair filled my nostrils. This reverie occurred and recurred at regular intervals and each time on waking up the feelings of loss were overwhelming and my sense of abandonment absolute.

Over time, I built up a picture of what was happening in the world outside. Some of this came from the news and some from hospital staff.

As far as events on the beach were concerned, the service SAPS had done me, by taking over the helicopter du Toit had hired, was about as much as they got right that day.

The SUV with Mira aboard turned tail and fled when the shooting started. Failure to secure a perimeter adequately at an exit from the beach allowed it to bludgeon its way through a roadblock and escape. It was found burnt-out eight kms away several hours later. Because of its armour, it would have taken something like an RPG to stop it. It had been stolen from the car park of a large corporate in Jo'burg days before. Mira and her captors were nowhere to be found. One SAPS officer had died after being run over. The other

SUV was shot up after its driver made the mistake of discharging a machine pistol into the dunes. He got the worst of the exchange and checked out at the wheel. The kidnapper who took the bullet that had ricocheted into me was dead before he hit the ground.

The recriminations in respect of these events started almost immediately. Initially, the blame was placed on the Special Task Force sniper who had acted without authority. If this individual had obeyed orders, senior operational commanders would have had time *to optimize the deployment of tactical resources consistent with maximizing targeted outcomes.* This crud came from an armchair warrior in the SAPS Press Office and was widely ridiculed.

One journalist particularly didn't buy any part of the police line and started asking penetrating questions. So penetrating it became clear she had inside knowledge of what had been going on inside SAPS on the day. The picture that subsequently emerged displayed confusion in the command structure because of blurred lines of demarcation. Within days a Captain from the Special Task Force was suspended pending an inquiry.

After that, the debate ricocheted into the political arena with African National Congress and Democratic Alliance politicians slugging it out with no holds barred. Each used Mira's kidnap as a proxy for a debate about serious crime in the Nelson Mandela Bay area. As the war of words intensified, Mira and her ongoing predicament rather disappeared under the weight of all the self-serving *kak* emanating from both sides.

Unfortunately, I wasn't left alone for long as regards officialdom. I had separate meetings with parties who descended on me from the Task Force and Detective Services, and later by the guy heading up the inquiry looking into the captain's suspension. Each time these people rocked up, I posed the same question about finding Mira. Each time, I was told there were lines of enquiry being pursued, the details of which they couldn't share with me. From this, I deduced the investigation was making no more headway than a greyhound doing circuits on a dog track.

Eventually, I got fed up and asked the staff to bar visitors by saying my health dictated the need for absolute peace and quiet. One Xhosa nurse who had a heart of gold but a face that would have stopped a charging hippo brooked no nonsense at all. On one occasion she shooed a cohort away along a corridor with an angry flapping of her hands. After that, I was left alone.

On a sunny afternoon, several days later, I took a call from du Toit. Any supposition that this might be a social call, perhaps an enquiry into my health and wellbeing, was quickly shattered.

'Mr. Nemo,' he said, without preamble, 'I've found you at last. You should comprehend this is the fourth call I've had to initiate to ascertain your whereabouts.'

'You have my sympathy.'

'I think a statement of contrition would be more to the point.'

'Contrition? -What are you talking about?'

'I'm talking, Mr. Nemo, about your remarks to the police regarding my activities on behalf of my client Franco Zarakolu. They are under the impression I was somehow involved in his wife's kidnap.'

'Any such impression, bro, didn't come from me.'

'Then please explain their line of questioning.'

'Since I wasn't there, I can't. What I can tell you is that a good interrogator will approach the subject of an inquiry from different angles to see whether things stack up. I guess maybe . . .'

'Inexactitude doesn't facilitate this discussion,' du Toit interrupted angrily. 'Do you know SAPS detectives have come to my offices twice. Feculent little men with broken fingernails who arrived unannounced and asked impertinent questions . . .'

And so it went on. I let his verbal diarrhoea wash over me until my feeling was one of drowning. At that point, I put the phone down.

I'd seen Frank several times before the abortive exchange on the beach. But the news that it was him who'd alerted SAPS shortly after Mira was kidnapped came to me from a young Sergeant in Detective Services. So much distress did this cause that I bawled the guy out of the room in my furious disbelief. When I later recovered from a prolonged coughing fit, I was assailed by a spectrum of emotions that swung violently between betrayal and rage. But more than either of those was the blow this information dealt my self-esteem. It said much that I evidently didn't enjoy Frank's confidence even though the course of action he'd pursued had been the one I'd begged him to take in the first place.

I had messages from Frank at regular intervals but put off seeing him for more than a week. I had to get my head round what had happened and to shift my thinking to a place where I accepted that whatever he'd done made no difference to the way things turned out.

When we did meet it was on an afternoon when the sun was streaming into my room through the large plate-glass windows. I was sitting in an easy chair and had been reading before nodding off. I wasn't aware of him until a thin voice called my name.

Startled, I looked up. 'Hullo Frank,' I said dully, clearing my throat. I motioned him into the only other chair in the room.

'Hello Sol,' he said heavily.

I watched him shuffle towards the seat and was shocked by his appearance. True, he was over 70 but he was moving like a man two decades older.

'How are you?' I asked.

He sat down wearily. 'Should be me asking that question.'

'I went first.'

Frank tried to smile but his face muscles were in rebellion. His features were set into corrugations of worry and for the first time it registered with me that his trademark Zappa moustache was now completely white. 'I'm OK,' he said. 'They started me on a programme of cardiac rehab.' It was only then he lifted his eyes to mine. 'Look, Sol, I wanted to . . .'

I cut across him. 'It's not important,' I said, anticipating what was on his mind.

'But it is. You could have been killed. SAPS didn't want . . .'

'Why Frank?' I interrupted again.

'I-I didn't want you in harm's way.'

'That's not what I asked.'

The old man looked confused. 'I'm sorry, Sol. I don't understand.'

I spelt it out for him. 'Why didn't you say you'd contacted them? For fuck's sake, Frank, it was what I'd advised all along. I don't get why you left me out of the loop.'

Frank stared at me woodenly and looked uncomfortable. 'It was the advice I had,' he said. 'SAPS told me you'd be looking over your shoulder all the time if you knew.'

'That's bullshit!' I exploded. 'Like I was some rookie who doesn't know zip. I do understand how these things work. I think you might have had a little faith.'

Under my onslaught, Frank shrank back and was close to tears. I realized soon enough directing my anger and hurt at him served no purpose.

A silence grew between us and to break it I shrugged and said, 'What's done is done, Frank. We must look forward. There's no place else to go.'

The old man nodded his agreement. 'SAPS fucked up,' he said. 'They told me the whole thing was under control. It seems their idea of control is everybody else's idea of a total screw-up.' Exhausted, he slumped back in the chair.

With my rational mind working once more, I sympathized. 'Whichever way it played out there were no guarantees,' I said. 'There never are in kidnapping cases.'

'But I let you down, Sol, and upset you. I see that now. Can you forgive me?'

I did a double take. I couldn't recall a time when Frank had ever asked me that. Given my debt to the man, I fast became embarrassed and tried to make amends. 'What's there to forgive, Frank? You've always had my best interests at heart from way back. I remember yours was one of the few faces that didn't look right through me

20

all those years ago. And yours was the place I called home when I needed it. Hell man, you were my safety net. I wouldn't have got this far without you.'

'You were worth it.'

That made me feel like an arse. Abruptly, I changed the subject. 'What news from SAPS?'

Frank heaved despairing shoulders. 'They've told me they've some lines of inquiry, but that means nothing. I think they're waiting to be told when the kidnappers next contact me.'

'What about du Toit?'

'What about him?' snapped Frank. 'I suppose he'll let me know if he's contacted, but he says he won't act for me again. He was pretty pissed I'd gone to the police and not told him. Said he'd have to review the efficacy of our working relationship or some such horse shit. I explained he was my financial adviser, not someone to tell me what's in my wife's best interests.' Frank breathed hard and became reflective. 'Of course, the way it's turned out,' he went on, 'du Toit was absolutely right. Bringing SAPS in was a huge fucking mistake.'

My curiosity overcame an expression of support for his viewpoint. 'How did you meet du Toit in the first place?' I queried.

'At one of those Chamber of Commerce lunches. He came along to give a talk about minimizing capital gains on disposal of business assets. Mira was with me, and we got talking to him when he finished. After that, I met him a couple of times. Mira was supposed to have been there as well. Somehow, she was never around.'

The poignancy of what he said struck Frank and I saw tears start in his eyes.

I steered him away from unpleasant thoughts. 'You had an accountant in Jeffreys, didn't you?'

The old man nodded. 'But du Toit's in another league,' he said. 'He saved me a stack of money last year. He's an exceptional accountant.'

And a considerably less than exceptional human being I thought to myself. 'Did the kidnappers get the first payment?' I queried.

Frank nodded. 'The remaining 40 million's waiting to be collected.'

I saw something like hope flame in his eyes as he calculated the chances of exchanging all that money for Mira's life. It was a no-brainer, wasn't it?

For a moment, I too persuaded myself it could be a done deal but then reality kicked me in the balls. Two dead kidnappers and the ongoing police investigation couldn't be ignored. The chance of there being a replay seemed small indeed; at least in the short term.

'Most of the money was raised from Zap-it,' Frank volunteered. 'Du Toit found private investors in Cape Town.'

Zap-it Armed Response was Frank's domestic and commercial security business which he founded over 40 years ago before. It was his life's work and probably the substitute for the son he never fathered. 'I'm sorry,' I said.

Frank shook his head and pulled at his moustache. 'Don't be,' he said. 'Mira and I had been talking about my taking more of a back seat for months. That was why du Toit was of particular interest. He had the skills and connections to make it happen.'

The old man paused as a great sadness fell upon him. 'I didn't see a sale taking place like this,' he said. Then he raised teary eyes to mine and asked fiercely, 'Do you think I'll get Mira back?'

What was I to say to him? Tell him he needed to be patient. Tell him to take it a day at a time. Tell him not to lose hope. Or be honest and tell him it was probably over. That there'd been one attempt at an exchange, and it hadn't worked out. It was tough to accept she was gone, but there it was.

I did neither of these things. It seemed to me that my opinion wasn't helpful. It's often said there are two types of people in this life. There are those who sit on their butts, and frequently talk out of them, and there are those who get off their butts and get going.

'I can't tell you what's going to happen, Frank,' I said. 'What I can say is that I'm going to see what can be done to get Mira back.'

CHAPTER FOUR

I left hospital early one Friday morning when the air was still fresh and cool. It was a pleasure to be in the open again and feel the sun's new rays on my skin after nearly three weeks in a sterile, air-conditioned environment.

I took a taxi to the Ford dealers on the Expressway who had the Mustang. They recovered it as the wheels had been stolen after I transferred to the rental on the day of the aborted exchange. They gave me a cup of coffee and took me to the car. The new polished alloys showed very well and complemented the car's gleaming blue paintwork.

After retrieving my wallet from the Mustang's cubby-hole and checking my Glock, which had lain untouched beneath the driver's seat, I drove away. I stopped at a Pick 'n' Pay for some groceries before heading home.

I have a single storey place in Seaview to the west of PE. It's discreetly located behind high walls which match the house's face-brick construction. Once through the electric gates, I parked and took the neat, white-pebbled path to the front door.

Despite employing a maid who comes in twice a week, the inside of the house felt stuffy, the air heavy and stale. I opened everything up, ate some cereal, and made French toast that I washed down with fruit juice. After that, I brewed a pot of coffee and sat on the closed-in stoep. After the morning's strenuous schedule, I dozed off like those geriatrics you see slumped in the day rooms of church-run, old age homes.

When I woke up the weather had changed. It had clouded over, and a breeze was ruffling the fronds of the palms that stand overlooking the ocean. But, as the coffee pot was still warm, I lingered a while and refilled my cup.

Later, a bout of painful coughing and an unpleasant pulling sensation in my chest drove me back inside.

I retreated to my small study at the rear of the property, settled into my office chair, and hoisted my legs onto the desk. For a while, I caught up with paperwork. It took me longer than expected but, when I was done, I made a call.

Later, and after eating again, the evening stretched out before me. I hadn't been resident in the place for three weeks but, even before my hospitalization, concluded the house was a poor buy. It was too remote and much too quiet.

I bought it in the frenzy of spending that ensued after learning of the size of the inheritance from my birth father. I think it was his way of trying to make amends for having failed to acknowledge me publicly when he was alive.

He was a wealthy Boer farmer who traced his ancestry back to the Dutch founding fathers. My mother, on the other hand, was of Indian origin and out of Durban. She worked on one of his farms as a domestic help and was 30 years his junior.

Given this, and the political climate of the time, it would have taken courage on my father's part to acknowledge his bastard, half-caste son. And if this makes me sound bitter, it's not my intention. The truth is I've lacked for nothing in my life. Absolutely nothing.

I went to bed before midnight but woke up within a couple of hours. I was trembling, sweating heavily, my pulse racing. I got up and worked hard to regulate my breathing before walking up and down the living room focusing on no more than putting one foot in front of the other.

I confront this problem from time to time, usually at night. I don't want to know what triggers it, but the fact is the silence in the house unmans me. It leaves me feeling stranded in some alien time and space where there's no longer any connection or communication with the living world.

Frankly, there's not a lot to be done about this situation. In all conscience, you can't call a friend at three in the morning to say you can't sleep for some reason they'll likely find unintelligible.

On these occasions, my thoughts often turn to Ayesha, but she lives 300 kms away in East London. Most definitely, I have to say that ours is an ambiguous relationship but, even if it wasn't, the same considerations regarding convention would apply.

So, if the walking therapy doesn't work, I often leave the house and drive the Mustang up past the site of the Seaview Game Park to the N2. I can go west towards Cape Town or east towards Durban. It really doesn't matter as I load the CD stacker and, with the volume turned up high, hurtle along the deserted highway, topping out at around 200 kph on the long straights, with nothing but the beat of the music and the roar from the engine in my head.

The trick cyclist told me this is risky behaviour. But my response is to say that what I do beats everything else I've ever tried, short of drinking myself into a stupor. And to be honest, what they think is irrelevant if what I do stills the demons in my brain and settles the seething cauldron in my stomach.

CHAPTER FIVE

'*Hoe gan dit, Sol?*'

'I'm fine, Arnie,' I said untruthfully. My chest was sore, and I was doing the breathing exercises they showed me in hospital. I broke off when the house phone rang.

'Hey man, I got your message,' said Arnie. 'Sorry I didn't get in to see you. There was stuff to do. I think you know how it is.'

I did know. Warrant Officer Arnoux Coetzee was attached to SAPS Detective Services. He had a wife called Esme and two children; a brother without work, but with a girlfriend who had a baby; and an aged mother with incipient dementia whose means didn't cover the cost of the care home where she lived. The responsibility for providing for all these souls fell on his shoulders. As a result, Arnie was constantly juggling work, family, financial, and filial responsibilities. It was a stage act that required the skills of a choreographer and the footwork of an accomplished dancer.

'Of course, I understand. I wanted to talk to you about the Mira Zarakolu kidnap.'

At the end of the phone, I sensed Arnie's defensiveness. 'Sol, the case is as hot as a Natal curry. Did you hear the news yesterday?'

I said I hadn't.

'There are moves to suspend the Provincial Commissioner.'

'For what?'

'The comms at the beach malfunctioned. Apparently, they were trialing new equipment.'

'What's that got to do with the PC?'

26

'His brother-in-law works for the supplying company,' said Arnie. 'Questions have been raised about SAPS procurement. And why new equipment was being tested on such a sensitive op.'

I became impatient.' What the hell's that got to do with finding Mira?'

There was no answer for I heard a raised voice at Arnie's end. 'I am sorry, Sol, but I have to go. There's been trouble with my mamma at the home. Apparently, they've just rung, and I need to get over there.'

I commiserated but this didn't help me any. I was about to suggest calling back but instead Arnie asked me over the following day. It was his son's birthday and a *braai* had been arranged for friends and family. If I got there mid-morning, we could have some face time and catch up properly.

The suburb of North End lacks civic amenities, but its transport infrastructure is second to none. It has freeways on three sides and is bisected by the railway which terminates down at the port. The place even has its own railway station.

Arnie's house was located half way up a steep rise and on a corner plot. It was difficult to miss as the exterior elevations were painted canary yellow. This was the one colour left over in sufficient quantity after a building job his cousin had completed a couple of years back. But the paint was now peeling on account of the sun and the dwelling's proximity to the salt air of Algoa Bay.

I approached up a treeless, crumbling road and parked beneath the two-storey end wall of the house and at 90 degrees to the displaced kerb. A few metres down the hill a storm drain was partially choked with weeds and a retaining wall farther along bulged like a woman in the last stages of pregnancy. I watched a skinny cat survey all this from a sunny patch across the road and yawn. It was evidently no more bothered about the state of the local environment than the politicians at City Hall a short distance down the road in Govan Mbeki Avenue.

I hauled the stuff I bought en route out of the boot and made my way round the corner to where steps led up to the porch. At the top, a floor-to-ceiling metal grille was unlocked, and the door stood ajar so I called out.

As if from nowhere, a small boy appeared and looked at me quizzically. 'Who are you?' he asked.

'I'm Sol,' I said bending down and smiling. 'I think you must be Taki.' The boy grew shy and began to back away. 'It's your birthday today, isn't it? Or maybe it's your sister's?'

Taki stopped and looked at me fiercely. 'It's *my* birthday.'

'And how old are you today, Taki?'

'I'm five.'

'Are you sure?' I asked with a grin. 'I thought maybe you were turning four.'

Before he could answer, Arnie appeared and scooped up the boy in one strong arm. 'Hi Sol', he said, giving Taki a kiss. 'This little monster really is five years old today. I guess it's a while since you saw him last.'

'It's got to be a year or more,' I said.

Inside, I watched as Arnie sent Taki through a side door in search of his mother. Then I followed him through the living room where worn leather sofas occupied one side and a wall-mounted TV plus a bookcase and two DVD racks took up the other. Everywhere was spotlessly clean, an observation reinforced by the smell of lemon polish.

I dumped the bags on the breakfast bar at the back at which point Arnie noticed them for the first time. He stepped forward and opened each of the carriers in turn. 'This is too much, Sol,' he said.

'Ach, the boerewors *It* comes highly recommended, so it was a must-have and I put a couple of bottles in as well. It's no big deal.' I drew an envelope out of the pocket of my shorts. 'Before I forget, this is for Taki's birthday. It's a voucher because I've no idea what you buy for someone who's only five.'

Arnie seemed lost for words and so busied himself removing the box containing the sausage and the spirits from the bags. I hadn't seen him for a while, and he struck me as careworn. There was tension in his face and for the first time I saw grey hair at his temples. He and I had worked together in SAPS for several years and often as part of the same Detective Services' teams. At that time, he wore his responsibilities more lightly.

'How's your mother?' I asked.

Arnie shrugged powerful shoulders. 'Physically, she's fine,' he said, 'but mentally not so good. When she becomes forgetful, she gets frightened, and sometimes lashes out. There was another incident yesterday which was why I was called over.'

'Can the home cope with her?'

'It's OK for the moment,' said Arnie, 'but I worry for the future. If she gets worse, they may ask her to leave. I don't know what would happen then.'

I sympathized but my mother was long gone and my father's attempts to establish a functioning relationship with me had come far too late to be of any significance.

'Best not to dwell on it,' I said, clapping him on the back. Quickly, I changed the subject. 'But what we might dwell on,' I continued, 'is the drink you're about to offer me.'

Arnie smiled. 'What can I get you? Coke, fruit juice, tea, coffee?'

I looked pained. 'The brandy's not half bad,' I said. 'How's about a shot of that?'

Arnie pointedly looked at his watch, but I ignored him. Then he unscrewed the brandy, fetched a glass, and retrieved a large bottle of Coke from the fridge. He poured out the drink and passed it over to me. He watched me take an appreciative sip.

'To hell with it,' he said smiling and pouring himself one as well.

We took the brandy bottle and Coke down the steps into the small backyard. It was more or less square with a bedraggled palm in one corner that sheltered a quantity of roof tiles stacked against its trunk. The *braai* was set up on the far side of the parched grass and a glass-topped table stood adjacent with fold-up chairs scattered around.

I watched Arnie start the BBQ with firelighters and kindling you buy at the roadside for 15 bucks a bag. As he added larger pieces of wood to the flames, he turned back and said, 'I need to be careful what I say about the case, Sol. There's a lot of crap flying around at the moment. The message from the top is don't talk to anyone unless it's official police business. If you don't savvy, we'll chop you off at the ankles.'

'I'm not going to breach confidences,' I said. 'You know that as well as I do.'

Arnie looked at me askance. 'Come on, Sol. That doesn't cut it. Too many people know of the connection between us. If there's blowback as a result of something I tell you, the first guy who's going to get his nuts chewed is me.'

I couldn't fault his logic. Arnie liked the job he'd got and more importantly he needed it. An unemployment rate north of 25% concentrates the mind wonderfully. 'OK,' I said. 'Let's play it that I ask some questions and you blank any you don't like.'

Arnie was in the act of adding charcoal to the burning wood and was silent. I took this as an invitation to ask away. 'What's new?' I asked.

Arnie pulled a face.' There's been no contact from the kidnappers we know of. And for the moment we've run out of leads.' He sat down and took a long pull on his drink. He looked at me seriously. 'I don't wish to sound unfeeling, but you know she's dead, don't you?' He saw the expression on my face and went on hurriedly, 'I'm sorry to say it, Sol, but the world moves on. Ten days ago there was a gang rape in Booysens Park. After they'd finished with her, the fine citizens responsible set her on fire. She was 14 years old and died in hospital. In the last week there've been two murders and three armed robberies. All separate incidents. We're stretched every which way, Sol. Hell, bro, you can't really have forgotten how it is.'

I hadn't, but I wasn't on the inside now. I was simply another guy with a beef about something which intruded into his personal life.

The difference was I wasn't looking for somebody to take away my responsibility. All I needed was pointing in the right direction. 'Tell me about the man who picked me up,' I said. 'He made me put the kidnappers' cell in his cubby-hole. Did you find it?'

Arnie shook his head. 'We didn't. When he was asked, he denied seeing a cell. He was stopped about three kms from where he dropped you. The roadside was searched thoroughly between the two points, but nothing was found.'

'And what was his story?'

'He said he was paid to drive you around before dropping you off at a beach party.'

I looked incredulous. 'And whose party was this supposed to be?'

Arnie grinned 'You'll love this,' he said. 'Apparently it was for your birthday.'

'That's just crap!'

Part of my outrage in learning this was because SAPS had said so little when they me visited in hospital. All they wanted was to ask questions. What I now understood was where some questions had come from.

'You're not going tell me anybody believed his garbage, are you?' I asked.

Arnie raked the charcoal until it glowed red before turning to face me. 'SAPS has nothing on him. Our only record is that he holds a firearms licence. We sweated him for four days, Sol. We had to get a court extension to do it. We also turned his place upside down and poked round his finances. His story never changed. Not once. And the other thing is he never complained. Not once. It was like he'd been briefed as to how to play it. Forensics went over his pickup with a fine tooth comb and came up with zilch. He had 400 bucks on him when he was arrested which he says was what he was paid to drive you.'

'What about the person who gave him the money?' I asked wearily. Weary, because I had a good idea as to what the response would be.

Arnie shook his head. 'That was where his story got a bit vague. Apparently, he met some guy in a club and they got talking. You

31

know how it is. He says he was asked if he wanted to earn some easy money. He was told to drive to Walmer and pick you up. You'd be wearing a green T shirt with a black smiley face.' Arnie broke off when he saw my angry expression. 'No, before you ask,' he went on hurriedly, 'he didn't get a good look at the guy in the club. The lighting wasn't great and besides he'd had a few drinks. He said he was sure we understood. He was so sorry he couldn't be more helpful. Perhaps if there was some CCTV . . .'

'Spare me,' I said, lifting a hand. I took off my sunglasses and knuckled my eyes. After that, my gaze strayed to the brandy bottle. I looked at it for a moment and I swear it gave me a come-hither look. 'Perhaps another drink?' I suggested.

Arnie thought the idea had merit, so I poured out two new measures and dumped Coke on top. I passed him one and said, 'Where can I find this guy?'

'I'm sorry Sol, I can't tell you that. And I can't give you his name either. As far as SAPS is concerned, he's no longer in the frame. We had nothing we could charge him with, so we let him go. He's now no more than a private citizen.'

'You don't seriously buy that?'

'In an ideal world, I'd have put him under surveillance,' said Arnie, 'but you know what's needed to do that. SAPS doesn't have the resources and that's the end of it.'

'Come on, bro, give me something.'

But the fact was Arnie was a worried man. He didn't want to be put in a position where he might later have to justify actions which he knew left him out on a limb.

We talked for another half hour at which point Esme brought the two children into the garden with the food for the braai. Later, Arnie's brother turned up with his girlfriend and baby, closely followed by a couple of friends from adjacent houses.

In retrospect, the company was good, the sun shone out of an azure sky, the drink flowed as readily as people wanted to imbibe it, and I was pleased the *boerewors* was so well received.

But it was all small compensation for my feelings of frustration. At the point where I came to leave, I knew no more than that the two dead kidnappers were a couple of low-lifes from Manenberg in Cape Town. They had various drugs and firearms convictions but there was nothing recent against them and they were considered no more than foot soldiers in Mira's kidnap. As far as du Toit was concerned, and despite vociferous protestations, he was temporarily deprived of his tablet and his cell phones to see if any useful information could be gleaned from them. Forensic Sciences took charge and one of their IT people undertook the software interrogations. But few people had any confidence that anything of use would emerge and so it turned out after several days' effort. Whatever tracks might otherwise have been left in cyberspace, it seemed they'd been magicked away.

As I was about to climb into the car though, Arnie caught me up. 'Thanks for coming,' he said, 'and thank you very much for your generosity. Esme opened the envelope for Taki. There's enough there to take care of his birthday and his sister's for a couple of years. I can't tell you how much it's appreciated.'

'It's nothing,' I said. 'I was glad to be here. You must all come over sometime soon.'

'That would be great.' Arnie hesitated before making up his mind about something. 'Let me ask you one question,' he said firmly. 'When you were ordered to put that cell in the cubby-hole do you recall seeing anything?'

I cast my mind back. It seemed like a very long time ago. 'There were some score cards,' I said slowly. 'Done out in various colours. What of it?'

'They're from a gun club,' said Arnie. 'Our friend in the *bakkie* likes to shoot. And it seems he does it locally and often.'

CHAPTER SIX

The gun club was situated beyond the western outskirts of PE and on the far side of a mess of roads that connected with the main highway. I drew up in a cloud of dust, climbed out and crossed to a blockhouse built in the Brutalist style of architecture.

I was accosted before taking a dozen steps. 'That's a fine set of wheels you got, son,' said a voice that sounded like it had been squeezed through a centimetre-wide pipe. Its owner looked old enough to have known Methuselah.

'I guess,' I said, lifting my shades onto the top of my head and turning to face him.

A couple of shooters carrying rifle cases crossed my line of sight. 'Night, Hennie,' they called to the old man.

Hennie waved a stick-like arm in their general direction, but his gaze was still fixed on the parked Mustang bathed in the rays of the setting sun. Behind it stood a tall fence surmounted by barbed wire. 'What's under the hood?' he asked.

'Five litre V8 producing around 450PS and over 500 Nm.'

'Uh-huh. What'll it do flat out?'

'Around 250 but it's speed limited.'

'And what would I pay for a fine machine like that?'

'About the same as for a detached house.'

Hennie whistled and shook his head sadly. 'It's like I'm always saying,' he said. 'Country's gone to the dogs.' Then it occurred to him he might have spoken out of turn. 'I meant no offence, son,' he added hastily.

'None taken,' I said flashing a smile. I surveyed the single storey blockhouse from which Hennie had emerged. 'Would I be right in thinking these premises belong to the Voortrekkers Club?'

'That's what it says on the sign by the gate: Voortrekkers Rifle and Pistol Shooting Club.'

'The sign's been somewhat attenuated,' I pointed out, 'on account of the number of bullet holes. It's kinda difficult making out the words.'

Beneath a cap advertising a beer that had vanished from supermarket shelves 15 years before, Hennie's wizened expression didn't alter. He was as thin as a straw, wore a creased check shirt and had around his waist an ammunition belt from which hung a holster made of ballistic nylon. The gun it housed probably exceeded his overall body weight, though not by much. 'I'm the Manager here,' he said firmly. 'What can I do for you?'

I drew breath, but not without wincing slightly, and plunged in. 'I was here with a friend of mine a few days ago. He was on the range while I made some calls from his car. Anyway, this guy came out and crossed to a Toyota *bakkie*. As he got in, he dropped his wallet. I wasn't fast enough picking it up. By the time I did, he'd hightailed out of here. Anyway, I didn't see anybody who looked like they were in charge. If you were around, I missed you.'

'Mondays and Tuesdays are my days off. You wanna give me the wallet for safekeeping?'

'Actually, I'd like to return it personally. Unfortunately, I don't know who the guy is.'

Hennie looked at me quizzically. 'You got the item with you?'

I fished in my pocket, drew out a black leather wallet I'd bought that morning, and handed it over.

The old man made a point of putting the wallet to his nose and smelling the leather. 'It's brand new,' he said.

'It is. And if you look inside there's 25 new bills. That's 2500 bucks. I reckon it might have been a special birthday present. Or maybe something like an anniversary gift.'

Hennie looked inside, saw the notes and reluctantly, I thought, handed the wallet back. 'What did the guy look like?'

'He'd have to shed a few kilos before being thought anorexic.'

The old man cackled, and I swear false teeth slipped and slid around his mouth for a few seconds. 'I'm sorry, son,' he said, when he recovered himself, 'but most of the boys here would benefit from being able to hitch their pants with shorter belts.'

I smiled. 'I was trying to be polite. This guy was easily 120kg plus. Balding head, grey stubbly chin, mid-forties or thereabouts.'

Hennie's eyes rested again on the Mustang. 'What colour was the *bakkie*?' he asked.

'Midnight blue, but dirty and pretty old.'

A dim light came on in the old man's faded eyes. 'That sounds like Heinz,' he said.

'Heinz?' I asked casually.

'Heinrich Mueller. He's a regular. Always here at weekends and often comes in Tuesdays.'

'Have you a number for him? Or better still an address. I'd imagine he's upset at his loss, particularly if it was a present.'

'I can't do that, son. Give you an address I mean. That's confidential information. I can probably find you a number.'

It took him ten minutes rummaging amongst a whole lot of rubbish that had been shoved into a filing cabinet marked, 'Property of South African Army-Do Not Remove.' I transferred the number to my cell and made to leave but Hennie followed me outside.

'You mind if I ask why you're taking so much trouble over this,' he said.

'I guess there could be a reward.' I watched Hennie's eyes run over the Mustang before shifting back to me. It was only then I laughed. 'You think I don't need the money, right?'

'It did cross my mind, son.'

'The wheels aren't mine, man,' I said. 'I'm just looking after the car while my boss's out of town for a few days.'

CHAPTER SEVEN

What's in a name?

I knew one Heinrich Mueller from history lessons. SS-Obergruppenfuehrer Heinrich Mueller to be precise. He served as head of the Gestapo in Nazi Germany and disappeared at the end of WW2. Lack of evidence of his death led to decades of speculation as to his whereabouts. Curiously, he was neither indicted nor tried *in absentia* at Nuremberg.

Clearly the Heinrich Mueller I sought couldn't possibly be this man, but it got me thinking about the burden that may be carried by a namesake. This must be one good reason for changing your handle.

In my case, I was deprived unilaterally of my birth name early on and, while I could now reclaim it, I see no point. It has no relevance for me, either today or in the future. In fact, I've become fond of the air of mystery that my present moniker sometimes conveys. I guess this stemmed from my appreciation of Captain Nemo in the Jules Verne I read.

I didn't discover though what the word meant until I was 13 years old and was approached by a classmate. He and I shared only one thing in common and that was our mutual loathing of one another.

'Hey Nemo!' he shouted at me. 'I bet you don't know what your name means?'

I smelt a trap and went on the offensive. 'I bet it's more appealing than whatever Swanepoel means,' I retorted.

'You don't know, do you?' crowed Swanepoel. 'You really don't know!'

At that point, I was lost for words and stood there dumbly waiting for whatever embarrassment his explanation was likely to cause me.

'Nemo means nobody in Latin,' exclaimed Swanepoel. 'How does it feel to be nobody, Nemo?' By that time, a group had gathered round wondering what all the fuss was about. 'I say everybody,' shouted Swanepoel, 'I think we've just found out what we've known all along. Master Nemo here is a nobody, and he even has the name to prove it.'

Swanepoel laughed for no more than the few seconds it took my brain to activate my fist and drive it into his mouth. He didn't expect that, and his head jerked backwards before blood started to spill from his lip.

Nevertheless, it took me a while to get past the incident. My contemporaries, at the exclusive boarding school to which my father had consigned me at the age of seven, were the sons of politicians, government officials, and successful business people amongst which were generously sprinkled the offspring of doctors, accountants, advocates and other professionals. All I could say about my father, who had never been more than a smudge in my waking consciousness, was that he was a farmer.

In retrospect, this episode was just another station along the road towards the alienation I felt towards an environment in which it seemed I'd been placed in order to punish me. But don't run away with the idea I lacked the resources to fight back. The incident with Swanepoel, and a couple of others like it, served to establish my reputation as someone with whom you didn't take liberties if you valued the shape of your face. And that was A-OK as far as I was concerned. But it left me marked out as the student with a skin colour that had nothing to do with too much sun; the student who often stayed on at school when everyone else went home at the end of term; and, of course, the student with the strange name.

*   *   *

There were seven Muellers in the telephone directory. To find the right one, I got in touch with my network of agents. I use the term 'agent' loosely as they're drawn from the ranks of the unemployed who act as car park guards in PE. They hang around, if necessary, all day, and keep an eye on your car. When you come back, it's customary to give them a few bucks for their trouble.

I made several calls from home and recruited the individuals I needed. In each case, I passed on the name Mueller and a unique address. I stressed urgency and asked that everyone bearing the name be identified and described to me. This method of working, which could be highly effective, had occurred to me after reading about Sherlock Holmes' Baker Street Irregulars, street boys who were sent all over London by the great detective as intelligence gatherers.

Some results came back within 12 hours, but they weren't the man I sought. I paid the agents off and provided reassurance I'd use them again when the need arose. Such assignments though were *ad hoc* so I was unable to make promises.

Next morning, I was out on the verandah when my cell vibrated.

'Sol, my man, how you doing this fine day?'

I'd had a rough night, this time because of my chest, and had been up since before dawn. 'I'm good,' I said. 'You got something for me?'

'I gotta a slam dunk, my man.'

'OK,' I said, my tone neutral. 'First, tell me who you are.' I was waiting on Mustafa, Alex, and Ignatius at that point. The rest had already reported in.

'Sorry Sol, it's Iggy. Like I was saying this guy's real fat. He gets any fatter you could use him as a ball.'

'Describe him,' I said with some sense of excitement, my eyes scanning the list in front of me to refresh my memory as to where Iggy was calling from.

'I guess he's older than me and maybe a bit shorter,' said Iggy. This wasn't very helpful, but the info soon got a whole lot better.

'Like I was saying he's huge and he drives this blue Toyota *bakkie*. Looks like it's been doing Round Africa rallies.'

'That's great,' I said warmly. I'd withheld the information about the Toyota as I didn't want my informers putting two and two together and making five. Besides, Toyotas aren't an uncommon sight. 'What's the situation as of now?'

'He drove away, Sol, just before I called. He had a couple of bags with him so maybe he's out shopping.'

Iggy was about half an hour away in Summerstrand, so I asked him to wait. In the meantime, I got myself organised. I stood Mustafa and Alex down and arranged to pay them off. After that, I assembled an overnight bag including a couple of T shirts and base-ball caps of different colours. I also collected a light top for night wear and selected food and drink. I fetched the Glock from the Mustang before garaging it and putting everything into my white Ford Fiesta. It's about as distinctive as a golf ball on a driving range which makes it perfect for surveillance work.

I left mid-morning and took the road east which runs through Lovemore Park, dropped down to the coast and followed the seaboard until it turned inland. From there I joined Marine Drive and ran up past the Humewood Golf Club before making a left into Admiralty Way. I followed this and stopped a few minutes after-wards on a piece of waste ground defined by broken-down, chain-link fencing and encroaching scrub. Parked beneath bushes that provided shade from the midday sun and partially obscured from the road, I settled back after taking a long pull from a water bottle.

Iggy joined me ten minutes later. He was a rangy guy and had about as much meat on him as a half-starved stick insect. Dreadlocks framed a face which was thin and pinched but when he spotted me his features broke open in a large grin.

'Hi, my man,' he called as he opened the passenger door and sat down. We exchanged a high five and I watched as he took a drink of water. Iggy was a user of *dagga* which went much of the way to explaining his sometimes odd and unpredictable behaviour.

Nevertheless, he was as gentle a soul as was ever placed on God's earth.

'So,' I said with some impatience 'what am I supposed to be looking at?'

Iggy pointed through the windscreen with a thin finger towards Happy Valley and a six-storey apartment block that overlooked it. 'Mueller came back about half an hour ago,' he said. 'Toyota's in the car park. Do you see it?'

I couldn't at first but then spotted the pickup's bonnet peeking out from behind the bulk of an estate car. From this vantage point though, it would be difficult seeing anyone enter or leave the vehicle.

Iggy read my mind. 'Everything going in or out has to pass this spot,' he said.

'Good. I don't suppose you know which apartment is Mueller's?'

Iggy was triumphant. 'Top floor on the right-hand side.'

'How did you work that out?'

'There was an old lady doing some tidying up. I asked her where I could find *Mrs.* Mueller as she had some gardening work. She said there was nobody of that name, but there was a *Mr.* Mueller. Did I mean him? I sort of . . .' Without warning, Iggy broke off. 'Say, you got anything to eat? My belly's emptier than ANC promises.'

I laughed at that, got out of the car, and went to the boot. I fetched the carrier bag with the food and passed it over. 'You help yourself.'

Iggy began urgently rummaging amongst the contents. 'You got *biltong* Sol?'

'Bottom of the bag.'

Iggy found the dried meat, opened the wrapper, and crammed his mouth. I didn't like to ask when he'd last eaten a decent meal. The purblind tell you there's no malnutrition in our Rainbow Nation. Worse than them are the mothers who say it's all the fault of apartheid; like white rule ended around six months back.

'Great,' said Iggy when he'd had his fill. 'That was real nice.' But he wasn't finished as he dived into the bag again and found feta

41

cheese and bread rolls. I tried to be patient but at last prompted him, 'You were telling me about Mueller's apartment.'

'Right, my man, I was. Thing was the old lady told me Mueller lived on the top floor. There are three apartments on each level. The top end one's empty and being done out. You can see paint tins on the balcony. There are a couple of girls in the middle who I saw sitting out early on. Mueller's next door. He came out and smoked a cigarette while he made a call.'

I was curious. 'What happened with the old lady?'

'I said my information must be wrong. Then I asked her if there was anything she wanted doing. She said there wasn't, but she gave me 20 bucks. That was real nice of her.'

The mention of money made me dig deep into the pocket of my shorts. I drew out some 200 Rand bills and passed them over.

Iggy's eyes widened. 'So much,' he gasped.

'You got me a result,' I said. 'And you got it quickly so there's a bonus.'

'I guess this job's important.'

'It is, but it's more than that. It's personal.'

Iggy chatted a while until I let him go. He said he'd walk down Second Avenue and I knew what he meant by that. With the money given him, I thought he might buy beer, find somewhere quiet, and perhaps smoke a spliff or two.

I asked Iggy whether he could come back that night if required, and he agreed if I paid for a taxi. That way he could cover me for maybe four or five hours overnight while I slept, assuming Mueller didn't move. If nothing happened by the following morning, I'd have to get other people involved. There was one guy I'd had dealings with in the past who was in my line of business. On a speculative basis, I gave him a call to see whether he might be around, but he was too non-committal for my liking. For the moment, I decided to let it go. Sufficient unto the day . . .

Iggy had chosen my observation point well. It was unobtrusive yet had a good view over the apartment block below. With the aid of a small pair of binoculars, I glassed Mueller's apartment and the car park at regular intervals but saw no sign of life.

Mueller's balcony was narrow in depth and accommodated no more than a circular table and a couple of chairs made of white moulded plastic. Curtains beyond the glass at the back of the balcony were only partially drawn but reflected light gave no clue as to what was going on inside.

I had time to kill, and maybe a lot of time. I ate a slow meal of pita bread, ham, and some feta which Iggy had left and washed it down with Ceres cranberry and kiwi fruit juice. I propped a book of Housman's poems on the steering wheel and read in a desultory way; tinkered with a Sudoku puzzle until my patience evaporated; and tuned in from time to time to Algoa FM. At one point, a couple of wagtails visited and hopped about on the hood. I offered food but what I had wasn't to their taste and they soon departed. A few vehicles passed up and down the adjacent road and there was some footfall back and forth as the hours limped past.

At around 5 p.m. Mueller came out and sat on the balcony. He was cradling a glass of spirits and soon lit up a cigarette. I watched as clouds of blue smoke drifted lazily away from him. With his shirt off and exposing a white belly of vast proportions, I was reminded of nothing so much as the curved backs of the whales you see surface on those marine cruises out of Cape Town. His attention though was focused on something he was viewing on an iPad, something which evidently required gentle stroking in the area of his groin.

CHAPTER EIGHT

Later, as the sun fell behind a line of trees, so the lights along Marine Drive and Beach Road gained prominence. Beyond them, the ocean darkened and became black. In the streets of Humewood, I saw lights start to come on in the houses and apartment blocks as people returned from work. There would be single people of course, but also couples and families settling down for the evening in at least some spirit of amity. Despite knowing nothing of their circumstances, I envied them their intertwined lives. It is ever thus we delude ourselves as to what we perceive to be others' good fortune.

I switched to infra-red bins when night set in. By that time, Mueller had disappeared and all that indicated he might still be around was the light burning in the room behind his balcony. At that point, I focused on the car park, illuminated by a single spot-light mounted high up on an exterior wall. His *bakkie* though was in darkness.

I was getting close to summoning Iggy, when I saw headlights down below. This had happened several times, so I didn't react immediately. By the time I got the bins up to my eyes, a vehicle was already well clear of its parking space and heading out of the block's grounds. As it passed under a streetlight, I saw it was the Toyota.

All the stuff in my lap got chucked into the foot well. I transferred the Glock to the passenger seat, fastened my seat belt, and started the engine. Slowly, I moved the unlit Fiesta away from the bushes and to the side of the road. Seconds later the pickup tore past me. It was heading for Admiralty Way and the coast.

I kept Mueller in sight without drawing his attention. There was little traffic and, with one tail light out, it wasn't difficult tracking his progress. But my quarry was as nervous as a first-time burglar. It wasn't traffic cops he feared because he frequently had little regard for speed limits. What dictated his actions was evidently concern about being followed. As a result, he seemed more interested in travelling than in arriving.

It was nearly one o'clock when he turned into a housing development near Glenroy Park. I let his tail light disappear as I drew up. I knew there was only one road in and out of the estate. If I were to keep Mueller in sight, the Fiesta would stand out and risk my surveillance.

I pulled into the kerb and went after him on foot. Or rather I jogged in the direction he'd taken. The road made a wide left-handed loop. The houses on either side were large, many with high walls topped with wire. Soon, up ahead, I saw the stationary Toyota. It was parked on a rectangle of grass overhung by silver birches. As I watched, its lights went out and Mueller emerged. Slowly, very slowly, he looked about him and seemingly scented the air for danger. As there was a half moon, I shrank back into shadows thrown by acacia bushes. Somewhere far away a dog barked and one closer by soon joined it in a duet.

I thought my quarry would make for one of the houses but instead he retrieved several bags from the Toyota. Then, without warning, he disappeared. The next thing I heard was a car door open and shortly afterwards slam shut. Evidently, he had another vehicle.

I didn't wait but turned and sprinted for the Fiesta. I've a fair turn of speed but I ain't Usain Bolt. Before going far, I heard an engine behind me. It came up fast. Once again, I melted into the shadows. Mueller passed me in a dark saloon, making for the junction with the main road. I was still a couple of hundred metres from the Fiesta. I could only watch helplessly as his indicator light flashed prior to turning.

But suddenly brake lights came on. After that his car slowed and finally stopped, the indicator still flashing. The reason why wasn't obvious. I made the most of this advantage and ran flat out. In seconds, I was back behind the wheel. Winded, I started my engine.

Up ahead, Mueller was stationary and now I saw why. Spotlights mounted above a cab lanced the night. They belonged to an artic that was trying to turn. Because of the restricted space, it was a slow process. All I heard was the repeated squeaking and hissing of air brakes.

I watched for a few seconds in the rear-view mirror. After that, I did some manoeuvring of my own. I turned the steering wheel to the left and gently pressed the accelerator. Without touching the brakes, which would have advertised my presence, I steered the car until the wheels bumped the far kerb. Then I reversed and drove forward again, so I faced in the right direction. Ahead of me, the saloon remained stationary, its engine idling.

By the time Mueller was able to move, rain had started. Initially, it was drizzle but soon it turned into a stream and that became a deluge. Visibility was poor and soon got worse, but lack of traffic helped me.

I followed Mueller across town to the Old Cape Road, watched him pass St. Albans prison, and keep heading west. Eventually, we left the houses behind and drove on through open country. The rain gradually eased but the air that blew in through the top of my window had turned cold.

I stayed well back from Mueller as we drove for perhaps 25 kms. Next, without warning, his one taillight vanished. I doused my lamps and coasted to where, I reckoned, he must have peeled off. Fortunately, I was in time to see him before he was swallowed by a fold in the ground. He was somewhere away from the highway on my right.

I pulled off the road, picked up the Glock from the passenger seat and climbed out. A dark, peaked cap and a lightweight top over my T shirt gave me weather protection. The infra-red bins went into one of my pockets. I stuck the gun into the waistband of my shorts.

After that, I made for where Mueller's car disappeared. The ground was rough and wet underfoot with patches of low scrub. The rain started up again along and with it a stiff breeze sprang up.

I stopped where the ground fell away into a wide valley. As I watched, Mueller came into view below me, the car having made a detour around rocky outcrops. It was slowly following an old concrete road. It wasn't that though that held my attention. His headlights picked out broken walls, shattered roofs, and piles of rubble. A single chimney, solitary as a ghost, looked out over the surrounding devastation. What sort of settlement this had been, I didn't know.

His car though was still rolling, and I needed to get closer. Heedless of the scratches to my legs from thorn bushes, I scrambled down the slope.

At the bottom, I jogged past a line of roofless buildings. At the end, I peered round the corner of a tumbledown wall. Mueller's car was picking its way cautiously over rough ground. Then it stopped, apparently uncertain where to go. I crept closer.

Mueller made up his mind. He dabbed the accelerator, and the car descended a slope. It rolled past a line of unkempt palms and swung right. Brake lights vanished when he switched off his engine. Standing beneath the palms, I heard the wind rustle the fronds. I watched Mueller step out of the saloon, retrieve his bags, and walk away.

I crouched down and moved crab-like seeking a view beyond the bulk of his car. I found a rock to one side and peeked out to see Mueller navigate the short distance to a dilapidated house.

It was a small place and partially roofless. To protect what was open to the sky a tarp had been rigged. My bins confirmed the canvas was anchored with large stones. Panes of glass in the two front windows were mostly broken.

I was now wet through. Water streamed off my cap, fell onto the long hair at the nape of my neck and dropped down my back. With bare legs scratched and my feet sodden, I stopped and took stock.

CHAPTER NINE

Mueller had disappeared into the house an hour before and not reappeared. I was a short distance away and would have moved closer, but the intervening ground was of loose broken stone. Besides, the cover wasn't enough to hide a Cape hare.

Impatiently, I continued to wait until there was a noise from the house. As I brought the glasses up to my eyes, the front door was flung open. Three men spilled into the rainy night. One was carrying a storm lamp. Another had Mira handcuffed to his wrist. The third was Mueller.

Some disagreement caused raised voices but too far away for me to understand what was being said. Their dispute though worked to my advantage. I seized the opportunity to draw the Glock and racked the slide to chamber a bullet.

The group started to move off. Evidently, Mira needed physical support because she struggled to put one foot in front of the other.

I stood up and stepped out. I closed the distance to half what it had been. To keep my eyes adjusted to the dark, I didn't look at the lamp. Meanwhile, the dispute continued. It was between Mueller and the other two.

'You got a problem, Heinz, take it some place else,' said one of the kidnappers.

'Fuck you,' said Mueller. 'I gotta a right . . .'

'You got nothing,' another voice interrupted. 'Yash calls the shots. You count for shit.'

I was now standing ten metres behind them. I extended my arms, the Glock anchored in both hands.

'You should listen up, bro!'

As startled as a nervous buck, three bodies spun in unison. Mira slumped against the guy to whom she was handcuffed as he jerked round. Momentarily, he was wrong-footed. But I was more concerned about Mueller. For a tub of lard, he reacted fast, a gun emerging from his pants.

I didn't hesitate but put two slugs into his huge chest and saw him go down

I swung the Glock back and saw another arm rise in my direction. I fired twice more, heard a yelp and then the clatter of a dropped gun. It was followed by a crash as the shot kidnapper dropped the lamp. Its light went out.

That left the guy with Mira. But, swinging the gun again, I lost my footing. Trying to regain my balance on loose stones, I tripped and fell, the Glock flying from my hands.

When I looked up, I saw three figures in retreat. One guy was staggering and holding his shoulder. The other kidnapper had his hands full with Mira. It wasn't apparent my intervention had even registered with her.

Desperately, and on my knees, I searched for the Glock. It had skidded into a cleft of rock and took far too long to find. By the time it was back in my hands, I heard a powerful engine start up.

I tried to stand but fell again. I'd turned my ankle over my foot, and it wouldn't support my leg. I got up on the other leg and started to hobble. As I did so, headlight beams picked me out for a few seconds. After that, they veered away across my line of sight. The vehicle was a large SUV. Mindful of Mira, I shot at its tyres as it hurtled past. Since it neither slowed nor changed direction, my effort was wasted.

I limped over to Mueller's car, but the keys were missing. After, I crossed to the dead man and looked down. His chest was a mass of spilt blood diluted with rainwater. I felt for a pulse but knew he was dead. A search of his pockets yielded nothing.

I got out my cell. It was a toss-up whether to call the police or Arnie for back-up. As it turned out, it didn't matter as there was no signal.

I started to make my way back to the road. Hurrying along, I found my foot painful and, man, was I suddenly weary. The adrenaline rush was now over leaving me as limp as wet paper.

But, in the bat of an eye, everything changed. Mounting the last rise before the main road, I looked up and spotted the SUV. It was off the track in a gully, its engine idling in the night air. The headlights threw their beams across a rocky terrain till they morphed into darkness.

What to make of this, I didn't know. Drawing the Glock, I crouched down and watched. But nothing stirred and the engine beat was as regular as a healthy heart.

I edged forward behind the vehicle, my gun pointed. The rear windows had privacy glass so told me nothing. The other windows were closed. I moved a few metres to the left and saw the front tyre was shredded. At least one of my shots had found its mark.

I screwed up my courage, the Glock fused to my wrist and my finger curled inside the trigger guard. With trepidation, I reached out and opened the front passenger door. The interior light flashed on, picking out every detail. Suddenly, my nose was filled with a strong coppery smell.

Mira was upright in the front seat and covered in blood. It was in her matted hair, on her face, and it spilled down her filthy dress. Her left hand was in her lap, and it too was wet with blood. But in that small hand she clasped a small screwdriver of the type found in vehicle toolkits.

The horror before me was all so far removed from my recollection of her. What I remembered was a beautiful coquette, a gorgeous butterfly as fickle and insubstantial as a summer zephyr.

I put my gun on the hood and looked across to the kidnapper in the driver's seat. He was slumped over the wheel, his head turned towards me. His eyes were open, the expression in them one of deep shock.

For him, the attack Mira mounted must have come from nowhere. There was no doubting its frenzy, born of desperation. Perhaps she'd found the screwdriver in the passenger door bin. I saw the puncture marks in his neck and chest where she repeatedly stabbed him. I guessed he'd braked and raised his left arm, cuffed to her right, to ward her off. It was to no avail. Maybe, she got lucky with her early blows and quickly overcame him. It was his bad luck to have been up front. He should have sat in the back with her. It was the other guy who was the wheel-man. But now, with roles reversed, it was the driver who was in the rear. He was slumped unconscious, his breathing ragged and shallow.

Mira slowly turned her head towards me. Her eyes were as big as the trauma I discerned in them. She didn't recognize me and simply stared. Then her gaze fell to her lap and the screwdriver she was holding. Without warning, she dropped it as though it was on fire. After that, she wordlessly searched my face.

'Mira,' I said softly. 'It's Sol. You're OK now. I'm going to look after you.'

I reached out a hand in reassurance, but she shrank away. Next, she was struggling to breathe and started to shake uncontrollably. I grasped her shoulders and drew her towards me. She smelt bad and her breath was foul, but I gathered her into in my arms.

'It's OK, Mira. It's all over. You're safe now. Nobody's going to hurt you any more.'

After a while, her breathing began to steady and the shaking abated. It was then she whispered in my ear, her voice strained. 'I-I had to do it,' she said. 'You understand that, don't you S-Sol? I-I had to make them stop. M-Make them stop it. I-I just had to.' She lapsed into silence and her body relaxed in my arms.

Exhausted, she drifted off. I hoped it was to some happier place, her oblivion a consequence of fatigue or drugs.

I looked over the front seats to the other kidnapper. His breath-ing remained uneven, and his face was mud in colour. His upper chest and shoulder were a bloodied mess. Without attention, he'd soon die.

I stepped away, crossed to the driver's side, reached in and switched off the engine. Then I tried to call again. It was now after two, but I opted for Arnie. I reckoned things would move faster if he summoned the cavalry. This time I got through.

Given the time of night, I didn't get the reaction I expected 'It's OK,' he said. 'I wasn't asleep. You likewise I guess. What's up?'

Quickly, I brought him up to speed. 'Where are you?' he asked.

'Not sure, but I reckon around 30-40 kms from PE along the Cape Road. I used the Fiesta to track Mueller. It's parked up on the hard shoulder pointing west. It won't be difficult to spot.'

'I'll call an ambulance first.'

'That's good, Arnie, but they need two. Mira's in bad shape. Not a good idea for her to have to share back to PE.'

'OK. I'll get to it now. Then I'll get on to SAPS in Mount Road. They can coordinate response. Anything else?'

'Not that I can think of. I'm going to try and get Mira up to the road. It'll be quicker transferring her when the ambulance arrives.'

Arnie said he'd call me back when things were in train.

Moving back to the SUV coincided with the rain stopping. The guy in the back was now making gurgling noises. Experience told me this wasn't good, but I didn't give him much thought. Mira was my priority.

I went round to the driver and put my hand into the pocket of his shorts. I found the keys to the handcuffs soon enough. But to release Mira, I had to trail back to the passenger side. When the cuffs were off, I saw ugly wheals on her wrist where the metal had chafed her skin.

Then I shook her gently and watched her eyes flutter open. There was panic until I smiled and said, 'OK, Mira. It's me again. You remember, don't you?' She didn't respond and with no physical reaction either I pressed on. 'Look, Mira, I'm going to take you up to the road. There's an ambulance on its way. My car's there and we can sit until it arrives.'

I took her lack of reaction as acquiescence and reached in to help her. I reasoned that if I could get her out of the vehicle and standing, we could walk together to the highway. Hope springs eternal. But hope's a fickle friend. Mira didn't stir and was just dead weight.

Wondering what to do, my eyes fell on the Glock. Distracted, I retrieved it from the hood and stuck it back in my waist band. After that, I stretched across and, making an effort, lifted Mira bodily. Obligingly, I got her to put her arms around my neck.

Mira was maybe five foot three and weighed no more than 50 kg. Good things come in small packages. Good, until you're faced with having to lift them.

The first 25 metres was almost a doddle. But, after that, the track started to ascend. My arms quickly grew tired and so did my legs. More, there was an unpleasant throbbing in my foot where I'd turned it over. But I knew once stopped, I'd never get started again. My clothes, already clinging to me from the rain, stuck some more as my body heated up and sweated. It might have helped if I'd removed my top before picking her up.

The pain in my arms became acute. Maybe I could put Mira down and then try a fireman's lift. I dismissed the idea and decided not to stop for a breather. But soon my legs started to register their own protests as I felt a pulling on my hamstrings.

I soldiered on, the sweat pouring off me, the pain in my arms acute until finally I was there.

I propped Mira against the side of the Fiesta with one hand and found the car keys with the other. I opened up, flung the door wide and gently manoeuvred her inside. As I settled her into the passenger seat, Mira's hand found mine and squeezed. Looking back, I think it was her way of confirming she was safe, her ordeal over.

After that, I leaned exhausted against the Fiesta and sucked in great mouthfuls of air. I lifted the cap off my head and tousled my sodden hair. Then I wrestled to take my top off as the material was stuck to my wet arms. With that done, I stretched several times to relieve aching muscles.

Checking my phone, I found a text from Arnie. It had come while I was ascending the track. It confirmed both ambulance and police services were on their way. There was no ETA.

When my heart rate returned to the low hundreds, I hobbled round the car and dropped into the driver's seat. I placed the Glock on top of the dash and looked across to Mira. She was curled up with her eyes closed, her features partially obscured by locks of dirty and knotted hair. I noticed some bruising to her chin and several marks on her legs. I wondered when she'd last had a change of clothes.

None of it mattered now. She was safe with me. It was just a question of waiting for help to arrive. I settled back in the seat and let the tension drain from my body. With little power to resist, I closed my eyes.

CHAPTER TEN

Huge distances between settlements in our Rainbow Nation means traffic, in the depopulated regions between, is almost nil in the small hours.

I don't how long I slept, but my awakening was violent. The cause was the thunderous passage of a juggernaut that rocked the Fiesta as it hurtled along the highway a few metres away.

That event though was soon eclipsed, my attention caught by a gleam from distant headlights. At this point, the road stretched in a straight line to the far horizon and whoever was coming my way was closing the gap fast.

Or they were, I believe, until they spotted my car. At that point, a transformation took place. Lights that had been growing ever brighter became no more intense signalling the vehicle had slowed.

I watched for a long minute until it finally pulled off the road in front of me. But, by that time, I was standing outside, Glock in hand. Moving a few metres, I chose the dark shadows above a deep gully.

The vehicle came to rest head-on 30 metres away. But, with lights full on, I was none the wiser as to its identity.

I watched as someone stepped out and heard a door close. It was followed by the scrape of boots on tarmac. A man appeared in front of the headlights. I recognised the SAPS uniform of blue shirt and pants, the regulation brown belt, and the holstered pistol. His voice was directed at the Fiesta.

'I phoned a while ago,' I called to him.

The policeman hadn't noticed me because he swung round fast and began walking in my direction. He was stocky and well-set-up. Like 100 kgs of well-set-up hard muscle. 'Don't know anything about that,' he said. 'We pulled over when we saw the car.'

'Nice of you to oblige.' In the distance came the wail of a siren.

The policeman heard it too because he stiffened, but he kept coming. 'If you're carrying, better give me the piece,' he advised. 'Don't want no accidents.'

What he said implied foreknowledge. 'I'm fine,' I said, my voice raised. But that was only because I was competing with the siren. The SAPS guy was now no more than a few metres off.

At that instant, out of the corner of my eye, I saw another figure emerge from the police car. He made no move in my direction. On the contrary, he began running towards the Fiesta and Mira. Distracted, I turned and was about to shout something. I never got the chance because the policeman rushed me. Full tilt, he cannoned into my chest. It was like being hit by a truck. Smashing one fist into my solar plexus, he pushed me hard. I fell back over the edge of the gully and tumbled down. The ground was strewn with rocks and thorn bushes too small to break my fall. But they gave me cover when he began shooting.

Bullets zipped and zinged all around me. I kept my head down and my body curled up. I came to rest on my side with thorns pressed agonizingly into one thigh. After the shooting stopped, I flexed my leg with difficulty. Above me, the wailing siren became as maddening as a buzzing mosquito. When it was silenced, an eerie calm descended.

I sat up and checked myself over. I ached in various places but found nothing broken. The punch to my torso though made breathing painful; I wondered if my surgery had been compromised.

I started back up the gully with a feeling of dread. In the dark, it took a while to skirt the thorns and negotiate the loose rocks. When I reached the top, I was huffing and puffing like a 60 a day nicotine junkie.

There were two ambulances parked up. I ignored them and limped over to the Fiesta.

Mira wasn't there.

It was a fact no less distressing than if I'd found her dead. Yet I could hardly count my discovery a shock. The bombshell for me had been getting slugged and pushed down the gully. What followed afterwards had been wholly predictable.

My priority now was Arnie. As I keyed his number, I saw a paramedic hurrying towards me. Middle-aged and dressed in a boiler suit, she looked kinda irritated. 'You wanna tell me what's going on?' she demanded. 'We got a call . . .'

I put up a restraining hand. 'First,' I said, 'did you see anything on your way here?'

'Like what?'

'Cars, SUVs-that sort of thing'

'At this time of night? -We saw nothing, excerpt one large truck. Look . . .'

'Did both ambos come from PE?'

'They did.'

'OK. I need to make a call. After that, we'll talk.'

She would have said something more, but my expression silenced her. Only the cast of her shoulders conveyed her disapproval as she stepped away.

I called Arnie. He picked up at once. 'Listen,' I said. 'I was jumped by two guys in SAPS uniforms. They took Mira and went west. I repeat west. Not sure if the vehicle they're using had SAPS livery.'

'How long since?'

'Ten minutes tops.'

'Leave it with me. I'll get back to you.'

I hobbled towards the medics. Before I'd taken a few steps, the paramedic was back in my face. 'I've got two crews here,' she snapped. 'Apparently, this was an emergency. We pitch up and all we find is an abandoned car. Then you appear from nowhere. You mind telling me what the hell's going on.'

I explained as best I could. But that was after telling her where the wounded kidnapper was to be found. She dispatched one of her crews and they drove off down the track.

In a kindlier frame of mind, she turned back to me. 'That must be painful,' she said, looking down at my leg.

'I tripped and turned my ankle over. Really, it's nothing.'

'Maybe, but we'll take a look anyway.'

She led me across to the open door of the remaining ambulance. Light spilled from the interior and revealed a young coloured guy sitting on a gurney. His nose was buried in what I took to be a textbook. His disinterested glance in my direction turned to a stare as he took in my appearance. 'You look like you've had a bust up with Tyson Fury,' he said.

I gave him a tight smile and would have replied but the woman butted in. 'Out Josh,' she said abruptly, 'and give a body space. I can't work with you sitting there swinging your legs and looking superior,' She gave him and me a grin. 'He wants to be a pharmacist,' she explained, 'and give up all this excitement. Sad in one so young, don't you think?'

'Get away with you,' said Josh. 'Right now, I'm about as excited as a corpse at his own funeral.' With a good-humoured grin, he climbed out and strolled off.

I took his place on the gurney. For the first time, I looked at my arms and legs. They were a mass of scratches, cuts and abrasions. My T shirt was torn in two places and my shorts, originally khaki, were stained and spattered with blood.

My new friend checked me over paying particular attention to my chest area and my ankle. Apart from extensive bruising, she confirmed me fit. 'Might be best if you don't drive for a few days,' she advised. 'Give your ankle a rest.'

'But I need to take my car back to PE.'

'The only way that's going back to PE is on a trailer,' she said flatly. I looked puzzled. 'Didn't you notice, man? -You've got two flats.'

In my anxiety to locate Mira, I'd not taken anything else in. Perversely, this information gave me some comfort. Even had I been able to get to the car quickly enough to mount a pursuit, it was unusable. Without wheels, there was nothing further I could have done for Mira.

My lacerations were attended to using alcohol-free wipes and a pad of tissues. While this was being done, Arnie called me back. He said roads west of my location would be patrolled and there'd be spot checks, but his voice betrayed little hope of a result.

I was beginning to feel the same way about when SAPS might show up. 'What's with the back-up, Arnie?'

My friend sighed. 'Priorities got changed round. There was stuff elsewhere. Their ETA's now around ten minutes.'

That left me thinking what might have happened had the good guys rocked up before Mira was snatched back. Conjecture of that sort though torments the rational mind.

As it turned out, by the time the cavalry appeared, the paramedic was done with me, and the other ambulance had left for PE. It took with it the one surviving kidnapper whose life hung by a fraying thread.

CHAPTER ELEVEN

It was said of Captain Francoise Bezuidenhout of SAPS Detective Services that his police enrolment dated from the time of the Sharpeville massacre. This was nonsense as that atrocity occurred in 1960. Less easy to dismiss was the statement that he'd been on the payroll since the Soweto uprising nearly 20 years later. I knew him by name, of course, but he spent his time working out of Bethelsdorp, so our paths had never actually crossed during my period of service.

Bezuidenhout arrived in an unmarked, 15-year-old Beamer. I assumed it was his personal transport unless SAPS procurement policies had altered since my day. He was followed by a couple of police units that initially parked on the roadside. But, at the captain's insistence, they moved off down the track and out of sight of the highway.

'No point advertising,' Bezuidenhout said to me, after we exchanged preliminaries. 'The Zarakolu case continues to attract a lot of attention. Most of it unhelpful.' He paused and fastened a pair of baby blues on me. 'I had a chat with Warrant Officer Coetzee about you,' he went on, 'and he says you're reliable. He also says I should trust you. I know Coetzee by reputation and respect the man so what's good for him is good for me.'

'Thanks for the vote of confidence.'

Bezuidenhout responded with a quizzical look. 'I have to say, Mr. Nemo, I don't understand your interest. Who exactly is Mira Zarakolu to you?'

'It's not about Mira,' I said. 'It's about her husband Frank. And as he's the closest thing I have to a father, you'll understand my motivation.'

The captain invited me to sit with him in the Beamer. Climbing in, I was surprised to see the interior's leather seats and facings were the colour of freshly spilled blood.

'It was spec'd by one of those stock trading nerds in Jo'burg,' explained Bezuidenhout. 'People tell me it rather clashes with my image. What image? -I don't know what the hell they're talking about.'

But I did. While the car's interior might call to mind banquette seating in one of those old New Orleans' bordellos, the captain's charcoal-grey suit, with narrow lapels and a pencil tie, called to mind a Calvinist Sunday service where you might hear a homily on Total Depravity.

Bezuidenhout changed the subject. 'I reckon you could use a cup of coffee.'

I said he reckoned right and watched him reach over the seat and produce a silver flask plus a couple of mugs.

The drink poured, he lit a cigarette and drew on it thoughtfully before blowing smoke out of his open window. He looked like a man at ease with himself and with all time in the world.

Me, I was impatient. 'So, when does this two step get started?' I asked.

Skin at the side of Bezuidenhout's face crinkled in a smile. 'Sun-up's at around five,' he said talking to the windscreen. 'Forensics will be here at first light. I'm the CSM/IO so we'll do a walk through together. That way you can show me everything. In the meantime, let's take it from the top.' He turned towards me. 'Might be an idea if you start by telling me how you found this guy Mueller.'

I cast my mind back. It seemed like a long time ago. Slowly, I began to talk. And while I talked, he smoked, one cigarette after another, lighting each new one off the butt of the old. For the most part, he didn't interrupt but then I was experienced in conveying a witness account just as he was at evaluating what he was hearing.

Besides, both of us knew I'd have to make a written statement in due course so the whole thing would get re-visited.

We left the car as the sun, no more than the size and colour of a fried egg, peeked above the far horizon. Walking across to where I'd been shoved into the gully, Bezuidenhout bent down and viewed a few shell casings.

'9 mil,' he said disgustedly. 'I doubt we'll get much from these. Seems every fire stick nowadays uses this ammo.' He looked up at me. 'You really think the guy who slugged you was SAPS?'

'Given the timeline, it's difficult to credit anything else,' I said. 'Sure, I dozed off after getting Mira back to the car, but I wasn't out that long. My best guess is the vehicle turned up no more than a half hour after I called Arnie.'

'OK,' said Bezuidenhout. 'I'll dig around that and see what emerges. The roster sheets will tell me who was out and about at the relevant time.' He turned back to the gully. 'You reckon your gun's down there somewhere.'

I followed the inclination of his head. 'Somewhere,' I repeated. 'It kinda flew out of my hand when I was pushed over.'

We found the track and walked down to where the two police units had parked. There were three uniforms, two men and a woman. They saw us approach and straightened up, one of the guys replacing the cap on his head.

'Any update on Forensics?'

'About half and hour Captain,' said the woman consulting her watch.

'OK. You stay here and wait. Forensics is not to move in until I get back and do a briefing.' He turned to the men. 'You two are to search the gully below the road. You're looking for a Glock. I want it bagged as evidence. Start from the top and work down. It shouldn't be that difficult to find. Any questions?'

There weren't so the Captain and I moved off again and descended as far as the SUV. From a distance, it looked nondescript enough except all its doors were open.

I directed Bezuidenhout to the nearside and he looked into the face of the kidnapper behind the wheel. Daylight didn't make him any prettier but the shock I'd seen in his eyes had vanished as they were now glazed

'Where's the screwdriver she used?' said the captain.

'It fell down. It should be in the foot well.'

But it wasn't visible, so I crouched and peered in at seat level. For a better view, I had to get on my knees. 'It's wedged under the seat,' I said, after a moment. 'I can see the end of the handle. It could be tricky to recover.'

'I'll warn Forensics.'

Bezuidenhout gazed into the back but all he saw was a large wet bloodstain in one corner.

Following him round to the driver's side, I looked again at the figure slumped over the wheel. 'Was he carrying?'

I shook my head. 'He'd nothing in his hand when I saw him outside the house and there's no sign here.'

'Could be something in his waistband at the back.'

I shrugged. 'Maybe. They'll find out when they move the body.'

I led the captain away and we dropped down into the wide valley overlooking the shattered settlement. The single chimney was stark against the vault of the sky and was the only thing intact amongst the surrounding devastation.

'Do you know this place?' I asked.

Bezuidenhout admitted he didn't. 'Whatever it was, it hasn't been occupied in a very long time. The brickwork's at least a century old. And they don't make the tiles you see here.'

We passed through and dropped down the slope on the far side. I took in again the line of palms and beyond that the spot where Mueller had parked his car. Farther back was the house from which the kidnappers had emerged in the rain the previous night.

Mueller's body rested where it had fallen, the gun he'd drawn close by. His corpse lay cold and desolate in the early rays of the sun, but I was unmoved. It had been him or me and it wasn't like this was my first experience. For me, it had always been an occupational hazard. It went right back to the days, 20 years before, when I was employed as a guard by Frank's security company, Zap-It. After any incident of violent confrontation, it was easy to justify myself if I was mentally upbeat.

But when tested by feelings of being weak and alone, uncertainty would creep in. At those times, I could be undermined by guilt. These emotions often then triggered the flashbacks, the nightmares, and all those unpleasant physical side effects that came as part of the package. A SAPS psych assessment, carelessly left in view when I'd once applied to transfer to the Special Task Force, summed it up: '*Subject's tolerance to stress suspect. Evidence of underlying trauma. Reject.*'

'I wouldn't waste any regrets on him,' said Bezuidenhout breaking in on my thoughts. 'He got what was coming to him.'

'My guess is he has another ID,' I said. 'Maybe you'll get something on him this time round.'

Bezuidenhout looked askance. 'This time round?'

'This was the guy who drove me to the exchange. He was picked up afterwards. SAPS sweated him for days but got zilch.'

'Coetzee didn't tell me that. Maybe we'll find something on the body.'

'Or in the car,' I said. 'It looks like a rental, but I couldn't find the key. His Toyota's back in PE.'

'Thanks for the reminder. I'll have it picked up.'

While we'd been speaking, Bezuidenhout had been searching the ground but now he turned back to me. 'I can't see the other gun,' he said. 'Are you sure there was one?'

'I heard it drop.'

'OK. I'll flag it up, so it's not missed.'

That left the house. The tarp I'd seen was pulled over a single room at the front that would otherwise have been open to the elements. Beyond, as we drew near, I saw an interior door standing ajar. On the floor close by were two cans smelling of petrol. This suggested the kidnappers had been in the process of not only

65

vacating the place, but also setting it ablaze. But where had they been planning to take Mira?

Bezuidenhout stepped as far as the doorway and looked into the room. I saw an expression of revulsion etch itself onto his features. Then, muttering under his breath, he stood aside for me.

It was a large open-plan space with a kitchenette in one corner piled high with unwashed plates and crockery. Above, there was a begrimed window that allowed the morning sun to cast its rays in a solid rectangle of colour on the threadbare carpet. Two bedsteads stood off to one side each with a new mattress still in its plastic wrapping. On the other side were easy chairs and an ancient sofa. A large low table was covered in discarded food packaging and empty cans while carrier bags and a collection of boxes were scattered on the floor. The only source of lighting appeared to be from a couple of storm lamps whose illumination couldn't now match the strength of the rising sun.

But it was the scene visible through the open door at the back of the room that held my attention. Framed against a picture window, mostly covered by tacked-on sacking, was a single metal bed frame. A pair of handcuffs with the bracelets open rested on top of the headboard. It was evidently the means by which Mira had been secured, her arms stretched above her head, the rest of her body defenceless against whatever abuse her captors' imagination might deem diverting or entertaining. It was no wonder that when Mira had the opportunity she'd struck back with such desperate savagery.

I turned away and rejoined Bezuidenhout who was taking off his jacket. Together, we walked back silently to where the police units had parked. While we'd been away, more vehicles had arrived and from them a disparate group of men and women had emerged. It was they who would take responsibility for safeguarding evidence by taking photographs, dusting fingerprints, searching for DNA, and collecting exhibits.

The captain took me to one side. 'I need to keep your car,' he said. 'I want the slugs from the tyres, and we'll fingerprint everything.

Incidentally, you'd better have your dabs taken. After that I can arrange a lift back to PE.'

I thanked him and stuck out my hand.

Bezuidenhout took it and we shook. 'I'm grateful for your help,' he said. 'When could you give us a statement?'

'I'll be in touch in the next day or two.'

CHAPTER TWELVE

SAPS dropped me at Sunridge Park with all my stuff from the Fiesta after which I took a taxi to Seaview. Despite changing my clothes before getting into the police car, my appearance drew some curious looks as I waited to be picked up.

I don't remember the exact time of my arrival home, but the maid was in because the vacuum cleaner was in action. Dumping my bags in the hallway, I went into the living room. The floor-to-ceiling plate-glass windows with ocean views were great but I despised the pretentious Doric columns built into each corner at the back. Sight of them always reminded me of Julius Caesar's assassination; a memory dredged up from a production of the play at boarding school where they deigned to let me paint scenery.

I stood in admiration of the seascape for a minute or two oblivious to the vacuum cleaner's silence. It was only when I heard footsteps that my reverie was broken.

'Morning, Sol,' said the maid standing by the door to the passage. 'I was just . . .' Her voice died when I turned, and she took in my appearance.

'Hi Buhle,' I said. 'How you doing?'

'*I* was real fine. But seeing you I ain't sure no more. You look like you ran into a hippo with toothache. Maybe a couple of them.'

I laughed. I never quite knew how to take Buhle as she always spoke her mind. This characteristic had caused her problems when she was younger, but she was now of an age where her candour was usually viewed as harmless eccentricity. Or that was my take on it.

'No hippos,' I said, 'with or without toot
worry about me.'

'Ach, but I do. What you been up to, S
water kayaking? Cave diving?'

'Nothing so dangerous.'

'You're not gonna tell me it was som
shook my head. 'Whatever it was, it must
shindig.'

'That's one way of describing it.'

The maid gave up. 'All I can say is, I'n
here. I wouldn't have the energy to set the

But Buhle would have done that for m
That was how she was. I wished she could li
able maid's quarters a short distance from
sure me knowing she was close by, thoug
during one of my panic attacks.

Buhle offered to make me something, bu
ate to shower and wash away the sweat a
there'd be time to think about food.

I went through into the bathroom and
above the shaving mirror. Under the gla
nance looked sick and dispirited. Pouches
black as my matted hair and the muscles
with fatigue. One cheek was badly scratch
gash at the side of my neck. Discarding my
of bruising at the base of my sternum. Eve
of my skin, I discerned the bluish tint of
large welt.

I stripped off and walked into the shower
play over me for a long time. When I finally e
was of bed.

Sleeping for too long made me ravenous
then, Buhle had left for the day and the shac
lengthening. I snacked on *biltong* and gorg

grillers. After that, I made coffee and took it back to the
ɔm so I could dress.

ing something to Frank had been nagging me for a while. But
:t was I had no stomach for the task and so it got shelved for
st of the day. I'd talk to him the following morning.

when the new day came indecision still ruled. It wasn't helped
: fact that Bezuidenhout had been successful in peddling to
ess a line about a shoot-out between what were suspected to be
l rug gangs. Given it all happened a distance from PE itself,
ι the early hours, helped to minimise the news hounds' inter-
:sides, there was plenty of other serious crime to report. There
: is in the happy, carefree world of our Rainbow Nation.

ιe of this helped me as far as Frank was concerned. Sure, I
give him an account of what had occurred but at the end of it
ɔe no better off. He would still be in limbo not knowing
er he should ready a celebration or organize a wake.

er, I went to the SAPS station at Bethelsdorp and made a
s statement. It was a long and tedious process conducted by a
ıble whose slow wits were only outshone by the leaden pace at
he moved a pen across innumerable sheets of paper.

ιn, less than four hours after leaving the station, I was
ıoned back by someone whose manner on the phone was so
ı she didn't bother to volunteer her name.

my arrival, I was kept waiting 20 minutes before being
ed by a large guy wearing an olive-green, short-sleeved shirt.
ɔse to my feet, he planted himself so closely in front of me I
ιe opportunity of working out what he'd had for lunch.

ι Nemo?' he demanded.

ısn't in the best frame of mind as my guts were churning and
:art was pounding. Maybe it had something to do with the
ιons I received and the manner of its delivery. 'Who wants to
ɔ' I asked.

ι asking the questions.'

ζ, have it your own way. My name's Nemo.'

'I need to ask you some questions.'

'I deduced that from your earlier remark,' I said, wondering what was afoot.

But it wasn't that which he grabbed. Clamping powerful fingers in a vice-like grip on my upper arm, he propelled me along a corridor and into an interview room. 'Wait,' he said.

The door closed behind him, and I was left in a windowless space with a single table and a few unmatched chairs. As the minutes ticked by, my mouth dried up and I became breathless. To regain control, I focused on one part of the wall in front of me where there was a long and jagged crack. With my eyes fixed on it, I began to inhale slowly and deeply with one hand, the palm sweating, placed on my stomach.

It was in that attitude the guy found me when he returned. From his manner, it seemed he thought my behaviour denoted guilt in respect of some as yet unspecified offence. So it was, with a triumphant gesture, he thumped a heavy evidence bag onto the desk. 'What do you think of this?' he barked.

Even had my eyes not been fixed on the wall, I'd have refused to take any interest in the bag. 'Let's backtrack,' I said, my voice cracking from dryness in my throat. 'I'd like to know who I'm talking to.'

Very deliberately, the guy leant over me resting two hirsute arms on the tabletop. His face came in close to mine again, giving me another shot at identifying his stomach contents. 'I don't like smart-arses,' he said.

'Nor me,' I said. 'Particularly when they don't have the first idea as regards basic procedures.'

I thought the guy was going to hit me, but something brought him up short and instead he sat down opposite. But his was a lowering presence, so I drew back out of reach of fists the size of a grizzly's paws.

'What about this?' he said, inclining his eyes to the bag.

'What about your name?' I countered.

'Fourie. My name's Fourie.'

'Detective Services?'

'SAPS Reservist.'

'Uh-huh,' I said. For the first time, I looked down at the evidence bag which contained a gun. To be precise it was a Beretta Tomcat. 'I think you're going to ask me if that's my piece.'

'Is it?'

'I don't know. I'd have to compare the serial numbers with the licence I hold.'

'Don't bother,' said Fourie. 'We've already checked. This heater's registered to you.'

'Thanks. It was stolen several weeks ago. Where did you find it?'

'Did you report it missing?'

'No, I didn't.'

'Why was that?'

'I was taken off a beach by helicopter shortly after it was stolen. I'd been shot. I was in hospital for about three weeks. Where did you find it?'

'Is there anybody who can verify that?'

I showed my annoyance, but my dry mouth didn't help. 'A-Are you talking about the helicopter, being shot, or spending time in hospital?'

Fourie ignored that. 'Your gun was found in the house used by Mrs. Zarakolu's kidnappers. Your statement makes no mention of your having been inside.'

'It's not in the statement because it didn't happen.'

'So how do you explain your prints?'

'Obviously they were there from when the gun was originally stolen.'

'The prints are more recent than that.'

I was incredulous. 'Says who?'

'I've seen the fingerprint report.'

I looked at Fourie who clearly believed every word he was telling me. But belief isn't always truth and I try to keep abreast of developments as regards some of this techie stuff. 'Dating fingerprints is in its infancy,' I said. 'If memory serves, work's been done in the USA using an imaging mass spectrometer. It's hardly field kit. Samples analysed, I seem to recall, were single prints off polished surfaces. This isn't real world stuff. What exactly did the report say?'

The reservist's eyes slid away. 'It talked about a possibility,' he admitted.

'Somebody's flying a kite or making mischief,' I said, before a thought occurred to me. 'Captain Bezuidenhout doesn't know you're speaking to me, does he?'

Fourie started to look uncomfortable. 'No, he doesn't. The report's just come in. I happened to see it and . . .'

'You thought you'd use your initiative,' I interrupted, 'and have a few words informally. And that's what you've now done. Of course, if you think it's appropriate you should inform the captain of our discussion. I'm ready to answer further questions but there are no prints of mine in that house. In the meantime,' I went on, pointing to the evidence bag, 'I guess you'll want to keep this, but I'd now like my other gun back.'

That earned me a look as cold as a Siberian winter. But I got my Glock back and then I got outta there.

CHAPTER THIRTEEN

But I had no apology from him and no relief from my anxiety.

I went back to the Mustang and, after drinking some water, put a stick of gum in my mouth. The afternoon was fast advancing but the prospect of going home filled me with apprehension, the long hours stretching into a longer night.

I was fortunate though. Money gave me options and I began weighing the alternatives. As I worked through a short list a further possibility struck me and, on a whim, I found my cell and punched in a number. It rang several times before voice mail kicked in. But I didn't want to leave a message so tossed the instrument into the passenger seat.

Slowly, I warmed to the idea of a long and leisurely meal at the Coachman on the waterfront. I might have to wait to eat but it would be worth it as their Dover sole is unsurpassed. Maybe, I'd get lucky and have a table on the deck overlooking the ocean.

As I went to press Start, the screen on the phone lit up. I grabbed it and heard a voice say, 'Sol, *mon ami*. How very nice of you to call.'

'Hi Ayesha. It's been a while. How are you?'

'I'm well and enjoying all the good things this life brings.'

'I'm pleased for you. I was kinda wondering, Ayesha, if you're free for dinner tonight.'

'What time had you in mind?'

I looked at my watch and calculated rapidly. 'Would 8.30 suit?'

'That's fine but I'm on a plane to Cape Town in the morning. Where shall we meet?'

'There was that little place we went to a while back. It was near the Regent Hotel.'

'You mean Homer's Garden.'

'You're right. That's the one. You have a great memory, Ayesha.'

'And you are always so charming. *A bientot*, Sol.'

My date was 300 kms away in East London but I made good time and passed the Amalinda Nature Reserve at around 8.15. After making the loop at the Nahoon River Interchange, I went south on the R72 and drove towards the ocean. I pulled over close to the five-storey, sand-coloured elevations of the Regent Hotel. Appropriately, The Boss was singing *Human Touch* as I switched off.

Homer's Garden was in a thoroughfare nearby whose street entrance had bevelled glass panels. I walked through to a small courtyard where there were circular wrought-iron tables painted white and cane chairs with well-padded cushions. The back wall was almost obscured by a mass of purple bougainvillea.

Ayesha wasn't there but had sent a text to say she'd be a few minutes' late. I ordered an espresso and a bottle of still water before working through my other messages. There was nothing of significance except one from friends who said they'd like the chance to catch up. But there was no suggestion as to when and, with three children under five, I thought maybe they were being no more than polite.

I began composing a reply when Ayesha interrupted me, my first intimation of her arrival being the heavy scent filling the air.

'Hi Sol., may I sit down?'

Momentarily flustered, I rose awkwardly to my feet. 'Of course. Please . . .'

She silenced me by touching a finger to my lips, gave me an amused smile, and planted herself in a chair to one side of me. She placed a silver, clasp-lock clutch bag on the table close to her. It matched a strapless black dress that was tastefully etched with silver sequins at the hem.

I sat down and turned to face her.

She was statuesque, with long black hair, skin tones a few shades lighter than mine and expressive eyes the colour of amber. It was said, long before the birth of Jesus Christ, that amber originated as a liquid produced by the sun's rays. In Ayesha's eyes I recognised the same limpid quality.

'It's good to see you,' I said. 'It's been quite a while.'

She ignored my implied criticism and instead scanned my face. 'It's good to see you too, Sol. But *mon ami,* you seem to have been in the wars since last we met.'

The scratches on my cheek had faded somewhat but the gash on my neck remained unsightly. 'You know how it is,' I said, shrugging it off.

Catching the eye of the waitress, I ordered drinks and, because the place was busy, detained her while we also chose food.

After that, we settled back to talk though conversation with Ayesha always inclines to the one-sided. This is deliberate as she knows everyone loves to talk about themselves. 'What happened to you, Sol?' she persisted when the waitress left.

'Did you read about the high-profile kidnapping in PE a few weeks ago?'

'Kidnapping? -I'm not sure I remember.'

'It concerned a woman called Mira Zarakolou,' I said. 'An attempt to ransom her went wrong and the kidnappers escaped, even though SAPS had been tipped off.'

'OK,' said Ayesha slowly. 'And you were involved in this?'

I nodded grimly. 'Mira is Frank's wife.'

Ayesha's eyes widened. 'Ach, now I see the connection. I didn't recognize the name Zarakolu. Whenever you've talked about Frank, you've always referred to him only by his first name only. So, what happened?'

I'd explained the sequence of events by the time our food arrived. As Ayesha began eating a *vetkoek* filled with mince I said heavily, 'Personally, I think Mira's dead. There was a chance, but I blew it.'

Ayesha put down her knife and squeezed my hand. 'You don't know that,' she said. 'Besides, from what you told me, I don't see you had much choice about the way you reacted. You said the men who turned up were dressed as police. Shooting first and asking questions later wouldn't have been a great idea. Suppose they really had been SAPS?'

But I wasn't so easily appeased. 'I shouldn't have let the one guy get so close. I was distracted and he barrelled in. Maybe I'm getting slow in my old age.'

'You're always so hard on yourself,' she countered. 'My guess is you were exhausted. And the good guys were way too long getting there.' She smiled supportively. 'Come on Sol,' she added. 'I didn't come here to eat on my own.'

I looked at my food and without enthusiasm began forking it into my mouth.

'Have you spoken to Frank yet?' asked Ayesha a few moments later.

'N-No, I haven't.' With an effort, I organised my thoughts. 'I don't know what to say. Sure, I can explain what happened but that resolves nothing. He's simply left in limbo and in his state of health that's unhelpful. I wanted to sort this, but I can't.'

Ayesha turned those limpid eyes of hers upon me. 'Don't beat yourself up,' she said. 'You've done more than anybody else would have done. Way more.'

I made to interrupt, but a look silenced me. 'I know what this is about,' she said firmly. 'You see this as a means to repay the debt you think you owe him. But I doubt he sees it the same way. Remember, he never had children. You being around all these years has been something he probably wouldn't have had otherwise. Relationships are a two-way street, Sol.'

'I understand that. But what I owe Frank isn't something that can ever be repaid.'

Ayesha took that under advisement but only for a moment. 'I know why you think like that,' she said softly.

I was taken aback. 'You know?'

'Yes, I do.'

'Ayesha, I haven't spoken to anybody about this for ... Well, forever. What did I say? And when?'

'It was a couple of years ago. It was very late one night. You got rather emotional, and it all spilled out.'

'I don't recall.'

Ayesha laughed. 'Well, you'd had rather too much to drink and when you didn't bring the subject up the next day, I saw no point revisiting it.'

'But what did I tell you?'

'Does it serve some purpose to dredge this stuff up?'

'I guess not,' I admitted. 'But we've known each other a long time. I suppose I'm curious.'

Ayesha pushed her empty plate away and took a sip of wine. 'The way you told it,' she began quietly holding my gaze, 'you were 18, maybe 19 years of age. You left school after matric and went to university in PE. But things went wrong for you. Badly wrong. Boarding school at least gave you some framework you told me, but in PE you had nothing. You said you went to pieces. There were problems with drink and drugs. It all led to you trying to jump off a bridge. It was lucky Frank happened by and found you. But he did more than that. He took you in and straightened you out. After that he gave you a job in his company. Eventually, you went back to university.'

Throughout her account, Ayesha's tone had been as lacking in emotion as a coroner's report. Maybe that was the reason I struggled to accept that her words related to me. And, because of the intervening years, they were from a time with which I no longer felt any connection. The child is father of the man though and resonances from the past frequently haunt me.

When I offered no reply to what Ayesha had told me, she added quietly, 'Your memories must be painful.'

'Actually,' I said, 'I have no specific recollections at all. Frank said I was completely out of it when he came upon me that night.'

Ayesha squeezed my hand again and gave me a big smile. 'Do you think you could eat dessert?'

I looked at my neglected dinner and decided food wasn't an overriding priority. 'I've got a better idea,' I said. 'Maybe you've something just as sweet back home.'

Ayesha's place lay close to Nahoon Beach and the Mercedes-Benz Pro Driving Range.

I woke up there at about six the following morning. Ayesha though was gone as I suddenly missed the warmth of her naked body against mine. But her absence was explained when I heard sounds from the kitchen. I put my pants on and padded down the stairs to find her.

She was standing by the central breakfast bar in a man's blue shirt and holding a glass of fruit juice. She had loafers on her feet but her long brown legs were bare.

'How did you sleep?' she asked with a grin.

I yawned and stretched. 'I slept very well,' I said. 'In fact, I haven't slept so well since the last time I was here.'

'That's good. What do you want to eat?'

I helped her fix breakfast and together we took our plates out onto the deck with its view over her small but immaculate garden. An ibis strutted its stuff on the well-watered lawn, occasionally casting a wary eye in our direction.

We were sharing a cafetiere when she said, 'Maybe, Sol, we could spend more time together. It's always like we're ships passing in the night.' She turned towards me, and her amber eyes were so deep and limpid I could have drowned. 'You know I'm very fond of you, don't you?' She took one of my hands in hers.

'I know,' I said automatically.

But the fact was I didn't know. Just as I didn't really understand what she did for a living. Ostensibly, she was the in-country marketing executive for a French perfumery company and often flew out of East London to Cape Town and to Jo-burg/ Pretoria. It meant she was away much of the time and as a consequence our meeting up was infrequent. Suggestions I'd made in the past about getting together elsewhere than in East London had always been politely but firmly rebuffed as impractical given her work commitments. Nor would she have been able to accommodate me, she said, as she was occupying company lets in the cities she visited, and her employers were unsympathetic in matters regarding her personal life. The justification for this was that she was very well paid for committing herself body and soul to their commercial interests. Of course, I accept that South Africa isn't exactly a place where many employees have a whole lot of bargaining power given our ongoing economic woes. Even so, some of what she told me I found difficult to credit, but then my background had never been in the corporate world.

All in all, what she was now telling me was a significant departure from the *status quo*. On that basis, I had to wonder at the reason for it. The most obvious one that sprang to mind was my dramatic change of fortune as a result of my inheritance. That had moved the dial in terms of what I could afford from being part of the McDonald's and Coke hoi-polloi to membership of the Dom Perignon and Beluga caviar set. It was irrelevant that I neither liked champagne nor salt-cured roe, but it was highly relevant to the way Ayesha saw life generally. She liked the good things and her house, and the F-TYPE Jaguar parked in her double garage were evidence of that.

This left me in Catch-22. She was everything any man might dream of. No, let me rephrase that. She was everything this man might dream of. But could she be trusted?

The answer was that I wasn't sure. And that was despite having known her ever since she'd had some hassle with a guy who'd been stalking her. That had been back in the days when I was with SAPS on a temporary secondment to East London. Warning the guy off, even though it hadn't been done in any official capacity, had been easy. It had required a robust, no-nonsense approach that I found simple to execute. It was some of the other stuff regarding relationships I struggled with.

'Spending more time together would be great,' I agreed with her. 'Perhaps I could come here for a few days, or you could come over to PE. What do you think?'

'I've never seen your place in Seaview. I'd like to visit.'

'When are you back from Cape Town?'

'Should be no more than three days.' Ayesha glanced at her watch and winced. 'Wow, is that the time? I'm on a flight in less than two hours.'

I drove her to the Airport via the Biko Bridge and walked with her into the terminal building. I hung around while she checked-in which took an age.

'I hate goodbyes,' she said when she was done, reaching up and kissing me.

'Me too,' I said, already feeling the icy sensation of incipient abandonment.

'You'll call me soon, won't you?'

'I will.'

'Bientot amant.'

'*A bientot*, Ayesha.'

I watched her walk away. Her black hair, gathered up on top of her head, matched the sobriety of her trouser suit and pumps, the only compromise being the flashes of red and blue in the neck scarf she was wearing. Her get-up made her look every inch the part of a marketing executive from a French perfumery company but was it just a brilliant disguise? For the first time, I was left wondering about what she might really be up to.

CHAPTER FOURTEEN

I took the slow road to PE so I could stop at Port Alfred. On arrival, I made for the clapboard, Cape Cod style Halyards Hotel. It has views over the Royal Alfred Marina and promotes itself as being casual in style. That suited me as I thought the place ideal for a casual acquaintanceship with coffee and cake.

I found a spot at a table overlooking the water and hoisted my feet onto the chair opposite. Behind me there were splashes and shrieks from the glassed-in, outdoor swimming pool. With the tang of the sea in my nostrils, I gazed across the tidal lagoon and man-made islands in the Kowie River. I'd thought of buying property there because it was so pretty, but the houses were too large and were often occupied by holidaymakers or retirees. More than that, when I found out that boats and boating were a constant topic of conversation, another reason for not proceeding presented itself. Boating to my mind has but two red-letter days: the one when you get a boat and the one when, with jaw-sagging relief, you get shot of it.

I started on a slice of chocolate cake ruminatively, my thoughts turning back to Ayesha before they seamlessly and inevitably tuned in to the subject of my money.

The inheritance I received from my father changed my landscape out of all recognition. After the estate agents, land surveyors and bean counters had sucked their pencils, scratched their heads and dismissed some flights of fancy, the overall figure they arrived at was a value of 800 million bucks, give or take. This sounds like a lot of money particularly when expressed in Rand which, in international currency terms, has about as much resilience as a rice pudding skin. Translate it into US dollars or Euros and the numbers are ones you can get your head round. Just. But in whatever currency, the size of my inheritance was beyond the dreams of avarice as far as I was concerned.

The guilt set in quickly. Not so quickly that I didn't go mad for a while with extravagant trips and holidays worldwide; the purchase of timeshares in property in PE and elsewhere; the frequent buying and selling of sports cars; and some dabbling in both the art and stock markets. Then there were the watches from the likes of Chopard, Hublot, and Omega; the gold and silver bracelets from Cartier; the flying lessons; the clothes from Versace, Gucci, Armani, Prada *et al*; and those expensive, and ultimately unused, club memberships in Cape Town and Jo-burg.

But then it dawned: what the fuck had I been I thinking? -After all, a very expensive education had left me well attuned to the musings of philosophers like Rousseau, Locke and Hobbes on the subjects of equality and justice, the rights of man, and not forgetting either the Christian precepts of humility and service.

Hell, you don't have to look far to find grinding poverty and mind-numbing deprivation writ large within the borders of our Rainbow Nation. Every settlement of any size usually has its shanty town or location where ramshackle dwellings, thrown up with whatever material is to hand, exist almost within walking distance of the preserves of the uber-wealthy. Lack of employment, lack of education and lack of means breeds every form of vice including a murder rate which deprives 50 people of their lives every day of the year. The disingenuous or self-deluded will tell you it's no different elsewhere and, for instance, the murder rate in the RSA is no higher than that in the USA. This is true but conveniently ignores the fact that America has a population six times larger than ours.

Giving away most of my inheritance wasn't difficult. I chose ten charities with care, informed their either startled or bemused trustees what I wanted to do, and after that set the wheels in motion. Of

83

course, much of what I inherited wasn't in cash form. There were two game parks, several farms, and portfolios of residential and commercial property in all the major centres of the country. There were investments in stocks and bonds, shareholdings in private companies, and even an incubator fund which provided seed capital to start-up enterprises. To superintend all this, I hired firms of accountants and lawyers with sufficient geographic reach to be able to do the work required. Beyond that, I left them to get on with it. It took months and there were some issues along the way but at last it was all done, and I walked away with sufficient means to ensure I would never have to worry about paying the bills again.

But my new-found wealth couldn't fail to resonate with somebody like Ayesha. It was a route by which she could escape her workaday existence and aspire to a life which would give her security and comfort. I couldn't criticize her for that given what she'd told me in the past about her upbringing.

My problem was that I wasn't good on trust particularly regarding my willingness to trust women. According to the psychiatrists, this was because the loss of my mother at an early age had imbued in me a degree of cynicism. I wasn't qualified to comment on this, but my profound sense of insecurity pointed to where the truth lay.

Resolving how I felt about Ayesha wasn't going to happen quickly. Indeed, it might take a while longer than the guys out on the water in front of me who were attempting to cut something fouling their boat's propeller. They were using a blade on an extension handle and were making heavy weather of it. I doubted this was an example of synchronicity, but I was prepared to accept it was proof positive of the foolishness of being a member of the boating fraternity.

I finished my cake, drained my coffee and left.

It wasn't yet noon, but the interior of the Mustang was oven hot from a baking in the sun. I dialled the lowest setting for the air-con and pressed Start. I was rewarded with the usual burble from the V8 which increased in volume when the throttle was blipped. I like tapping the accelerator, though not in any showy sort of way, but just enough to let you know I'm around. I was about to pull out of the car park when my cell sang out.

'Hi,' I said.

'Mr. Nemo?'

'Speaking.'

'It's Bezuidenhout.'

'Hi Captain. How are you?'

Bezuidenhout ignored me. 'We have a development, Mr. Nemo. I've been asked to call by Colonel Ndosi. He sends his compliments and . . .'

'Ndosi? -Compliments? -What are you talking about?'

'A body's been found,' Bezuidenhout ploughed on. 'We believe it's Mrs. Zarakolu. Given the current state of her husband's health, the Colonel and I agreed we'd ask you to make the initial identification.'

So distracted had I been by Ayesha, I'd not given Frank a thought since the previous night's discussion. Now the issue was back staring me in the face, along with a multitude of feelings and emotions. 'Of course,' I said, my mouth suddenly dry. 'I can be back in PE in a couple of hours.'

'May I ask where you are?'

'Port Alfred.'

'I see. Colonel Ndosi assumed you'd be in PE. On that basis he said to tell you he can send a car.'

'Why would Ndosi assume anything about where I am?' I asked irritably. 'And I don't need a car to take me to the morgue.'

'The body's not in PE. It's on the far side of Mossel Bay.'

I was taken aback. 'That's five hours plus by road.'

'Hence the offer to send a car.'

'I have transport,' I said. 'What's the timeline?'

'Colonel Ndosi's already left. He'd appreciate it if you could join him ASAP.'

This all sounded very hands-on for the Ndosi I knew who'd spent his time during my service endlessly pontificating regarding a wide variety of trivia in the belief this amounted to frontline policing. He held the rank of Station Commander, but it was my opinion, derived after much focused deliberation, that he was incapable of locating the source of his own farts. 'Why's Ndosi gone personally?' I asked.

'There are jurisdictional issues with the Western Cape,' said Bezuidenhout. 'A positive ID from you will hopefully sort those out. We can then recover the body and . . .'

'Recover?' I interrupted.

'My understanding is the body's at a game park. There are some complications over retrieving it. That's all I know.'

'OK,' I said. 'I guess I'll meet you there.'

'Unfortunately, not. I've too much to do here. Maybe we can catch up when you get back.'

'That would be good. By the way, I'd appreciate the return of my Tomcat.'

As to this suggestion, Bezuidenhout made no comment and confined himself to giving me the game park's co-ordinates. I fed these into the sat-nav and rang off.

After that, I filled the tank and bought food and drink for the trip before heading for Grahamstown and the N2.

CHAPTER FIFTEEN

It's one thing to blast along empty highways in the dead of night but quite another to undertake the same trips by day. There were baboons playing tag in the road near Clarkson and traffic cops enforcing speed limits on the far side of Knysna, amongst other things. All told, I lost more than an hour and so reached my destination after five o'clock.

Bezuidenhout had told me to avoid the road to the main house and take a track on the right. Apparently, it was marked Feed Stores and I should follow it for 200 metres to a fence that was at the western extremity of the Reserve. Terrific, except he didn't know the area and was conveying instructions already made cockeyed by two or three retellings.

I drove a sunken trail for half a kilometre with the dust thrown up fashioning a curtain behind me in the hot still air. Apart from a few bucks in the distance and a hyena close by which lifted its head and stared balefully, I had the landscape to myself.

A distance on, the trail forked but there was no indication which way to go. One track though had a better claim by reason of wear, so I took it.

It was the wrong choice for it became deeply rutted and I feared for the Mustang's sump. I turned the car with difficulty and went back. This time I chose the road less travelled, and it did make all the difference. Rounding a rocky shoulder, a couple of minutes later, I saw a chain-link fence, a metal gate, and a SAPS *bakkie*.

The vehicle was parked sideways on and the young cop inside was smoking a cigarette. He didn't get out but raised a limp hand in an excuse for a greeting.

I understood why when I left the Mustang. The heat hit me like a slap from a hot towel. It must have been over 40 degrees and in the hollow where I stopped there wasn't a breath of air. I stretched and walked stiffly towards the police vehicle lifting my shades onto the top of my head. The intensity of the sun though was blinding and made me knuckle tired eyes.

'Man, you're way off the right road,' called the cop. 'Main house is north of here.' He looked across to the Mustang, its blue paint mostly hidden by a thick veil of dust. 'I reckon you'll get it in the neck when they see the state of it.'

'I'm not delivering,' I said. 'I'm looking for . . .'

'You mean the rig's yours?' the cop interrupted.

'Yeah, I . . .'

'You must be one rich dude.'

I hadn't time for this. 'I'm looking for Colonel Ndosi,' I said pointedly.

The cop stepped out of the *bakkie*, ground out his cigarette, and strolled across to me. His blue shirt was ringed with sweat under the armpits and there were beads of moisture on his forehead. 'Who's asking?' he said.

'My name's Nemo.'

'You expected?'

'I've come from Port Alfred. You can reckon I'm expected.'

'Got any ID?'

I fumbled in the back pocket of my shorts and gave him my driving licence. The guy stared at it for all of two seconds.

'Wait,' he said abruptly before walking to the vehicle. As I rummaged in the boot for fresh water, I heard him call in. The next thing I heard was his voice saying to me, 'They don't know no Ndosi.'

In the act of taking a swig of water, I lowered the bottle. 'Ndosi is

SAPS Eastern Cape. Tall bastard with hard eyes and a superior look. Please ask again.'

I listened to more backwards and forwards on the radio, but I didn't understand the Xhosa he was speaking. Eventually the interchange ended, and the cop gave me a smile. 'They found Ndosi,' he said. 'Arsehole, is he?'

'Grade A,' I said.

I followed the cop's directions which meant another half kilometre throwing up dirt along a track that ran in a semi-circle past a wood. My passage disturbed a fish eagle that took off and flapped its wings a couple of times as it sought to distance itself from my dust cloud. Beyond the trees, in a flat area of baked scrub, I spotted several uniformed and plain-clothes police standing around vehicles drawn up in a protective screen. Among them were a couple of unmarked white SUVs. But my attention was grabbed by a guy sat cradling a rifle on one of the roofs. His attention was focused on something away to my right. I looked in the same direction but, from behind the Mustang's wheel, saw nothing.

I pulled up and shoved the gear lever into Park. Blipping the throttle a couple of times, before hitting the Stop button, caused the doors of one of the SUVs to open. It disgorged four men in white shirts and blue ties. They looked reluctant to give up the cool of the air-conditioned interior and to step out into the fierce heat of the sun. One of them detached himself from the party and strode towards me.

Easily identifiable, I recognized the lanky figure of Lt-Colonel Ndosi. As his body language was stiff and unfriendly, I matched mine to suit the occasion. It wasn't difficult as, had the invitation from him been in respect of anyone else but Frank's wife, I'd have declined it summarily.

'You got here, Solo,' he said.

'As you see,' I retorted. My dislike of him was deep-rooted and an element of that was he was one of the few people who'd ever called me Solo. I was convinced he'd always done it to make me feel like an outsider, some lonely guy who went his own way and wouldn't play the game.

'I was told you made out,' Ndosi said, casting his eyes in the direction of the Mustang. 'Must be nearly a million bucks' worth. Assuming it's paid for.'

'There was change,' I said. 'Look, I've come a long way so how's about we cut to the chase.'

Ndosi didn't like that, and his black eyes flashed. Maybe I shouldn't have been surprised by this behaviour from a man who'd tell you with a straight face he was directly related to Shaka, the Zulu monarch. Only my information was Shaka had no known or recognised issue, a fact I'd pointed out in company on one occasion.

'Come with me,' the Colonel said.

He moved off and I followed but one of the men Ndosi had been with in the SUV broke off a conversation and approached. He was a big man running to fat, his saving grace being avuncular features.

'Colonel, I'd be grateful if you'd introduce me,' the stranger said.

Ndosi stopped and turned back to me. He tried to smile, but he didn't try very hard. 'Solo, this is Brigadier Joubert representing SAPS Western Cape. Brigadier, my former colleague, Solomon Nemo, who left us a while back to take up new challenges.'

If I'd wanted to say anything to counter this travesty of the truth, I didn't get the chance because Joubert darted forward and extended one paw of a hand. 'I'm pleased to make your acquaintance, Mr. Nemo,' he said. 'Colonel Ndosi tells me you've come across from PE to help us. That's very public-spirited of you.'

'It's not a problem,' I said. 'I've a strong personal interest as Ndosi here may have explained.'

I'd no idea what the Colonel had explained but I caught a look from him as sharp as a stiletto. That was because I'd failed to use his rank when referring to him. He'd always been a tad precious about stuff like that.

Joubert placed a fatherly hand on my shoulder. 'I'll take you over in a moment,' he began, indicating an area on the far side of the screen provided by the vehicles. 'But first let me explain what we have here. Over there is a crocodile pool. Apparently, it's part of the safari experience this place offers. A body's been thrown into the pool. In fact, it's landed on a small island rather than in the water. For the moment it's marooned there. As you may imagine, it's an unattractive sight.' He looked at me sympathetically. 'You OK with this?'

I said I was OK with this and so the three of us walked between the parked vehicles to the far side. The guy with the rifle sitting on the roof of a police vehicle was as watchful as before.

The pool was perhaps 60 metres in length and maybe half as wide. It was surrounded by a waist-high, chain-link barrier. The banks were shallow earth and a horizontal fence of barbed wire, strung between closely spaced metal stakes driven into it, was designed to keep the crocs from climbing out. Even under the early evening sun, the water was opaque, its colours ranging from dark brown to olive green. It wasn't all water though as there were several islets supporting no more than scrub and thorn bushes. It was on one of these, at the far end, that I noticed an incongruity. It was a difference in colour that drew attention to something that wouldn't normally be there.

'We'll go to the other end,' said Joubert. 'You'll be able to get a better view.'

We walked abreast with the chain-link fence on the right. The pool seemed devoid of life until suddenly I saw an ugly snout and a pair of eyes break the surface. Seconds later, the croc was gone, a swirl in the water being all that marked its passage.

The body was on an islet at sufficient distance from the bank to make retrieval problematic. It was lying face down and suspended about a metre and a half from the ground, support being provided by a thorn bush into which it had been thrown. The head with matted black hair was turned towards the bank and the side of the face was burned a livid red through exposure to the sun. The bare arms and legs were in the same state.

I'd no idea what my reaction to this sight would be. In my experience what makes death horrific is where a corpse looks lifelike. I thought of the baby I'd once seen who suffered a cot death or the young guy who'd come home from work, sat in an armchair, and died without uttering a sound.

It wasn't like that here. What I observed looked like a shop-window mannequin after some catastrophe like a fire or flood. Sure, there was human shape but nothing which gave it human characteristics or personality.

'Well?' asked Ndosi impatiently, breaking into my thoughts.

I turned and faced the two of them. 'It's Mira,' I said flatly.

'Are you sure?' This time it was Joubert who spoke.

I nodded. 'I just about recognize her face but there are other things. The height and build are right. She's wearing the same clothes as on the night I found her. Those were heavily bloodstained as these are here.' I paused and then added with my arm outstretched, 'You see the silver bracelet with the charm on her left wrist? -She told me it was a gift from a favourite aunt when she completed matric. It's not been taken as it had no value, except as a keepsake.'

'OK,' said Joubert. 'That's good enough for me,' He looked at Ndosi. 'Once we've recovered the body, we'll authorize its release to Eastern Cape. I'm sure we can help by providing transportation to PE.'

'That's most kind of you Brigadier,' said Ndosi with a suitably servile expression on his face.

'Why's the recovery's taking so long?' I asked.

'That's hardly any of your business,' snapped Ndosi.

'No, no Colonel,' said the Brigadier. 'I'm happy to explain the situation to Mr. Nemo. After all, he's made a considerable effort to assist us.' Joubert turned to me. 'At the moment, there's a stand-off with the safari park owners,' he began. 'Apparently, there are 14 crocodiles in this pool. I don't have to explain how dangerous they are. Anyway, when some of my men arrived this morning, they had to shoot one of them to keep the rest from taking too close an interest in the body. The park's owners weren't pleased and instructed . . .'

'What the hell were you expected to do?' I interrupted.

Joubert gave me a small smile. 'That apparently is my problem, as I was told in no uncertain terms. Now, we've got SAPS lawyers talking to some smart-arse lip in Cape Town who's threatening everything from mounting a private prosecution under the Animals Protection Act to instituting a claim against SAPS for loss of business profits. You know what lawyers are like. They might get something sorted out between them by next Mandela Day, but I wouldn't bet the farm on it.'

'So how does this play out?'

'I'm not prepared to attempt a recovery unless I can protect the men doing it. As far as I'm concerned that means shooting any croc that looks like a threat. But that . . .'

Joubert suddenly broke off as something grabbed his attention. I followed his gaze and saw the water eddy within a short distance of where Mira lay. After that, a few air bubbles broke the surface of the pool.

'You there,' the Brigadier shouted to the constable sitting with the rifle. 'Keep a sharp eye out. You see a crocodile close to, you fire. Do you understand?'

'Yessah.'

Joubert turned back to me. 'Earlier today, I contacted the Air Wing,' he said. 'Mrs. Zarakolu will be retrieved by a helicopter fitted with a winch. But restoring the dignity of the dead can't be allowed to jeopardise the urgent needs of the living. My advice is the recovery will now take place at sun-up tomorrow. Overnight, we'll light the pool and post snipers. In the circumstances, it's . . .'

'Brigadier?' called a voice. We looked up in unison to see a figure striding towards us. It was one of the two other men I'd originally seen in the white SUV. 'I've got the General on the radio, sir,' he said as he neared us, a little out of breath. 'He'd like a few words with you about the equipment budget.'

'Did he say anything about getting another helicopter?' asked Joubert.

'Sir?'

'Forget it.' The Brigadier turned to me and smiled. 'I have to go, but I'm most grateful for your assistance.' With that, he extended his paw again and we shook. 'I'm sure Ndosi will walk you back to your car.'

But Ndosi had other ideas and waited only until the Brigadier was out of earshot. 'We're done,' he said abruptly.

'Not quite,' I said. 'There's the matter of the guys who jumped me that night.'

'What about them?'

'But for them, I don't think we'd be having this chinwag.'

'What's your point?'

'Eastern Cape's got bent cops.'

'Says you. What you fail to realize is we've got criminals impersonating cops. It's a problem all over the country.'

'So these guys just happened by,' I exclaimed, 'and thought they'd grab themselves a kidnap victim? Whether or not they were SAPS, they sure as hell knew where to find me. You need to check who knew what and when on the night.'

'Screw you!' hissed Ndosi. 'The days are long gone since I'm prepared to put up with your crap.'

'Come on man, you're not making any sense,' I said. 'The wife of a very good friend of mine is dead. Do you seriously think that's the end of it? Do you think I'm going to let this ride? Frankly, I don't envy you explaining why your personal animosity got in the way of your professional judgment.'

'Are you threatening me?'

'You can read it anyway you like, Ndosi,' I yelled. 'You do nothing about what you've been told, and I'll bury you. In my book, you look like you could be an accessory after the fact. Whether that's because of negligence or incompetence will be for others to decide.'

With that, I turned on my heel and walked away, ignoring the shocked looks my outburst had caused. I was shaking with anger and my heart was racing.

I wanted to be away from the safari park fast but, in my haste, mashed the accelerator sending the Mustang into a long skid that kicked up as much dust as a herd of rampaging elephants.

Two minutes after that, I pulled up and almost fell out of the car. It seemed that whatever I thought horrific about death would have to be reassessed. Mira's body may have looked like that of a mannequin but the indignity of its display, the violence she had suffered, and my failure to save her all conspired to make me violently sick.

CHAPTER SIXTEEN

It hadn't been my intention to stop for the night but, as I slowed to a crawl over the White Bridge at Knysna, I reconsidered. On the far side, where the road ran at the side of the Estuary, there was a minor shunt involving several cars. The accident had been sufficient to block the highway heading east. In the fading light, I looked across the water to the lights of Belvidere Village. When I was still looking at them several minutes later, my decision to stop was easy.

As soon as the opportunity presented itself, I pulled off the road, drove a little way and drew up outside a lodge with letting rooms. Three weeks before, at the height of the holiday season, you wouldn't have been able to rent a broom cupboard, even if your name had been the late lamented Desmond Tutu. Now it wasn't difficult to visualise tumbleweed blowing across the wood-panelled reception area with its collection of bronzes, including a giraffe standing four metres tall by the main staircase.

They gave me a double room as a courtesy upgrade with a bed large enough to satisfy the appetites of an energetic polygamist and a balcony sufficient to seat a brass band. Actually, I felt lost in all that space so hastened to shower and change before making my way to the restaurant.

In deference to a stomach that still felt sensitive, I ate chicken with rice and some well-cooked vegetables. In one corner of the otherwise empty eatery, an elderly white couple loudly conversed in Afrikaans about the communist influences at work in government, this all being part of a conspiracy fomented by worldwide Jewry.

Sidelong glances in my direction seemed to have me taped as bearing some personal responsibility for this situation. It crossed my mind to pander to their prejudice by explaining I was related to Leon Trotsky. After all, he was a Jewish communist later exiled to Mexico who might perhaps have had a fling with a local girl and that would explain, three or four generations on, the coffee colour of my skin. But, as quickly as it entered my head, I dismissed the prank unconvinced they'd have any idea what I was talking about.

Depressed, I crossed to the bar, bought a bottle of brandy and took it up to my room. There was Coke in the mini-bar, and I took it with the liquor and a glass out onto the balcony.

I sat for a long while with only the sound of the cicadas in a nearby stand of trees to keep me company. Drinking steadily, all the stuff that had been spinning in my head gradually mattered less and less. Not Mira's murder, not the desolation Frank would experience, not my issues with Ayesha, and not my past. Particularly not my past. None of it registered anymore. It was like I was scanning story lines from somebody else's life because I was standing outside it all. Ultimately, I was relieved to be able to float away into time and space and make of myself an island fortress.

CHAPTER SEVENTEEN

Breakfast consisted of aspirin and plenty of water followed by a pot of black coffee and dried toast. Brandy may be good for settling the stomach, but it's not recommended for a clear head the following day. I should have drunk vodka.

I drove back to PE slowly. At two in the afternoon, I stopped at the halt by the Storms River Bridge and ate a cooked breakfast at Mugg and Bean followed by a cappuccino and chocolate cake. M&B make the best coffee in SA and their gateaux aren't a long way behind.

My speed hardly picked up as I continued my journey east. Dreading even the prospect of a discussion with Frank, the churning in my stomach and the pounding of my heart increased the closer I drew to home.

Once back in the City, I took a route via Circular Drive to Buffelsfontein Road along the southern fringe of Lovemore Heights. Frank's house was situated close to the reservoir and 19th century cemetery. His may not have been the biggest property in the area but to my mind it had the best views. At night, you looked down upon illuminations stretching into the far distance and if it was windy the lights seemed to dance like fireflies at play. I knew because it was my home for several years after my crack-up.

I parked the dusty and travel-stained Mustang on the steep driveway and walked up a flight of steps to the portico. Below me, an expanse of lawn swept round a large circular flowerbed and down as far as a dry-stone wall running parallel to the roadway. Security in this part of the City didn't reflect the prudence or paranoia, take your pick, observable elsewhere. In those locations, walled compounds topped with electrified wire or spikes weren't an unusual sight.

I rang the doorbell not knowing what to expect. I'd deliberated whether to ring Frank in advance of my visit but decided against. It only meant telling him of Mira's death by phone and that wasn't acceptable. I figured if he wasn't at the house, he might be at Zap-It's offices in Springfield. If it was necessary to go there, so be it. It wasn't as though I had anything more pressing to do.

Whoever was coming to answer the bell took an age about it. I heard tapping on the tiled floor inside and for a while it seemed to get no closer.

When, at last, the heavy door did open it revealed Frank's sister and with her appearance an explanation for the tapping. Isabelle used a walking stick because of a riding accident in her youth. I'd not set eyes on her for years and was now surprised to see her as she lived way up in the Transvaal.

'Hullo,' I said dully.

Isabelle first looked at me uncomprehendingly and then beamed. 'Solomon,' she said. 'We were expecting you to be in touch. But we didn't know when. Why didn't you ring?'

I ignored her question. 'If Frank's here, I need to see him.'

My tone caused the smile to flee from her face. 'Come in,' she said.

I moved past her, watched as she closed the door and then followed her across the reception hall. She took me into a room at the side of the house. 'Frank's out back by the pool,' she said. 'He won't have heard the doorbell.'

'I know,' I said, remembering the times when using my phone was the only way to get in having forgotten my house key.

'Frank hoped you might have been in touch before now.'

'I've been pretty busy,' I said without conviction. 'And there wasn't much to be said.'

'And now that's changed?'

99

Struggling to get the words out of my mouth, I managed to say, 'It's all changed.'

Isabelle grasped my arm and turned her face up to mine. 'Frank knows Mira's dead.'

'Knows!' I was taken aback. 'H-How does he know?'

Isabelle wasn't listening. 'She *is* dead, isn't she? I can see it in your eyes. And in the exhaustion in your face.'

I repeated myself. 'How does Frank know?'

Isabelle gave me a motherly look. 'He knows in the way something like that creeps up on you and settles in your heart,' she said quietly. 'He was talking to me a couple of nights ago and saying he thought she was gone. What happened, Solomon?'

I explained it to her in a few short sentences. By then we were sitting in a couple of carvers at the dining table. The room was one that had been rarely used in my day and it had the same air of neglect about it now.

Isabelle heard me out. 'If you take my advice,' she said, 'keep it simple when you tell him. Saying how close you came to her rescue isn't going to help anything.'

'That's good advice,' I conceded. 'How is he at the moment?'

'He's tired,' she said. 'Very tired. I've been here for the last few days to help out. And to keep an eye on him. His business though isn't bothered about constantly worrying him. He's supposed to be recuperating but there are lots of calls and he insists on taking all of them.'

'Frank always was hands-on,' I said. 'Maybe the distractions have been good for him.'

'I see that, but I'd like him to come home with me for a while. It'll be a change of scene for him.'

'What does Frank feel about it?'

'I think he'll need some persuading. Can you help me with that?'

'I can try.'

*   *   *

100

Isabelle asked if I wanted her with me when the news was broken but I declined. So, as she went back to the kitchen to prepare an evening meal, I made my way to the pool room. The table was still there recalling nights spent with Frank in the old days. Neither of us had been any good with a cue but that hadn't stopped us sharing some memorable times.

Sliding doors from the room led outside to an area enclosed on three sides by the house. At the centre was a small swimming pool with a mosaic surround composed of silver and gold chips arranged in alternating geometric patterns. Close by stood a magnificent palm that topped the roof line. The fourth side of the area was open and faced south. It was from this vantage point that the views over PE were to be had.

Frank was lying on a lounger facing the sun. His chest was bare exposing a mat of grey hair, shaggy as a dog's, and, on his head, he wore a navy-blue cap with the word Chief picked out in yellow thread above the peak. A pair of reflective shades protected his eyes and in one hand he held a large cigar that streamed smoke into the lifeless air.

I stood irresolute for a moment by the doors with only the gurgling from the filtration system to disturb my thoughts. Idly, I watched the crawler make its slow progress along the bottom of the pool. It was an image of tranquility I hated to shatter. Whatever premonitions Frank had about Mira, I was to be the messenger of death. Selfishly, I wondered whether it might affect our friendship. Precedents from Sophocles onwards told me there was some risk.

I moved with leaden steps towards him and tried to call out but found my voice reduced to a croak. On a table, pushed against one wall, there were bottles of mixers. Grabbing one at random, I unscrewed the top and took a long pull before realizing it was soda. Discarding it, I substituted a bottle of water.

I must have made a noise because Frank sat up and swung his legs onto the ground facing in my direction. He took off his sunglasses, folded them carefully and stared at me.

'Hullo Frank,' I said, half lifting an arm in greeting.

Frank put down his cigar and stood up from the lounger. 'Hello Sol,' he said slowly. He looked me up and down as though trying to figure out what I was about to say. The expression on his face was sad and his drooping Zappa moustache accentuated it. Slowly, he walked towards me, stretched out his arms and gathered me up in an embrace.

It was at that point I choked up. 'I-I'm so s-sorry, Frank,' I blurted out, my chest heaving. 'I-It's the worst news. M-Mira's dead.'

Frank said nothing but his body language told me plenty as he slumped in my arms. I had to hold him upright as sobs racked his body.

We stood like that for what seemed hours but can't have been more than a minute or two. After that, he broke away and retraced his steps to the lounger where he reached down for a whisky glass. He took a long slug out of it with his back to me. I watched and waited until at last he picked up the sunglasses and put them on.

'Let's go sit in the dining area,' he said carrying his drink and making his way to a short staircase at the side.

This led up to a steel-framed loggia with wooden decking. It was open to the sky as parallel joists were fixed to the frame. A glass-topped dining table with matching chairs occupied the centre space and on one side overlooking the swimming pool was a raised bed massed with rose-scented geraniums.

Frank didn't sit but walked as far as a chromium rail at the far end and I followed him. He rested his arms on the hot surface but, if he experienced any discomfort, it wasn't apparent. 'Did I ever tell you how I got this place?' he asked.

I did no more than shake my head.

'It was 35 years ago, Sol. In those days, I gambled a bit along the coast at Fish River. I won the place off a guy in a poker game.' He turned and saw the surprised expression on my face. 'Of course, when I went into it there was a hefty mortgage plus a string of secured charges. Against that, the location here was perfect and the views spectacular. The upshot was I sorted out the mortgage and paid off the debts.'

Abruptly, Frank dried up and I saw his shoulders heave as he was overcome again. He raised a shaking hand holding the glass and took another large gulp.

I put an arm round him. 'Why don't we sit down?'

But it was as though I hadn't spoken. 'L-Later I did some building work and general updating,' he went on. 'That was all before I added another storey. Hell, that was a job and a half, but my first wife was really happy with the result. I don't remember now, Sol, whether you ever met Maggie.'

'Briefly, a couple of times,' I said. 'But she was already sick and in and out of hospital when you took me in.'

Frank nodded but I don't think he was listening. His eyes were focused on something only he could discern. There was a long pause before he said, 'Tell me what happened, Sol.'

Contrary to what had been agreed with Isabelle, I told Frank everything including my abortive attempt to rescue Mira. It made sense to me because I didn't want him thinking I'd left hospital, done nothing to help and not even troubled myself to keep in touch. In retrospect, perhaps I should have stuck to what was advised. It would have been easier on Frank. But thinking back I don't believe anything would have turned out differently. Mira was dead and the reality of her death was inescapable.

Frank heard me out and drank steadily. I persuaded him to sit down at the dining table when he became unsteady on his feet.

I took a chair next to him and rested a hand on his arm. 'I got a call day before yesterday,' I said, resuming my account. 'They told me a body had been found.'

'So long ago?'

'It was located on the far side of Mossel Bay, Frank. I was asked to make a preliminary ID. They said they didn't want to distress you with it.'

I should have chosen my words more carefully because they made Frank explode. 'That's bullshit!' he exclaimed. 'They contacted you because they saw you as the easy option. The only contact I've now got with SAPS is through lawyers. They're chasing to get answers about the fuck-up on the beach. Looks like I can now add in the stuff that happened to you since.' Frank was breathing hard, his skin was a muddy colour and his forehead was wet with perspiration.

I sat with him silently and gave him time to regain his composure.

Eventually, he said, 'Give me the rest of it, Sol.'

'Mira was found in a safari park about 50 kms from the Bay. I made a positive ID yesterday. It means SAPS in the Western Cape will release the body and it'll be brought back to PE.'

'How did she die?'

'I don't know, Frank. They'll do an autopsy here.'

'Do you know when I'll be able to see her?

'I don't know about that either, but I'll find out.'

CHAPTER EIGHTEEN

I decided to stay with Frank. I was worried about him and wanted to be on hand to help, but I was also disinclined to go home. There was nothing for me there so, apart from a short trip down to Seaview to pick up clothes, I didn't move from Lovemore Heights. This made me think about the reasons for leaving Frank's in the first place. Of course, it was all about asserting my independence, but the truth was I struggled with living alone and had done so through all the years spent away.

Frank had no interest in going to stay with Isabelle and with me around she left within 48 hours. She didn't depart though without my asking her about Mira. I was interested in how she'd been perceived by her. It's often the case that women have better instincts than men.

Isabelle answered my question with one of her own. 'You knew her at least as well as I did,' she said. 'What did you make of her?'

My reply was guarded. 'What I thought wasn't important. For me it was about whether she made Frank happy.'

'And did she?'

I hesitated before responding because I was unsure. Fact was my opinion would forever be tarnished by the occasion when she'd made a pass at me. The incident left me outraged though at the time my rejection of her was tactful enough. It happened at the house when I went there one Saturday for lunch. Frank left unexpectedly as there was an incident involving one of Zap-It's armed response units. Mira never tried it on with me again because I never gave her any opportunity.

'It's my belief she made him happy,' I said at last.

Isabelle looked sceptical. 'One shouldn't speak ill of the dead,' she said, 'but I thought she was a gold-digger. For a start there was the age difference, and I didn't approve of that. Also, once she knew Frank had money there was no stopping her. He spoke to me on one occasion about his concerns and I gave him my opinion. Not that it counted for anything as three months later they married.'

I absorbed all this without comment but was discomforted by the way her words resonated with me. Potentially, I faced the same situation regarding Ayesha, certainly as far as the money angle was concerned.

Isabelle's comments though did have the effect of making me curious to find out more about how Frank had met Mira in the first place. My recollection was he'd always been rather vague on the subject.

The opportunity to tackle him arose a week or so later when heavy rain descended one afternoon, and Frank and I were sitting in the cinema room. With the phone switched off, we settled down to watch a movie. Frank had always been a fan of the Hollywood classics and, on this occasion, it was time for *Breakfast at Tiffany's* to have another outing. Later, when Henry Mancini's score had run its course and the credits rolled on George Peppard and Audrey Hepburn kissing, I asked Frank how he'd met Mira.

'I told you years ago,' said Frank. 'We got together in Cape Town.'

I smiled. 'That was the where,' I said. 'It wasn't the how.'

Frank hesitated. 'We met on the net,' he said shyly.

I was taken aback. 'Wow, you never told me that. Why did you do that? It strikes me as a strange way to find somebody.'

Frank gave me a wry smile. He was nowhere over his bereavement, but he was gaining traction, even though it was supported by an intake of alcohol that was worrying. 'For an old buzzard like me,' he said, 'it was pretty much a necessity. Besides, I wanted to meet somebody who wasn't living in PE. I couldn't do that except by accessing the net.'

'Why not meet someone here?'

'I've lived in this city forever, Sol, and know too many people. I wanted to spread my wings a bit. And it proved to be the right thing to do as I found Mira.'

Frank started to look reflective and with it sadness crept into his bloodshot eyes. As always, his white whiskers accentuated any hang-dog expression that came into his face.

I changed the subject. 'What was the name of that club where she sang?' I asked. 'You told me something about it once.'

'Bennie's.'

'In Camps Bay? -Yes, I remember now. It must have been four, maybe five years ago.'

'More like six, Sol.'

'I wonder if the place is still there.'

Frank shrugged. 'If it is, they won't have found anyone to replace her. She was something really special I can tell you.'

With the passing of the days, Frank became restless, so much so that he started spending time in the office. I was unconvinced he was strong enough but had to concede it gave him something other than his grief on which to focus. While he was away, it was my responsibility to organize the household.

I tried to contact Bezuidenhout on a couple of occasions but, despite leaving messages, heard nothing.

All this meant I took time out for myself. As ever, I found healing the body much easier than healing the mind.

Looking back, I had only one other significant conversation with Frank at the house and that concerned du Toit. Frank's relationship with him at the time of the ransom demand for Mira had been nagging away at me for weeks. Du Toit's name came up accidentally when Frank and I were sitting in the loggia one night having finished dinner. We were sharing a cafetiere and Frank was talking about Zap-It. The previous day he'd met the investors from Cape Town who du Toit had introduced. They wanted to get a better feel for his business having just acquired it.

'What were they like?' I asked.

'They're a couple of brothers in their thirties by the name of Trollip. Between them, they made a pile in commodity trading. They're now investing in bricks-and-mortar enterprises with sustainable cash flows and profits. They view security as having a bright future.' Frank paused a moment while he used a silver cutter to snip the end from a Montecristo cigar. 'We found a lot of common ground in our mutual dislike of Eugene du Toit.'

'How did he rattle their cages?'

'Apparently, he tried to charge for so-called consultancy work on Zap-It plus a finder's fee for the introduction. He behaved like he was dealing with a couple of kids fresh out of business school.'

I watched Frank light his cigar and draw on it several times to get it going. In the still air, blue smoke eddied lazily. I revelled in its rich aroma. 'Du Toit's involvement with Mira's kidnap has always puzzled me,' I ventured.

'How so?'

'Just that he seemed to pop up at the critical moment.'

'It's called coincidence, Sol.'

But I wasn't to be deflected so easily. I find it hard to believe in coincidence though accept it's even harder to believe in anything else. 'How exactly did it happen, Frank?'

'After Mira was snatched, I began to get calls from this guy. His voice sounded very strange. SAPS thought he was probably using a voice changer. Anyway, things went nowhere for days because of the amount he was asking for. I tried to explain I didn't have 50 million bucks lying round in loose change. But he didn't care about that and kept making threats. I didn't know what to do and couldn't get hold of you.'

I smiled ruefully. 'Two days tops in Windhoek turned into a fortnight. And my phone was stolen. Anyways, you decided to talk to du Toit?'

Frank shook his head. 'No, Sol, it wasn't like that. He rang me.'

'About what?'

'He was chasing invitations he'd sent out for a seminar to be held at his offices. I knew he'd call because a pal of mine at the Chamber of Commerce gave me the heads-up.'

'What happened when you spoke?'

Frank drained his coffee cup. 'I don't remember precisely. He seemed to pick up on the fact I was distracted and under a lot of strain. He must have heard something in my voice. I was at a pretty low ebb. Anyway, he asked if there was anything wrong and the whole story just spilled out.'

'How did he react?'

'Said he was sure he could help but wanted to be clear what I wanted. I told him I wanted Mira back. That was all that mattered. He said he could make enquiries about raising the ransom using Zap-It as collateral.'

'And it was after that you suffered a heart attack?'

'It was the day after,' said Frank. 'I was out of it and so du Toit took over.'

'How did he come to get your power of attorney?'

'He asked for it and I gave it to him.' Frank saw the questioning look in my eyes. 'Du Toit's a chartered accountant, Sol. A guy like that's got a lot to lose if he doesn't play straight. I needed to trust someone given the situation.'

I absorbed this without comment but asked another question. 'How did du Toit's involvement go down with the kidnappers?'

'Initially, they were furious and made all sorts of threats. Later, they came to accept the reality of the situation.'

'And SAPS?'

'After I told du Toit I wanted you to front the exchange and that it wasn't negotiable, SAPS said they'd watch you. They'd only move in at the appropriate moment.'

So now I knew how du Toit had fitted in. There was nothing there which was obviously amiss though the solicitude for Frank's distress after Mira had been kidnapped didn't chime with my assessment of the man. Nor did it chime with the way du Toit subsequently behaved towards Frank. But were my concerns anything more than trifles? -Frankly, I had no way of knowing.

A couple of days after that, Frank and I went our separate ways. He was going to be out of town as he was heading up a training/ team-building exercise with some of his people at a country hotel. It would be his last opportunity to be so hands-on. I thought he'd do better giving it a miss. I doubted he was fit enough, either physically or mentally.

Despite my reservations about his health, Frank gave me a broad enough smile as I loaded myself into the Mustang on the morning of my departure. But, when I looked in the rear-view mirror and saw him turn away from gazing after me, I saw how matters really stood in his shuffling gait and bent head. I admit I wasn't caught totally unawares when tears pricked my eyes.

CHAPTER NINETEEN

Late that afternoon, I stood with an estate agent in my front garden overlooking the white-capped ocean. A stiff breeze was agitating the fronds of the palms and already some of the dead stalks had succumbed and fallen onto the grass. 'So, you reckon a million and a half plus,' I said.

'Give or take,' she said. 'It depends how quickly you want to sell.'

'Cash flow's not really an issue. On the other hand, I don't want to be stuck with the place a year from now.'

'There's no way that would happen with our company.'

'The house was empty for two years before I came along.'

'Was it really?'

'Yes, it was,' I said. 'And it was your agency that had an exclusive mandate to sell it.'

My words made as much impression on her as darts thrown against steel plate. 'I wouldn't know about that,' she said dismissively. 'I've only been with the company four months.'

'Uh-huh,' I said. 'Let's leave it there, shall we? Perhaps you can drop me a line and advise how you think you can help. I'll be asking others to do likewise so I can pick one company to work with.'

The decision to sell Seaview had been made while I drove the short distance home from Lovemore heights. Nevertheless, it was the right thing to do. How long the sale would take to accomplish was anybody's guess, but at least the wheels were in motion. Now the decision was made, my relief was considerable.

*   *   *

I tried Bezuidenhout again and this time played telephone tennis with him for the best part of 24 hours. When we did speak, he informed me he was out at Baywest Mall investigating a robbery.

'I'll be here a while,' he said. 'I've got a DS I'm supervising. Everything's more or less under control so I can give you some time.'

'Can't you give me an update now?' I asked.

'Face to face is better.'

I didn't argue as Baywest's only a half hour from Seaview. 'OK, I'll see you soon.'

'Come to Entrance 4 and walk as far as the tapas bar. You'll see police tapes off to one side. I'll look out for you.'

Baywest Mall is but the first phase of a development plan to be rolled out over the next couple of decades to create Baywest City. As the suits in Jo'burg shelled out nearly two billion bucks to build a retail park with 250 outlets, I reckon they felt our Rainbow Nation had a long-term future. That fact alone lifts my spirits in a way that much else I come across doesn't.

I drove to Entrance 4 and parked the Mustang out of the sun. The Mall is busiest at weekends, so footfall was light, and the ice rink deserted.

I went as far as the bar and spotted the captain talking to one of his subordinates. He saw me out of the corner of an eye and raised an arm in greeting. I waited and reflected how out of place he looked in long dark pants, lace-up black shoes, a white shirt with short sleeves and a tie as thin as a length of liquorice.

Bezuidenhout finished at last, came over and shook my hand. 'We'll step outside-I could do with a smoke.'

I walked back with him to the entrance along the air-conditioned and marbled boulevard. On either side, the shop fronts gleamed under the light cast by halide lamps that made the area seem as sterile as a hospital operating theatre. In this place, a dropped sweet wrapper on machine-buffed floors was about as inconspicuous as a hornet on a sugar lump.

'What happened?' I asked, jerking my thumb back from where we'd come.

'Punk held up the jewellers. Got nothing as the assistant fainted. Panicked, hightailed out and fired at a guard on the way. Fortunately, he missed.'

'What was the point? CCTV must cover the place wall to wall.'

Bezuidenhout smiled. 'It does,' he said. 'If the footage's good and the perp's on file, we'll pick him up within a day or two. Seriously, I think some of these guys get a taste for prison food.'

The heat hit us as we strolled out beyond the entranceway, so we stayed in the shade. The captain produced a pack of Camel Lights, shook one out and lit up. For the first time, I noticed the heavy nicotine staining on the fingers of his right hand.

'Where do you want to start, Mr. Nemo?'

'Anywhere you like, Captain.'

He smiled and I thought there was something mischievous about his expression. 'I understand you had a robust exchange of views with Colonel Ndosi,' he said.

'He told you, did he?'

Bezuidenhout shook his head and exhaled smoke. 'I've friends in Western Cape. Some news travels fast. I got the intell within hours.'

'OK, so what?'

'So, suddenly Ndosi wants rogue cops given top priority. Not that he bothered telling me. I heard through the chain of command when they dumped responsibility for an investigation on me.'

'I guess the good Colonel was too busy.'

Bezuidenhout shrugged. 'Anyway, I felt vindicated,' he said. 'I flagged what had happened as a priority from the outset.'

'Uh-huh. I used to wonder whether Ndosi was corrupt or stupid.'

'Could be both,' said Bezuidenhout, grinding out his cigarette and selecting another. 'I agree with you he doesn't have the where-withal. If the system worked properly, they'd select people based on capability.'

From his name, Bezuidenhout was of Dutch stock and certainly his skin was a good deal lighter than mine. But black empowerment is the name of the game in the police as elsewhere, which is all fine and dandy providing those empowered know what they're about.

I changed the subject. 'What have you done so far?'

'I'm having all handguns collected for test firing. That way we can cross-match with the cartridge cases retrieved at the scene.'

'I assume there's some cover story.'

The captain smiled again. 'I agreed something with the techies in procurement. They drafted a memo out of Pretoria full of references to gas pressures, high temperatures and metal fragments to explain the possibility of malfunction. They cited a fictitious case where a gun had failed at a face-off. All I did was to attach a note ordering a phased recall.'

'Making weapons drawn that night a priority?'

'Not necessarily. I need to be circumspect as there's the possibility that the two you confronted weren't on duty. As I recall, you didn't know whether they arrived in a police vehicle.'

'You're right,' I admitted.

'Look, I know you're highly motivated to get results,' said Bezuidenhout, 'but I have to say we're not making a whole lot of progress. Mueller, it turned out, had another ID meaning we were able to trace an additional bank account. But it had been used on a strictly cash basis. So there's still no indication who's behind all this. The other guy you shot remains under armed guard in hospital. But he's not talking and like his dead companion he's also another lowlife from Cape Town.'

'Where in Cape Town?'

'Manenberg.'

I parked this. 'What's happening as regards Mrs. Zarakolu's autopsy?'

'Completed late yesterday. There was a backlog because of summer holidays. Death was caused by a single shot to the back of the head. I'm awaiting the report.'

I made no comment but was relieved that the end for Mira would have been swift and painless. 'And the formal ID?'

'As you know, that's for the next-of-kin.'

'I'm concerned about Mr. Zarakolu's health,' I said. 'But he's told me he wants to see her. What do you advise?'

'In your shoes, I'd dissuade him. Mrs. Zarakolu needs cosmetic work. We can work with your ID for the moment. There's no date yet for the coroner.'

'OK,' I said. 'I'm grateful for your time, Captain. You won't mind if I keep in touch?'

'I think SAPS would rather talk to you than Mr. Zarakolu's lawyers,' said Bezuidenhout grinning. 'By the way, you can pick up that gun of yours whenever you're passing. I was also asked to mention that your car's still in our pound.'

I did a double take. My use of the Fiesta was occasional, so I hadn't missed it. Even so, it was out of character for me to overlook something like that; too many things chasing round my head I guessed. 'I'll have it picked up,' I said, feeling stupid. 'Did you get anything useful from it?'

'Masses of fingerprints we can't identify so no surprises there. DNA samples from the passenger seat were matched to Mrs. Zarakolu. There are also other samples we've taken. They could be relevant if and when we have someone in the frame.'

We parted company after that. As Bezuidenhout walked away, I heard his phone's ring tone. I'm often surprised by people's tastes in music. On this occasion, I was nonplussed to hear the disco strains of *Stayin' Alive*. Given the captain's rate of cigarette consumption, I reckoned this might qualify as wishful thinking.

I'd hoped to get hold of Arnie but was unsuccessful. Despite then leaving messages, I still heard nothing and began to wonder if there was a problem.

When I finally caught up with him later, I cut to the chase. 'Hey man, where you been? I've been trying to reach you for a while.'

'I thought you were somebody else,' said Arnie.

Hardly a diplomatic answer from an old friend but at least it was honest. 'Who were you expecting?' I asked.

'No, no, it was my mistake. How are you, Sol?'

Notwithstanding his question, Arnie was distracted. Actually, it was more than that: he was apprehensive as there was a catch in his voice. 'I've been spending time at Frank's place. You'll have seen the news about Mira.'

'Yeah, I heard a while back. Look, Sol, I'm not involved with the case anymore.'

'That wasn't the reason I was calling.'

'Oh, I . . .'

'I met with Bezuidenhout earlier today,' I interrupted. 'He brought me up to speed with everything.'

'I see.' In the utterance of those words, I heard relief in Arnie's voice. 'What can I do for you Sol?'

'It would be good to meet up, Arnie. I haven't seen you in quite a while.'

'OK. You wanna come to the house?'

'Maybe somewhere else. How about Barney's?'

'Barney's is good. I'm on early turns this week. What about tomorrow around five?'

CHAPTER TWENTY

Barney's lies on the ocean side of Marine Drive close to Shark Rock Pier and Hobie Beach. I'd been going there for 20 years, ever since I first came to PE. It advertised itself as a tavern, but that didn't really say much. I liked it because of its laidback style; its steak and kidney pie; its views over the ocean; and the value for money it offered in the days when that was important. It was a place to hang out and chill and forget, at least for a while, all the *kak* in your life.

I left the Mustang in the car park at the side and climbed the wide concrete steps to street level. Passing through the cool, dim interior with its predominant dark wood panelling, I walked onto the deck. Bench-style tables were set out under sturdy red parasols because the sun was fierce, even though an onshore breeze might fool you into thinking otherwise. Maybe this was the reason why Barney's was so popular with pale-skinned tourists seeking a quick tan. But it wasn't the only factor because they also came to see the pods of dolphins that often leapt and dived metres from the beach.

I couldn't see Arnie, so I grabbed a table in the far corner by the rail. I dropped my shades onto the heavily varnished top and scrolled through my messages. There were a couple from the estate agents I'd met with, each expressing the hope they'd be favoured with the mandate to sell my house.

Arnie rushed in late, cast anxious eyes around the deck, saw where I was and crossed over. 'Sorry, sorry,' he said pushing bandy legs through the space between the seat and the tabletop opposite me.

'Busy?' I asked smiling.

'As ever, but I was held up. One set of lights at Humewood is out.'

I sympathized. 'You wanna share a tower?'

'Better make it a jug, Sol. I really can't stay that long.'

I caught the eye of the waiter and ordered a two-litre jug of Castle Draught. A tower's a three-litre container with a tap which is brought to your table and allows you to help yourself. Repeatedly.

'So, how's things Arnie? -Last time we met there were problems with your mamma.'

My friend made a face. 'Things didn't get better at the home, and we were asked to move her. We've found another place with better facilities.'

'Whereabouts?'

'Scottburgh.'

I had to think. 'That's near Durban, isn't it?'

'About 60kms this side.'

'So far away?' I asked as the iced beer and glasses reached us. Lifting the jug, I poured.

'Needs must, Sol. And her needs are a priority.'

Arnie took his glass and drained nearly half in one long gulp. An edge had crept into his voice which reminded me how he'd sounded on the phone. Perhaps he resented my questions but if he did it was for the first time ever. Ours had always been a relaxed friendship without aspects of our lives being closed off. And there was something else: Arnie had developed a tic beneath his left eye.

I thought changing the subject might help. 'I'm putting the house on the market,' I said.

'Really! -What decided that?'

'Place gets on my nerves and besides Seaview's much too quiet.'

'But you've only been there what . . . a year or so?'

'I know. I should have taken more time over buying instead of jumping in so quickly.'

Arnie shrugged. 'But money doesn't really matter to you, does it?' The question was rhetorical because he went on quickly, 'Where will you go?'

'I'll come back to town. But I don't have to think about that any time soon.'

'I suppose if the house went quickly, you could stay with Frank for a while.'

'In fact, I've been spending a lot of time with him over recent days. I wanted to stick around after the news about Mira.'

It was though I hadn't spoken for Arnie indicated the jug and his empty glass. 'You mind?' he queried.

'Of course not. You really don't have to ask.'

I watched Arnie fill up. For a moment, his dark eyes fastened on mine and, when I smiled, they slid away self-consciously. Something wasn't right and I asked him what it was. But he laughed it off, so I changed tack again and enquired about Esme and the children. Only then did I see some tension disappear from his face and his powerful shoulders relax. Even the tic beneath his eye ceased to jump like it was hot-wired.

I poured a further measure into my glass and said slowly, 'One reason I wanted to meet was to get your advice.'

For the first time, a real smile broke out across Arnie's features. '*You* want *my* advice? -Since when?'

'Since now.'

'OK, I'm listening.'

'Do you recall me talking about Ayesha?'

'You mean the lady in East London? The one you hook up with when she's not working?' Arnie made as though he was thinking. 'Yes, I do recall a conversation a while back. I said it might be wise to find somebody who has time for you and who doesn't live so far away.'

I ignored that. 'Thing is she's suggesting we make more time for each other and . . .' I suddenly stalled, uncertain how to continue.

'And what?'

'I'm not sure I know where she's coming from.'

'How do you mean?'

'I've known her a while now and previously everything's been on her terms. Now, suddenly, she's making this play.'

Arnie laughed out loud, and I noticed that now there was no sign of the tic. 'Maybe she's woken up to the fact you're a good catch,' he said. 'Maybe, she's starting to feel her age a bit and wants a different sort of existence. Maybe . . .'

'The key draw,' I cut in, 'is the fact I now have money.'

Arnie sat back and studied me. 'Maybe you're right, Sol. Only time will tell, won't it?' He reached for his beer and brought it half way to his lips before lowering it again. 'I know what this is about,' he said reflectively. 'This is about your fear of taking a risk. It's why you never settled down. It all goes back to childhood and the loss of your mother. You think if you make a commitment, it'll all go wrong for you.'

'Plenty seems to have done over the years,' I said, recalling a string of messy and ultimately doomed relationships.

'Life's a crapshoot, Sol. And you know as well as I do, there's a lot of crap in life. Give yourself a break, bro, and take it one day at a time.'

He was right and talking about it made me perceive the sense of what he was saying. But that was at the rational level. My problem was with an often irrational mindset. In any event, I thanked him for his advice.

As he got up to go, he said, 'I'm your friend, Sol. I really am. I think you should make the effort with Ayesha. Hell, you've got nothing to lose.' He hesitated for a moment and then added, 'On the other hand, Sol, the Zarakolu case is SAPS' business. Take my advice and stay out of it. Bezuidenhout's an old hand and knows what he's doing. He really does and I reckon he doesn't need you fouling up his lines of inquiry.'

Arnie had never talked to me like that before, but he wasn't at all self-conscious. In fact, I found his tone challenging and was taken

120

aback by his vehemence, particularly as Bezuidenhout hadn't intimated he wanted me out of the picture. I would have pursued the matter, but Arnie had to go and so I could only watch him give me a tight smile, turn on his heel, and walk out.

CHAPTER TWENTY-ONE

I considered what Arnie had said overnight and tried to call Ayesha first thing in the morning. There was no response, so I left a voice mail.

Ayesha rang me back less than an hour later. 'How are you, *mon ami?*'

'I'm OK. And you?'

'The same. I thought you were going to ring before now. I've missed you.'

'Likewise,' I said, before explaining what had been happening.

Ayesha was sympathetic. 'I'm so sorry to hear all this. How *is* Frank?'

'I think he knew Mira was gone before I confirmed it. Even so, it's been very tough. And he's not at all well. Anyway, at his insistence, he's now out of town for a few days.'

'So, with Frank gone, what are you up to?'

'Not a lot. In truth, I'm free.'

'Shall we get together? -Maybe tomorrow?'

'Sounds like a plan. Can I come to you?'

I didn't remind Ayesha of my suggestion that she visit me. Fact was I now found spending time in my house close to intolerable. The prospect of her being there for a while and then leaving was something difficult to imagine. Fortunately, she made no mention of what I'd said and so we agreed to meet in East London as before.

*　　*　　*

The things to be dealt with before I left PE took longer than antici-pated. Retrieving my Tomcat was a breeze, but getting the Fiesta back proved irksome. A spate of vehicle thefts from the police pound using forged paperwork meant there was a refusal to release the Ford without my producing three pieces of evidence indicating my ownership. After that, I went across town to sign a letter of authorisation so motor dealers could pick the car up. It needed new tyres to replace the ones shot out and I wanted the vehicle valeted to remove the fingerprint powder that caked it inside and out. They said I could pick it up the following morning.

After that, there was a choice to be made as regards the estate agent to use. I made the decision to go with one company because they could get out that afternoon to take photographs and sign off the paperwork. I was assured the marketing effort would commence within 48 hours. For me, it couldn't happen soon enough.

I slept better that night than had been the case for months. Maybe it was the prospect of seeing Ayesha that made the difference, or maybe it was because I was knackered. Whatever the cause, I over-slept. Muzzy-headed, I took a taxi and picked up the now sparkling and Fiesta. After garaging it and packing for my trip, I loaded every-thing into the Mustang and was on my way by 10.30.

CHAPTER TWENTY-TWO

I was ten minutes short of the Nahoon River Interchange in East London when it happened. My cell was on the passenger seat, though it's never answered when on the move. But, on this occasion, the traffic ahead had slowed to walking speed because of a breakdown and I saw the screen light up. The number displayed meant nothing as I lifted the phone and switched off the CD player.

'Hi there,' I said with something approaching lightness in my heart.

'Solomon? Is that you?'

'Hi,' I said again. The female voice didn't register. 'Who is this?'

'Solomon, it's Isabelle.'

'Isabelle?' Then I made the connection. 'Hi Isabelle. How are you?'

She didn't answer. 'Where are you?'

'In the car approaching East London. Why?'

'It would be a good idea if you pulled over.'

'There's no problem. I'm stuck in traffic.'

'I am so sorry, Solomon, but I've bad news.'

'W-What news?'

'I'm afraid it's Frank. He had another heart attack.'

I felt a constriction in my windpipe and my heart begin to pound. 'W-Where is he?'

There was a pause. 'I'm sorry Solomon. You don't understand. It was a massive coronary. I'm so sorry, but Frank's dead.'

Isabelle talked to me some more, but I'd tuned out. Finally, I cut the connection and dropped the phone. Pushing my shades onto the top of my head and with tears blurring my vision, I put my head in my hands. Struggling to breathe, a prickly sweat broke out all over my body. And there I sat, hunched over the steering wheel as my mind spun out of control.

I stayed like that until there was a rapping against my side window. Bemused, I lifted my head and looked at a man gesticulating. I opened the window and a blast of hot air hit me.

'You mind moving along, buddy. Some of us got places to be this side of midnight.'

Staring at him uncomprehendingly, I followed the line of his outstretched arm. A gap of 200 metres had opened in front of me. My mouth was as dry as ash. 'I-I had some b-bad news,' I stammered.

The man was unsympathetic. 'Not my problem. I suggest you take your bad news and your fancy car and park up out of the way. Then those of us who have . . .'

I shut the window, drove forward and pulled onto a strip of waste ground. I killed the engine and sat slumped at the wheel, my eyes gazing unseeingly into the distance. My cell rang several times, but I ignored it. There was no point answering because there was nothing to say and no one I wanted to talk to.

I was there a long while because the sun dipped until it started to shine in through the rear window. By then, I was hot and sweaty and dehydrated but felt no motivation to move. With little energy, I drifted in and out of a reverie but each time I surfaced it was with a start, my heart racing and my breathing strangled. Frank's death induced in me a rising sense of panic every time the reality of my changed circumstances hit me.

I got out of the car at last and, for the first time, saw the traffic had cleared. Fetching a bottle of water from the boot, I took a long drink too fast and gagged. My heart was still beating too fast, my breathing shallow and irregular. I knew one cure for those symptoms and that was to get going.

Climbing back into the Mustang, I hit the starter button and booted it over the N6 and the Nahoon River heading east.

CHAPTER TWENTY-THREE

It started to rain as I passed Durban International Airport, over 600 kms from East London. It turned into a downpour as I turned off onto the M4. Where the highway ran out, I took the road skirting the railway and the Bay of Natal before threading the Mustang northwards through the city centre. There were few people about because of the weather and the lateness of the hour so I drove unimpeded along streets normally notorious for their snarl-ups. The lit shop and store fronts I passed stared back at me, blank as the eyes of strangers.

I picked up the M4 again on the north side of the city and drove as far as La Lucia. I had some happy recollection of having been there before, but it was evident I was mistaken as the place was alien to me.

Choosing a hotel randomly, I retrieved my things from the boot and sprinted for the entrance through a heavy pulse of rain.

The woman at reception wasn't expecting anyone late on a rainy night and certainly not a travel-stained, coloured guy dressed in a creased T shirt and shorts.

'Yes?' she said, lifting her eyes from a laptop. The distaste in her face couldn't have been more palpable had she been calling out a drug dealer.

'I'd like a room,' I said.

'For how long?'

'One night.'

'You'll have to pay in advance.'

'Right,' I said, producing a credit card.

'Card machine's not working,' she snapped. 'It'll have to be cash. Assuming you have it.' Suddenly, she noticed my sodden appearance. 'How did you get here?'

'By car.'

She peered round me and into the wet night beyond the plate-glass window. 'I can't see anything.'

'It's the Mustang.'

'The what?'

'The Ford parked on the end by the BMW.'

She continued looking. 'Ach, that car,' she conceded. 'I see it now.'

'Terrific Can we get on with this? -I've come a long way.'

'You'll need to register.'

'Fine. How much for the room?'

'1400 Rand.'

I completed the registration form and counted out the notes. 'What can I get to eat?'

The woman pointedly consulted her watch. 'This time of night, the kitchen's closed. Ring down and see what they can do for you. Whatever your expectations, take my advice and lower them.'

With that, she shoved the key card towards me and turned her back. It seemed something of greater interest than a paying guest had caught her eye.

By the time I reached the room, my appetite had vanished, so I showered and went to bed.

I fell asleep exhausted, but my rest wasn't untroubled. During a fitful spell I saw the face of Mueller, the kidnapper, and imagined the pain in it after he was shot. More, I saw that belly of his, as large as the curved back of a whale, take the bullets and start to express streams of rich, red blood. Then his belly transformed itself into the scaly underside of a Nile crocodile. With no warning, the reptile launched itself at me, powerful jaws in a flat head open wide and green eyes fastened on mine. In horror, I struggled to get away but found myself paralysed with fear. Inexorably, I felt the croc's jaws lock around my torso as my arms flailed uselessly. After that, the air was sucked from my lungs by a force that suffocated me.

I woke up when I hit the floor, the sheets from the bed wound tightly about me. Fighting for breath, my heart was pounding fit to burst. Sweating profusely, I discarded the sheet with difficulty and staggered across the room to the window. It was still raining, and the streetlights were wet smudges of light against the impenetrable background of night. Standing there, it seemed I was the only person left in the world and that all time stood still. The thought made me choke up and suddenly I wanted to be somewhere else, anywhere else. Impulsively, I packed my things and left.

What happened next is jumbled in my mind. I didn't stay in a hotel again because many hours each night were spent on the open road. When I felt too tired to go on, I pulled over and slept behind the wheel. These rest periods ended when I awoke, usually after no more than a couple of hours, with my heart racing and my stomach in full-scale rebellion. Self-medicating with diazepam helped but only until the pills ran out. The common cause of my hyperarousal was the flashbacks I suffered with increasing frequency. This was stuff going back over the years both from my time with Zap-It and with SAPS; a tapestry of incidents that stitched themselves into a kaleidoscope of disturbed and threatening images. The most acute was when I was shot during the aborted exchange of Mira.

Over what was several days, I covered more than 4,000 kms. There was never a destination in prospect. I was simply moving from one town to another, one city to another and from one province to another stopping two or three times a day to fill up the tank. Often, I ate and drank on the move tossing bottles and cans and empty packaging into the passenger foot well, so it filled with debris. It also escaped my attention that I'd ceased to bathe or shave or change my clothes, or even run a comb through my hair.

It all came to a head late one afternoon as the sun was setting. Dog-tired and driving too fast, I misjudged the line of a curve on an empty road, skidded on loose stones and slammed the nearside rear quarter of the Mustang into a crash barrier. I climbed out shaken, but unhurt. If my response to the damage sustained by the car was philosophical, my reaction when I looked over the barrier overwhelmed me. Had it not been there, the car would have plunged into a deep ravine taking me with it.

In that moment, the realization hit me I didn't want to die. But, understanding my state of mind, I knew I'd need help to sort myself out. Chastened, I climbed back into the car and made for the nearest town. I found a hotel with Wi-Fi and, in return for purchasing an espresso, a bottle of water and a sandwich, researched websites on the PC they had set up in their lounge.

When I emerged into the open air once more, I knew for the first time in days where my destination was to be found. The sat-nav told me it was 556kms away.

One reason I had to drive so far was because the SA road network is based on the US strategic system of Interstate Highways developed by Eisenhower. Consequently, my journey consisted of a dogleg following the N14 to where it intersected with the N7 going south towards Cape Town.

I drove the route in 100 km chunks with stops when I was too tired to continue. As before, such sleep as I had was fitful leaving me stressed on waking up. By then, the flashbacks had taken a back seat but that didn't stop me fearing their return.

My destination lay close to Clanwilliam. The town was easy enough to locate but the Steinberg Clinic wasn't. Its signage on the highway was modest and the establishment itself was tucked away at the rear of a *rooibos* tea plantation. I gained access by following a track flooded from a recent downpour. The rain might have been unseasonal but farm workers in overalls and peaked caps using sickles to harvest the broom-like plants was routine for the time of year.

The clinic was a two-storey building of modular construction painted a shade of cream, presumably designed to enhance feelings of calmness. I pulled the Mustang across the front and found a parking space opposite a couple of tennis courts. On stepping out, I was surprised to find a smashed solar light by my back wheels.

I walked through steel-framed, plate-glass doors to Reception located at the rear of an atrium. Behind a long counter was a floor-to-ceiling mural depicting a wood of silver birch saplings in full leaf. At one side of the picture the words *SEIZE THE DAY AND YOUR LIFE* was stencilled in bold letters.

I approached a young black guy talking to someone on the house phone. Even though he was tall, he was dwarfed by the trees behind him. When he caught sight of me, he did a double take. But his recovery though was quick enough as he gave me a broad smile revealing perfect teeth. 'I'll get back to you,' he said to someone before putting down the receiver. Then he looked at me quizzically and, when I said nothing, asked gently in English, 'What can I do for you?'

'*Ek het hulp nodig,*' I replied in Afrikaans.

CHAPTER TWENTY-FOUR

'I need help,' I repeated.

'I understand. Can I ask if we're expecting you?'

I shook my head and tried to reply but the words wouldn't come because my mouth had dried out.

'It's OK. Take your time.'

'I-I'm stressed out. I have flashbacks ... Nightmares ... I can't sleep.'

The receptionist fixed eyes on me that were filled with sympathy. 'I'm really sorry to hear that. Can I ask if you have insurance?'

I fumbled in my wallet for the access card and with a hand that shook passed it over. Feeling dizzy, I put my other hand on top of the counter to steady myself. 'Please, can I have some water?'

'Of course.' I got another smile and watched the guy walk a few steps into a kitchenette located to the side. He returned with a small bottle and a clear plastic cup.

'Do you know what level cover you've got?' he asked, looking at my card.

I unscrewed the bottle and took a gulp before replying. 'For mental health it's limited. Out-patient only.'

'That's not a problem. Let me ring the insurers and see what the position is.'

'Fine, but I can pay.'

'Sure, but I must talk to the insurers anyway. Have you ID?' I gave him my driver's licence and heard him read out the words, 'Solomon Nemo.'

'My name's Sol. Just about everybody calls me Sol.'

'OK, Sol. Why don't you have a seat across the way while I call? I'll be back to you directly.'

I trailed across to a seating area comprising four settees in oxblood leather arranged to form a square. A coffee table sat in the middle and, leaving the water on it, I crossed beyond to a huge fish tank mounted on the far wall. It was very long and filled with tropical fish of all sizes and colours. With my hands tucked up into my armpits I hunched up in front of the tank and rested my forehead against the glass. Feeling the coolness against my brow, I peered into the tank and made eye contact with a large angelfish. It was canary yellow around the mouth and gills but its predominant colour was electric blue. I watched it as it swam in slow circles within my line of vision until transfixed my eyes began to close.

I was startled by a light touch on my shoulder. Turning round, I saw a middle-aged woman wearing a navy-blue jacket and matching skirt. She had a white plastic name tag fixed prominently to her chest. 'Hello Sol,' she said. 'I'm Beth.'

'Hi,' I said. 'My name's Sol.'

'Come and sit with me for a few minutes, Sol. There are a few details we need to sort out.'

I followed her across to one of the settees and sat down. Grabbing the water, I took a long pull. Meanwhile, Beth smoothed her skirt and a lifted a clipboard onto her lap. She passed me my medical insurance card and driver's licence. 'There's one other thing,' she said, reaching into her pocket and holding up my car keys.

I looked at them stupidly before looking at her. 'Where did you get those?'

'One of the gardeners found them, Sol. When you came in, you left your engine running.'

CHAPTER TWENTY-FIVE

I was in a bad way.

But that was why the privately-owned Steinberg Clinic existed. Its purpose was to take the distraught or broken and fix them, or at least attempt a fix by giving them its best shot.

From what I experienced, it pursued this objective through providing first-class accommodation and facilities; impressive clinical expertise; and what I would describe as a touchy-feely mindset. This last found its most obvious expression in the way in which all their staff were tutored in the art of smiling.

Consequently, they told me with smiles I was free to explore and try everything the Clinic had to offer; that I should adhere to the programme of treatment devised for me; and that I shouldn't leave the building and its extensive grounds without permission lest it inhibit my recovery. Kicking over the traces was second nature to me, but I was happy to comply with all this.

If I'm cynical about it though, the Steinberg reserved its biggest smiles for the occasions when it presented bills. There were four of them in all so I got used to the regular hammering my credit card endured.

But, in return, I learned my underlying malady was caused by something called Separation Anxiety Disorder. It was their opinion it stemmed from the early loss of my mother and that it was a condition that often spawned mental health problems in later life, typically depression and panic disorder. My line of work didn't help either as it made me prone to PTSD that could morph into suicide ideation. The shock of Frank's death had triggered a major event.

The time spent at the Steinberg rewired some of the circuits in my brain. This was down not only to the counselling I received but also the heavy dose of chill pills they prescribed. By way of follow-up, it was suggested I should meet regularly with a psychiatrist in PE who could monitor my mental health and fine-tune my medication. They recommended a couple of practitioners, and I undertook to look them up on my return home.

A day or two before my departure from the Clinic, I retrieved my cell from the Mustang and charged it.

There was a lot of traffic including messages from Bezuidenhout. He wanted me to call urgently. I rang, but his phone went to voice-mail, so I left a message of my own.

There were texts from Ayesha. They started by expressing concern at my failure to show up on time, and later worry as the hours had ticked by. Next, they became annoyed and after a day or two angry that I hadn't bothered to contact her. They ended by accusing me of cowardice for not telling her I wanted nothing more to do with her.

She was right about my cowardice but wrong about my reasons. I hadn't wanted her to see me in the state I was in. Running away from her was my way of dealing with things and everything else for that matter.

I wrote to her at length. There was no point in spinning a yarn and so I told her Frank's death had precipitated a breakdown. As a result, I'd spent time trying to get my head straight. I apologised saying I'd like to explain things face to face.

Isabelle had left message as well. She advised that Frank had bequeathed me his house in Lovemore Heights. This news brought home the finality of his death and left me choking up.

In that emotional state, I was relieved to note that my absence from PE meant I'd missed Frank's funeral by several days. Later, I came to realise it was just one more example of my cowardice.

CHAPTER TWENTY-SIX

Bezuidenhout called when I was in the car driving back to PE. I pulled off at the side of the N1 near Century City in Cape Town and activated the hazards. In the distance, part of the summit of Table Mountain was obscured by a white cloud in an otherwise cloudless sky.

'Hi,' I said. 'I saw your messages. How can I help?'

'Am I right in thinking you're away from PE?' he asked.

'You are.'

'So, you've not heard the news?'

'What news?'

'Four days ago, two of our officers were shot dead in Korsten, close to the Civic Centre.'

'I'm sorry to hear that. What happened?'

'It was an execution,' said Bezuidenhout wearily. 'They were sitting in a marked police vehicle at traffic lights. A motorcycle pulled up and the pillion shot them at point-blank range.'

'Really! -But what's it got to do with me?'

'Their side arms were due to be tested the day after they were murdered,' said Bezuidenhout. 'This was the ballistics test I told you about. After what happened, I recovered their weapons and have now had them examined.'

I was slow on the uptake. 'With what result?'

'Both officers had Vektors. I got a match from one to the casings we recovered.'

At that point, I caught up. 'Suggesting there's a leak inside SAPS.'

'More specifically inside Detective Services.'

'Or Ballistics.'

'Unlikely I think,' said Bezeidenhout. 'Someone on the take there would be motivated to falsify results. Obviously, that didn't happen.'

'Of course,' I said. 'All the time I was around, they were a tight-knit team. Long servers most of them.'

'They still are.'

'How many people knew in Detective Services?'

'Six, including admin support.'

'Plus Ndosi?'

'Plus Ndosi,'conceded the captain.

'Is Arnie Coetzee one of the six?'

'No-No, he's not. Why do you ask?'

'I had a strange conversation with him before I left PE. He warned me off any further involvement. He was quite pointed about it. But it wasn't as though I'd been particularly engaged in any way. The last occasion was when Mira's body had to be ID'd.'

Bezuidenhout paused before choosing his words carefully. 'I'm not going to warn you off, Mr. Nemo, but my purpose in calling was certainly to warn you.'

'About what?'

'Whoever masterminded the kidnap is now engaged tying up loose ends. The Korsten murders undoubtedly fall into that category. Seems to me you could be at risk.'

'How do you work that out?'

'Had you not traced Mueller and found Mrs. Zarakolu, it's possible the kidnappers could have got the rest of the ransom. You frustrated that and maybe panicked them into killing her. The result is you've lost them 40 million Rand. My point is they may look for a chance to pay you back.' He paused for breath. 'Tell me where you are now and let me help you.'

'I'm . . .,' I began to say, but for a reason that was instinctive rather than rational stopped. 'I'm working a case in the Northern Cape,' I lied, 'and may go to the Free State in a few days. It depends how things develop. Let me be clear, nobody knows where I am.'

'OK, but you should let me know if I can help in any way.'

'I will.' I paused a moment to summon my strength. 'Before you go, Captain, you should know F-Frank died. He had a further h-heart attack . . .' I tailed off as my mouth dried up.

'I'd not heard,' Bezuidenhout said. 'You have my condolences. Sounds like his death came as a great shock.'

'Thank you.' I was on hands-free and able to unscrew the cap from a bottle of water and take a drink. 'It was a very great shock indeed. I'm still trying to come to terms with it. I believe that whoever murdered Mira effectively murdered Frank as well. And right now, I'm wondering what to do about the situation.'

I don't think Bezuidenhout attached any significance to what I said, and, in truth, my rational mind didn't either. My remarks were something that welled up unscripted. How to give them any shape or form was something I hadn't even thought about.

I arrived at Seaview well after midnight. There was a substantial delay near Swellendam after a major accident involving an HGV towing a trailer and several cars. Even with the speed at which the emergency services clear vehicles off the highway, I was held up for several hours.

The enforced idleness gave me time to reflect and map out what I was going to do in the days that followed. There were several priorities but at the top of the list was the call I was going to make to my insurers. The damage to the nearside of the Mustang was a constant reminder of a time I wanted to forget as soon as possible. I reckoned restoring its bodywork could only enhance my new-found sense of something approaching a sense of wellbeing.

CHAPTER TWENTY-SEVEN

House	5,000,000 plus
Contents	1,000,000
Stocks	2,500,000
Bonds	1,250,000
Savings	1,500,000
Vehicles	1,000,000
Condo	2,500,000
Miscellaneous	500,000
Zap-It	????????

The figures were Frank's because I recognised his italic script in one of the margins of his desk diary. They'd been compiled within 24 hours of Mira's abduction judging by the date against which they were recorded.

I was sitting in the study of Frank's house in Lovemore Heights two days after my return home. That morning I'd been to Newton Park where an insurance assessor had looked at the damage to the Mustang.

Something had been buzzing around in my head for some time regarding the ransom for Mira and specifically du Toit's involvement. SAPS may have checked him out and found no hint of anything illegal as regards his conduct, but I was left uncomfortable. The problem was I couldn't say why I felt that way. What was clear was that it amounted to more than my profound dislike of the man.

I found the keys to the steel filing cabinets in Frank's cherry wood partner's desk. These were positioned against the far wall where there was a silver framed photograph of Mira hung above them. She was striking a coquettish pose with her hair done up and her lips rouged in a shade of red that brought to mind the archetypal scarlet woman. I guess Frank had thought her facial expression was reserved for him exclusively, but I knew the truth.

The filing system was as well-ordered as a company of troops on a passing-out parade. Nothing was out of place and the serried ranks of individual files were in alphabetical order, the contents of each followed a strict chronology. It was this ease of reference that prompted me to appraise Frank's financial affairs and become increasingly puzzled.

None of the assets he'd listed in his note had an up-to-date valuation. I'd have expected liquid assets like his stocks and bonds to have been appraised but there was nothing on file more recent than contract notes which were five years old. To test my theory, I went on-line and updated the prices of Frank's portfolio. His figure was two and a half million, but that value had more than doubled over the intervening period. So, this asset alone, plus Frank's bonds and savings, could have generated millions of bucks and perhaps been used as a bargaining chip for Mira's release. From my experience with SAPS, kidnappers' demands for ransom which might start at, say, ten million often ended up being settled at a small fraction of the original figure. There was no evidence here that any of this had happened and I wondered why. Nor was there any evidence of market appraisals being sought in respect of either the house or the condo which was in Cape Town. Again, this seemed such an obvious oversight and not one which was explained by reference solely to Frank's first heart attack.

Instead, it looked like the whole focus from the outset had been upon Zap-It. This by any measure was the principal asset in Frank's estate and maybe other possessions had been consequently ignored because collectively they amounted to little more than one third of the ransom demand.

But I had a further thought. Zap-It was, for obvious reasons, the least liquid of any of Frank's interests because it was a trading entity.

Any purchaser would want to ensure that key personnel were retained, that its physical assets were properly valued, that customer relationships were safeguarded and that the price paid for the name and reputation of the business was reasonable. Du Toit seemed to have been able to vault all these hurdles in a very short period. Yet I recalled when it had come to disposing of my father's business interests some of the deals had taken months to sort out.

I found a set of financial accounts for Zap-It covering the year to the previous 30 September. I was able to read the profit and loss account because that required no more brain work than deducting expenses from revenue to leave an operating profit. Where I came unstuck was in respect of the balance sheet. The terminology used meant little to me so my view about the state of the business was likely to be as informed as if a stranger asked me to comment on his or her health. But, in these situations, it's not necessary to possess any expertise provided you know a party who does, and you trust what they tell you.

I happened to be acquainted with such a person and so gave him a call. 'Hi,' I said to his receptionist 'Can I talk to Ralph?'

'Who's calling?'

'Sol Nemo.'

There was a pause and a couple of clicks before I heard the familiar voice of Ralph Rainier, Frank's accountant of 20 years before he was usurped by Eugene du Toit. 'How long's it been?' he asked.

'Quite a while, Ralph.'

'I was very sorry to hear about Frank.'

I dealt with that as best I could and then went on: 'Look Ralph, can I talk to you about Zap-It's accounts? I've found the last set in the house.'

'OK, but what's your interest?'

'I'm not sure. Perhaps you could talk me through them in terms I can understand.'

'You happy to come across to Jeffreys?'

'Sure.'

'I've got a cancellation late this afternoon. Tell you what, Sol, why don't we meet in Ocean Basket at around six? You can buy me a beer.'

Jeffreys Bay is about 80kms from PE and with a clear road I made the trip in well under an hour. I passed the Kabeljous Lagoon as the light was fading and drove south down Da Gama Road with the ocean on my left.

If you have small children who like sandy beaches shelving gently into the warm waters of an ocean, Jeffreys is a great place for a holiday. Great that is if you are prepared to accept that everybody else's children also like sandy beaches shelving gently etc, particularly over the Christmas and New Year periods. Consequently, the place is packed tighter than two coats of paint with all the tourists who stream south from Jo'burg and Pretoria, often in large white SUVs.

Happily, with the holiday season well gone, I had no such problem and ran the Mustang onto waste ground adjacent to the seafood restaurant. As ever, there were a couple of guys acting as unofficial parking attendants and I signalled to one of them. He acknowledged me with a smile, and, on that basis, we had a contract: he'd keep watch over my car and I'd give him something for his trouble later.

After ascending the restaurant's spiral staircase, I found Ralph sitting close to plate-glass windows overlooking the beach. He was tucking into Portuguese sardines washed down with a bottle of Windhoek and viewing Business Day Live on his tablet.

He looked up as I crossed over and gave me a gap-toothed smile. For a man of his means, the cost of the best in dental care was a bagatelle, but his morbid fear of dentists and their dark arts meant he had more cavities than a gruyere cheese. Hence, as Frank had informed me despairingly on one occasion, he suffered regular infections that needed treatment with antibiotics. If those didn't sort matters out, he occasionally had to resort to hospital extractions.

'Hi Ralph,' I said dropping into a seat opposite him and placing a brown envelope close to hand. 'Good of you to see me at such short notice.'

The accountant extended a hand, and we shook. 'It was an easy choice,' he said. 'I could spend another couple of hours in the office getting to the bottom of a claim for back tax or sit here and admire the view. Besides, I had no lunch to speak of.' He gazed at me, an expression of concern having crept into his heavy-bagged eyes. 'Again, Sol, I was so sorry to hear the news. Frank's death like that was a great shock. Must have been devastating for you, given how close the two of you were. I guess that was the reason you didn't make it to the funeral. In your shoes, I'd have done the same and stayed away.'

I hadn't expected this, and my lip quivered. Quickly, I brought a hand up to my mouth to hide my embarrassment. 'You know I'm really thirsty,' I said, abruptly getting to my feet. 'You finish your food while I go to the bar. You want another Windheok?'

Ralph looked askance. 'Is the Pope a very old man, Sol?' He tapped the brown envelope meaningfully. 'Can I take a *shufti*?'

I nodded and approached the bar. There was a guy there, but he was engrossed in conversation with a couple of teenage girls. He looked like he'd be prised away with a pneumatic drill. It gave me time to recover my composure before looking over to Ralph in time to see him tip out the envelope's contents.

Eventually, the bartender noticed me and accepted an order for a couple of beers plus a seared salmon salad.

By the time I returned to the table Ralph had finished his food and was wading through the notes to the Zap-It accounts. I poured out the Windhoeks before pushing one glass across the table to him. Sipping my drink, my gaze rested on the beach where there was a lone walker with a large dog. The streetlight across the road had come on and was creating a pool of increasing brightness in the gathering gloom.

I watched Ralph patiently for several minutes. He was cross-referencing the accounts to something he'd pulled up on his tablet.

144

Eventually, curiosity got the better of me. 'What's the verdict?' I asked

Ralph slowly lifted his eyes.' It's all very interesting,' he said slowly. 'The last time I did the accounts was two years back. Things have certainly changed since.'

'In what way?'

'Sales are up around 21% but pre-tax profits have fallen by nearly 10%.'

'How so?'

'Ach, for any number of reasons. Some of those are at work here but the predominant one is about how capex has been treated.'

'What do you mean?'

'Do you know what capex is?'

'Isn't it money spent buying something for use over the long term?'

'As an approximation, let's work with that. Usually, such expenditure will be written off over several years. But, if you shorten the period, the level of write-off increases and as a result profitability reduces.'

'Frank said something about du Toit saving him a lot of money. I guess that's what he was talking about. Is it legal?'

Ralph smiled, though the sight of his teeth wasn't pleasant. 'You can submit what you like,' he said, 'but you risk a challenge from the Revenue Service. And if they choose to be awkward it can cost you a lot of time and money. From what I hear du Toit frequently pushes boundaries.'

'You don't like him, do you?'

'No, I don't. He's an arrogant SOB and so sharp that one of these days he'll cut himself. As soon as he became aware Frank owned one of PE's prominent businesses, he made every effort to poach him from me. I once had it out with him on the phone. Not that it got me anywhere. Interestingly, Mira was dead set against du Toit from the outset.'

I pricked up my ears. 'Do you know why?' I asked.

Ralph shook his head. 'That was the funny thing,' he said. 'I remember she rang me up once. And that of itself was unusual. It was at the point where Frank had told me he was going to make the change. She wanted to know what I was doing about it. I told her it was a free country and Frank could do what he wanted. When I asked her to explain her attitude, I didn't get much sense from her. She simply said she didn't trust du Toit and that she had an instinct for these things. As I recall, she got very upset and slammed down the phone. It was all very peculiar.'

At that juncture, my food arrived. 'Can I get you something else, Ralph?' I asked as the waitress put a polished aluminum frying pan containing my fish and a salad in front of me.

Ralph shook his head. 'Maybe later, when you've caught me up.'

I squeezed lemon over the salmon and began to eat. 'What did you think of Mira?' I swallowed a morsel of the fish; as always, it was delicious.

Ralph turned his chair to one side to free up long legs. 'Can't say I ever warmed to her,' he said. 'She didn't strike me as having much substance. Of course, Frank was besotted with her, and she could do no wrong. But that attitude cost him plenty.'

'Was she a substantial drain on the business?'

'No, no, it was nothing like that,' said Ralph dismissively. 'The business could afford her, but it didn't really get value for money from her. Not that that is a unique situation by the way.'

'So, Zap-It's healthy?'

'Very. Nothing's changed in that respect in years. There's no debt and the company generates plenty of cash. From these accounts,' and Ralph tapped the papers in front of him, 'Zap-It could have funded significant expansion without borrowing.'

I laid down my knife and fork. 'After Mira was kidnapped,' I began, 'Frank got du Toit involved in raising cash for the ransom. Obviously, his principal asset was Zap-It and he needed to raise money fast.'

'How much are we talking about?'

'50 million.'

Ralph raised an eyebrow. 'And did he get the money?'

I nodded. 'Du Toit sold Zap-It to brothers who are Cape Town entrepreneurs. The payment showed up in one of Frank's bank accounts. What I want to know is what the business is worth. I mean was it a good deal, Ralph, or did Frank get ripped off?'

Wishful thinking made me ask the question so I really shouldn't have been disappointed by the answer. In my experience, people with qualifications as bean counters, legal beagles, deep divers and the like hedge their bets. It's all part of the mystique and having plenty of that means you can charge plenty of bucks for everything you do. Me, I like to cut to the chase, but they thrive on the exact opposite.

'It's difficult for me to comment,' said Ralph predictably. 'I don't do M&A work and you'd need to talk to someone who does. What I can tell you is that from the latest accounts, shareholders' funds stood at over 40 million. So, a figure of 10 million as a premium sounds a bit light.'

'OK, so if you were selling, what sort of opening bid would you look for?'

'I can't tell you that.' Ralph must have seen my look of exasperation because he added quickly: 'If it's any help Sol, I can say Frank got frequent approaches to sell up. He was never interested but I remember one party a while back who talked about a figure of not less than 80 million. And that was based on what he deduced about the scale of the PE operation. As far as I'm aware, he never got access to accounts or any internal management figures.'

CHAPTER TWENTY-EIGHT

I spent millions disposing of my father's business interests because of the legal and accounting issues that arose. It meant there were people in some of the largest professional services firms in the country who were prepared to give me the time of day. But I needed more than that, so I put in a call to Daniel Hetherington in Pretoria. He was a young guy and as bright as a newly minted Kruggerrand. He worked as a gopher for a corporate finance partner and he and I had spoken frequently about one transaction that proved problematic because of governance issues. I liked him for his friendliness and for his unassuming manner though we never actually met.

Unfortunately, Daniel wasn't around so I asked he contact me later at Lovemore Heights. I was told to expect a call by the end of the morning.

In the meantime, I looked through Mira's possessions. My justification for this, if any was needed, was that her duplicity raised questions as to her character. Of course, this was the policeman in me, but my SAPS experience had taught me you can always trust dishonest people to be dishonest. On that premise, I wondered if there was anything in Mira's past I should know about. Or anything that might specifically cast light on what had happened to her. Besides, I was doing nothing else that morning except waiting in for the pool man.

Frank and Mira had shared a bedroom at the back of house along with a large walk-in wardrobe. His stuff was on the left and hers on the right. His was well-ordered and tidy while hers looked as though a troop of baboons had enjoyed an hour or two of playtime. But 20 minutes spent rummaging through her collection of designer clothes, shoes and handbags revealed nothing of interest.

I moved on to her bathroom. The two of them had each had one of those; his on one side of the wardrobe, hers on the other. Dominated by a roll-top acrylic bath with white claw feet, my interest in hers was focused on the cabinets and cupboards surrounding the fancy wash basin. Once more, something near chaos reigned within each of these as I pulled open one door after another. But I was rewarded at last with the discovery of a jewellery box. It was hidden behind an array of Dermalogica skincare products.

Speaking of a time when different economic circumstances had dictated her life, the box was battered and covered in faux leather dyed claret-red. A cheap gold clasp had originally served to hold it shut but this was now bent out of shape and tarnished with age.

I went through what was there with care.

I found her birth certificate; a marriage certificate; *two* sets of divorce papers from the High Court in Cape Town; some old school reports; and assorted receipts, letters and postcards whose significance meant nothing to me. There were also a few small black and white photos and one which was considerably larger. But this had been torn into pieces and when I put them together, I found myself viewing the picture of an unknown woman who looked to be in her sixties. None of the photos, as far I could see, featured Mira.

Amongst artifacts at the bottom of the box were an amethyst ring, a necklace of fresh-water pearls which needed restringing, a thin silver bracelet, and an inexpensive man's watch with the initials DGS engraved on the back.

What was apparent once I ended my examination was that Mira had lied to Frank. She'd misrepresented her age; the fact she'd been married more than once; and the location of her birthplace. This last intrigued me, especially as Frank had said she'd been born and raised by well-to-do parents in Bloemfontein.

The reality was she'd first seen the light of day in the township of Manenberg situated about 20 kms from the centre of Cape Town. It

149

had been created by the apartheid government to house low-income coloured families under the Group Areas Act. More significantly, it was the place from which some of Mira's kidnappers had come. Was that coincidence or a viable lead?

I heard from Daniel Hetherington at 12.30. Because he was an affable guy, I regretted the tale I told him about Frank's business and the reason for my call because it was only as honest as a Chinese Rolex. It finished with my agreeing to send him scanned copies of Zap-It's last accounts with the details identifying the company's name and its location deleted.

'I'll await those with interest, Mr. Nemo,' he said. 'Do you know how your friend's business has performed since the year end?'

'The upward trend's continued.'

'That's most encouraging. It means the enterprise has momentum. When I get the accounts, I'll prepare an executive summary and circulate it internally. Of course, any price ultimately achieved is always down to what somebody is prepared to pay on a particular day. The most that'll emerge from this exercise will be an indicative figure. Or rather an indicative range.'

'I understand,' I said.

It was a few days before Daniel came back to me, at which point I was surprised to learn his indicative range was between 120 and 150 million bucks. 'How come so much?' I queried.

'Security's a hot area, Mr. Nemo. You've only got to look at the crime stats to appreciate that. Also, colleagues have said there are add-ons which can generate new revenue streams beyond the basic armed response service. The consensus is that your friend's business, if put up for sale, might well attract a bidding war.'

'Really' I said thoughtfully. 'My friend's close to retirement. If he wanted to continue working for a spell but release cash from a partial sale how would that affect the numbers?'

'But there's already substantial cash held in the business,' Daniel said. 'Or at least there was at the balance sheet date.' He paused and I heard paper rustling. 'There's a figure here of 9.3 million. If more was required, the business could borrow using its assets as collateral. The debtors' list would be the obvious place to start.'

'And if more than that was required, could a minority stake in the business be sold?'

'There are potentially a range of possibilities. Naturally, it's all predicated upon the desirability of what's on offer, but I think we've covered that already.'

I thanked Daniel for his time and rang off. Before I did, he told me his firm wouldn't charge for the time spent as they hoped to be tasked with the sale at some future date. I muttered something about that being unlikely in the near future.

The information from Daniel could have been used more quickly but I was distracted by a house move. Specifically, I'd decided to quit the property at Seaview and return to the City, but not to Frank's place: it was far too big and held a lot of memories I'd struggle to cope with.

My relocation wasn't as dramatic as it sounded. I left behind my furniture and decamped taking clothing plus some personal effects and transferred them into a two-bed furnished rental. The owners of the place were away temporarily, and my lease was for no more than six months. The decision to move had been easy as my house continued to unnerve me, particularly at night. It was all part of my being kind to myself, an idea sold to me by one of the psychiatrists recommended by the Steinberg Clinic. I'd seen him once since returning to PE and we agreed to meet at weekly intervals.

My new home was located close to St. George's Park which meant it was more or less in the centre of PE. It was in a five-storey building in a gated complex and viewed from the road looked like nothing so much as a fancy wedding cake with its tiered construction and white facings.

It was while sitting out one morning that my thoughts turned towards du Toit. Nothing I heard from Daniel dissuaded me from the view that he'd acted with the sole objective of taking control of Zap-It. Most disturbing was the revelation that the enterprise had apparently been disposed of for a fraction of what it was worth to a couple of individuals that the accountant had conjured up from somewhere in Cape Town. No doubt, du Toit would argue he was under pressure because of Mira's kidnap and in all the circumstances he'd done his best. But I was making assumptions about his views when I really needed to hear from the man himself. The decision to have it out with him was an easy one.

'Eugene du Toit please,' I said when ringing his office in the Cape Road.

'Who's calling *Mr.* du Toit?' said the male receptionist.

'Sol Nemo.'

There was a pause with the line open. Then the phone went dead as though I'd been cut off. A couple of minutes wait ensued before I heard a voice say, 'What's it about?'

'He'll know.'

'Nevertheless, you need to tell me.'

'Are you like this with everyone?' I asked irritably.

'Mr. du Toit is extremely busy, and I'm instructed to ensure his time's not wasted.'

'OK, try running Zap-It Armed Response up the flagpole.'

This time the phone went dead immediately. I waited and gazed out towards the park from my balcony. Far off, I saw a mother pushing a buggy with a small dog attached by its lead.

'I'm terribly sorry, sir,' said a new voice, 'but Mr. du Toit is unable to talk to you now. Perhaps you could call back later in the day?'

'What time would you suggest?'

'End of day is usually best. Will that be all, sir?'

I tried at the end of the day and again on the following day, twice, but to no avail.

In-between, I tried to call Arnie as we'd not seen each other since before Frank's death. But he wasn't around so I sent a text notifying him of my move to St. George's Park. As I was now back in town, we could meet up at short notice. Barney's, for example, was only ten minutes away.

I was also left a message by my insurers advising that the work on the Mustang had been approved. They asked me to contact repairers based near Despatch to book the car in. I rang and agreed a date for the coming Friday but, when they learned of my new address, said one of their apprentices could pick up the car on his way to work. They were pleased to tell me it was all part of their new, customer service offer.

It wasn't difficult for me to decide I couldn't just leave my questions for du Toit unspoken. That afternoon I took a walk from my apartment into the Cape Road and crossed the dual carriageway to access his office. It was in one of those converted bungalows set back about 50 metres from the highway. What would once have been the spacious front garden now served as a car park.

Black letters picked out on a gold metal plaque by the glass entrance doors announced my arrival at LE BUREAU DU TOIT and underneath in hardly less intrusive capitals the legend EUGENE DU TOIT B.COM (ACCOUNTING), CA (SA)-SENIOR PARTNER. The words 'and Associates' merited but lower-case italics on the third line. From this, it was apparent whose hand it was that slid the beads on the abacus.

But more than this what registered profoundly was the level of security at the place. Breaking in would have been out of the question as double-width armoured glass doors at the street entrance were duplicated at the end of a short internal passage. It was noteworthy too that every external window was heavily barred. It put me in mind of du Toit's home with its parallel lines of electric fences encircling his whole estate.

The reception desk on the far side of an expanse of deep wool carpet was fashioned from Italian marble the colour of ivory. The complexion of the receptionist behind it matched almost exactly as she lifted almond eyes to mine.

'My name's Sol Nemo,' I said before she could speak. 'I'm looking for Eugene du Toit. And before you ask, I don't have an appointment.'

'Perhaps you'd like to take a seat,' she said, 'and I'll enquire as to his availability.'

I was only a little mollified by her response. 'Tell him it's about a company called Zap-It Armed Response.'

'I'll be sure to do that.' She indicated a seating area on the left with a cool smile. 'Please make yourself comfortable.'

I had every intention of doing just that because my guess was the wait could be a long one. Helping myself to a cold drink from a bank of dispensers, I parked myself in one of several low leather chairs with chromium frames. It was positioned directly under one of the air-con units mounted in the ceiling. Leaning back, I was able to revel in the chilled air upon my hot face.

In the event, I sat for no longer than a few minutes before du Toit emerged and made a bee line towards me. He was wearing dark suit pants, a white shirt and a plain red tie. Seeing him again made me realize his face would struggle to wear any expression other than one of supercilious indifference. But I acknowledge he did try to alter it for me. He started by baring his teeth, in what he probably thought was a winning smile, and adopting a fawning tone of voice.

'I am so sorry to have kept you waiting, Mr. Nemo,' he said extending his claw-like hand. 'I believe you've been seeking a collo-quy for some days.'

I took the claw but briefly as it was strangely cold. 'Rather more by way of an explanation,' I said, 'than a conversation.'

'*Apropos?*'

'Zap-It Armed Response.'

Du Toit didn't bat an eyelid, but he did observe that an elderly couple who'd arrived moments before were hovering within earshot. 'I think we'll adjourn to somewhere private,' he said. 'Follow me.'

I trailed behind him along a corridor hung with framed pictures of a yacht. It was one of those rich man's playthings and I picked out the name *Alchemy* painted onto its pure white bow.

We ended up in a room where three chairs and a narrow table with a computer made the place look crowded. Du Toit waved me into a seat. 'Explanation of what?' he said without preamble.

'Why it was necessary to dispose of Zap-It.'

Du Toit looked puzzled. 'What exactly is your point?'

'Frank's main asset was the company, but it wasn't the only one,' I began. 'He had resources outside the business. By that I mean liquid assets. For example, he valued his stock portfolio at two and a half million but when I updated it was nearer six. Added together with the cash which could have been released from Zap-It, Frank had close to 20 million bucks to put on the table. Why didn't you negotiate with that?'

'The demand, may I remind you,' said du Toit, 'was for 50 million. I was dealing with some extremely difficult and unpleasant people who continually made threats. You also seem to forget I had my client's power of attorney. Everything undertaken on Mr. Zarakolu's behalf was sanctioned in writing.'

'Hardly,' I countered. 'What you may have had was a general authority. How was Frank to approve what you were doing after his heart attack?'

Du Toit evidently wasn't used to being questioned which was why the muscles in his jaw tightened. 'The legal position, Mr. Nemo, is unequivocal. So is the *de facto* one. Mr. Zarakolu wanted his wife back whatever the material cost. I informed you of that when we first met.'

I ignored him. 'Let me repeat my question,' I said. 'Why was it necessary to dispose of Zap-It? I believe other arrangements might have been worked out.'

'Such as?'

'Maybe, by giving up a minority interest in return for cash. Such an initiative would have preserved Frank's control.'

Du Toit's face creased into one of his smiles, only it looked like a self-righteous smirk. 'You clearly have no idea what you're talking about,' he said bluntly. 'The value of minority stakes in private companies is typically discounted by up to 90%.'

155

I wasn't to be put off so easily. 'Yet my advice is that security businesses are highly sought after. And that deals may be structured to mutual advantage and in many ways.'

'Whence derives this intelligence?'

I named the multinational firm who employed Daniel Hetherington and watched du Toit's high forehead acquire a sheen of perspiration. Nonetheless, he came back at me. 'And in absorbing this advice, did you explain all the circumstances?' he asked.

I had to admit I hadn't. 'How did you locate the guys who bought Zap-It?' I asked, changing tack.

'If it's any business of yours,' said du Toit regaining some measure of his self-assurance, 'I do work in the M&A space. That's mergers and acquisitions to you. In that regard, I maintain a database of clients looking for suitable business opportunities.'

'The deal went together remarkably quickly, didn't it?'

'Explained by the circumstances pertaining, Mr. Nemo, as we've already touched upon. Frankly, I think we've exhausted this topic so I'm going to terminate our discussion.'

Abruptly, the accountant stood up and would have made for the door, but my voice halted him. Despite himself, he turned back and sat down again.

'Based on the last set of statutory accounts,' I said, 'I'm advised the indicative value of Zap-It was between 120 and 150 million. You appear to have done a deal at a considerable undervalue. By doing so, you also chose to ignore Frank's other assets. Those could have been used to limit what needed to be raised from the business.'

'Ach, now I see what this is all about,' said du Toit. 'Are you perhaps speaking as a disgruntled beneficiary?'

For the first time *I* smiled. 'You're missing the point, du Toit. For your information, Frank has left me his house in Lovemore Heights. The bulk of his estate though goes to his sister and to her children. All in all, everybody's very well provided for, including me. Finally, let me assure you I don't need the house or the money that might be derived from its sale.'

At that point, du Toit decided to lose his temper. 'So, what sort of travesty has this performance of yours been?' he said, his voice rising. 'Don't you think I've better things to do than indulge your whimsicalities?'

'No doubt you have,' I retorted, 'but nevertheless you've seen me face-to-face today. I'm surprised you agreed to do that. It leads me to think you're feeling insecure.' I paused and saw the sheen of perspiration return to the accountant's forehead. 'A while back,' I went on, 'I disposed of several businesses owned by my late father. It took months and yet there you were within days of a kidnap able to find a couple of guys prepared to take over Frank's business lock, stock and barrel. Admittedly, at what seems to have been a knockdown price.'

Du Toit's countenance had paled while I was speaking, and some constriction afflicted his throat because he coughed noisily. 'What exactly are you implying?' he demanded in a strangled voice.

'I'm not implying anything. What I'm saying is that I spent years working for SAPS. I'm also saying that after a while you get a nose for something that's not right. And there's something here that's not right. I'm going to find out what it is because I owe it to Frank's memory.'

I stood up and made for the door. This time roles were reversed because it was du Toit's voice that halted me in my tracks. 'You would be extremely foolish to meddle in my affairs,' he said with an effort.

I turned and looked into his pale face. I saw the nervousness in his eyes and the sweat on his upper lip and I measured the threat. 'Uh-huh,' I said, before opening the door and walking out.

CHAPTER TWENTY-NINE

At about the time I was returning on foot to St. George's Park, my phone logged a missed call from Ayesha. I'd heard nothing from her since sending a long email during my stay at the Steinberg Clinic. I was disappointed not to have heard from her earlier, particularly as it wasn't infrequently that my thoughts turned in her direction.

I tried to get in touch but all that was available was her messaging service. I left a voicemail doing no more than acknowledging her call and saying it was great to hear from her. Given she'd taken so long to contact me, I figured it had taken resolve on her part to act as she had. I didn't want to scare her off by seeming needy.

I had another call from her two days later but couldn't pick up and so missed out again. Trying once more to reach her only resulted in further disappointment.

Communication on other fronts wasn't going well either. Isabelle got the names of the two guys who'd acquired Frank's company from the Operations Manager at Zap-It. Her reaction though to my misgivings about what had happened was muted as I don't believe she understood the issues. For my part, I did background research on the two investors which revealed nothing untoward. But my attempts to reach them at their business address in Cape Town proved unsuccessful. This wasn't surprising as I had no standing in the matter. Nevertheless, I left messages asking to be called.

Friday morning found me awake before dawn. I slept badly but there was no reason for my insomnia. A high, daily dose of chill pills now kept the demons at bay and most of the time reduced my level of anxiety to a mild unease. But I found nights difficult and often took a sedative to help me sleep.

I got up, dressed and from the living room watched the sun peep over the green domed roof of the cricket ground and infiltrate the branches of the palms standing outside. St. George's Park was quiet at that time of day and along the concourse leading to the arena the wooden seats mounted on their pre-cast concrete supports stood unoccupied and slicked with dew.

Feeling hungry, I made breakfast and contemplated how best to entertain my new neighbours. A housewarming had been suggested by my psychiatrist who was keen for me to engage on as many levels as possible. But, to my way of thinking, filling my place with strangers had considerable drawbacks. For instance, and from previous experience, disclosure of my line of work usually killed conversation as quick as an eyelid's blink.

So engaging was this topic that I must have dozed off because my phone vibrating on the coffee table didn't rouse me immediately. And when I did pick it up, it was without checking who was calling.

'Sol?'

'Hi,' I said.

'Sol, it's Ayesha.'

That got my motor running. 'Hi. Hi there, Ayesha. Sorry, I was daydreaming. It's great to hear your voice. How are you?'

'I'm good. How's things with you?'

'I'm OK. Moving back into town seemed the best thing to do. I've taken a rental for six months.'

'Makes sense after what you felt about the other place. I guess you'll sell it, won't you?'

'Already on the market. I think it could be a while though before someone bites.'

'Talking of time,' said Ayesha, 'I'm sorry I didn't get in touch sooner but . . .'

'It's OK,' I interrupted. 'I'm sure you had your reasons. I also wanted to apologize for . . .'

'Sol, you don't have to say anything,' she said firmly. 'I rang to see how you are and catch up. Light stuff, that's all. If we meet again, we can discuss how things might work out between us. Is that OK?'

'That's fine, Ayesha.' But it wasn't as the croak in my voice testified. That word *if* had dried out my mouth as fast as water squeezed from a sponge. I took a gulp of coffee and made an effort. 'So, what have you been up to?' I asked, trying to sound casual.

'I was away a couple of weeks.'

'Sounds good. Where did you go?'

'Europe.'

'Where exactly?'

'It was one of those tours of European capitals. You know the sort of thing. We did London, Paris, Berlin, Rome, and Barcelona spending a couple of days in each place.'

'Which city did you like best?'

Ayesha didn't get to answer because at that moment the bell rang, and I asked her to hang on. I walked with the phone to the door and opened it. There was a young black guy standing outside wearing an old golf cap. Long thin legs emerged from blue shorts and on his feet he wore white trainers that looked several sizes too large. I gazed at him blankly.

'I've come to pick up the Mustang,' he said with a smile, a gleam of anticipation in his dark eyes.

I stared at him for a few seconds and caught up fast. 'Of course, I'd forgotten all about it. Hang on a minute. I need to get the keys.' I walked towards the bedroom. 'Hi Ayesha, a guy's come to pick up the car.'

'That's fine, Sol. I'm not going anywhere.'

I went back to the door and gave the driver the keys. 'Take the lift to the basement garage,' I said. 'When you come out, it's in the corner bay. You can't miss it.'

'She driving OK?'

'She drives fine. She don't look too pretty though.'

'We'll soon fix that.' Then the guy was gone, and I closed my front door.

'Hi Ayesha. Tell me, which city did you like best?'

'I was thinking while you were talking. It's difficult to pick one. Maybe, I could pick two?'

'That's fine,' I said crossing the corridor back into the living room and opening the door to the balcony. 'You've my permission to pick two, but please not London.'

'What's wrong with London?'

'Didn't I tell you about my time there?'

'I don't believe you did.'

'About my four days of utter misery? -Surely, I did. Anyway, it rained most of the time. The courier lost some of my luggage. Everything was ridiculously expensive and on top of everything, I got food poisoning.'

Ayesha laughed. 'You're making it up, Sol.'

'Maybe the bit about the food poisoning,' I conceded, laughing with her. 'But the weather was lousy, and everybody looked so depressed. I liked Paris much more.'

Suddenly, I heard the burble from the Mustang's engine and from my balcony saw the car emerge from the basement onto the paved apron out front. Slowly, it rolled towards the exit and the security booth.

'So did I,' said Ayesha, 'but I didn't know what to make of the Parisians.'

She started to say something else, but my attention was elsewhere. In the morning sun, I saw the gleam of blue paint on the car's roof dissolve all at once in a toxic black cloud. At the same time there was the sound of a heavy detonation. On the fourth floor, I felt the force of the blast against my face and mesmerised watched the Mustang's bonnet claw its way into the air and fall back to earth somewhere out of sight. From the thick choking smoke, tongues of fire leapt skywards and engulfed the car from end to end.

CHAPTER THIRTY

Whether from the force of the explosion or from instinct, I fell back and collided with the rear wall of the balcony. Pain in my shoulder would register later but, at that moment, my attention was held by the smoke and fire raging below. Even though the roof of the car had been ripped open by the blast, there was no sign of the driver. But I did see the security guard rush from his booth towards the wreck, a protective hand held close to his face as he watched helplessly.

I stood there shaking until Ayesha's voice grabbed my attention. She was shouting down the phone: 'Sol! -Sol, what's happening? I heard a large bang. Sol please . . .'

'It's-It's my car.'

'What happened?'

'M-My car just blew up.'

'Blew up? What do you mean?'

'It was a bomb. It was meant for me.' With that awareness, panic took over. 'Ayesha, I must go. It's not safe. I-I'll call you later.'

'But shouldn't you contact the police?'

'I-I don't trust SAPS. I'll call you soon Ayesha. I will . . . I really will. Sorry.' With that I killed the connection.

I didn't linger, adrenalin fuelling my actions. Taking my Tomcat with shaking hands from the bedside table took seconds. Checking the clip and taking the safety off a few seconds more. In the palm of my hand, the gun was reassuring. Small and light it might have been, but it was effective and easily concealed. I'd have preferred the heavier Glock, but it was scrap inside the Mustang.

Pumped, I threw personal effects into a holdall and left. Gun in hand, I hurried down the steps to the basement. Seeing no one, I nonetheless heard shouts and raised voices from the garage ramp. I turned the other way and rushed an emergency door at the back. Emerging into the sunlight to the sound of sirens, I sprinted past well-tended borders and on through shadows cast by a carob tree. A moment later, I pushed open the street gate.

On the other side I took stock, my heart racing. The street was quiet until the air was shredded by a SAPS *bakkie*. It tore past me, quickly followed by an ambulance.

Shakily, I walked clutching the holdall, my other hand clasped round the gun. At the end of the road, I turned towards St. George's. As an empty taxi emerged from the hospital grounds, I hailed it and climbed in.

'Where to?' asked the driver.

'Just drive,' I yelled. The guy looked askance in the rear-view mirror. 'Just take off man. I need outta here.'

He drove and I tried to stop hyperventilating, but my breathing was ragged. Still shaking, I put the safety on the Tomcat and dropped it in the holdall.

The taxi's route took me as far as the Albany Road Interchange where it headed north. Shortly after, I knew where to head for and the road to Coega wasn't it. On my order, and avoiding the centre of PE, we turned and made a long anti-clockwise loop on the city's north side. Soon after, we headed south along Mission Road and from there it took only a little time to reach Seaview.

Maybe, I was being paranoid, but I had the taxi drop me half a kilometre from my house. I thought pitching up outside my gates might expose me to some new threat. But, in walking a circuitous route home, I observed nothing untoward. There were no suspicious vehicles and no human activity bar one woman who was trimming the edges of a rectangular flower bed. From beneath the brim of a battered straw hut with a light blue ribbon, she gave me a disdainful look and quickly turned her head away. My house was in an area of mostly white folks where elderly neighbours sometimes regarded me as they might their garden boys. Or maybe I was being paranoid.

My house was as quiet as the hush of evening. I let myself in and swiftly crossed to my study. I found two clips of ammunition and drew all my cash reserves from the wall-mounted safe. After that, I put additional clothes into the holdall and took the Fiesta out of the garage. I was in and out of the place within ten minutes.

Along the coast lay Blue Horizon Bay. Large houses built on the hillside have spectacular views over the ocean and beach. About half the properties are second homes occupied for a few short weeks each year. This makes BHB about as lively as a funeral directors' convention. But it suited my purposes well as I descended the steep road to the community centre and its car park at the back of the dunes.

A rain shower meant I was left undisturbed in removing the Fiesta's number plates and swapping them for ones from a parked Mercedes. Though wet through by the time the switch was finished, it was worth my time as I left driving a vehicle as distinctive as a paper cup and now displaying a false ID.

CHAPTER THIRTY-ONE

'Sol, you could have come to me.'

'A few hours ago, Ayesha, you were talking about *if* we met again.' I was sitting under a huge canvas awning at an open-air restaurant in Mossel Bay, the weather having improved as I drove west. I'd put in a call to Ayesha while I waited for my food. It was cooking metres away from me over a fire enclosed within a large circle of stones.

Ayesha sighed. 'That was then,' she said. 'This is now.'

Letting her get away with that wasn't an option. 'Ayesha, I don't understand what's changed.' I rubbed my left shoulder which was sore from its hard contact with the balcony wall.

'What's changed, dummy, is you could have been killed.'

'So, you do care?'

Ayesha was silent for a moment. 'I tried not to after you took off and disappeared like that,' she said. 'And now it looks like you're doing the same thing again. Why go to Cape Town?'

'Cowardice,' I said.

'I don't understand.'

'It's a good idea to be away from PE for a while.'

'OK,' she said slowly, 'but I'm guessing that's not the only reason.'

I turned away from a family of five sharing my long bench table and said seriously, 'All this began with Mira's kidnap. I'm puzzled as to why she was targeted.'

'Because she was married to a man with money?'

'That's fine as far as it goes,' I said, before explaining to Ayesha what led to my suspicions about du Toit's involvement and that he'd threatened me.

'I still think you should tell the police and let them handle it.'

'I don't believe they'll get anywhere. Unless there's real evidence, they don't stand a chance with a character like du Toit. He's smart enough to keep himself out of trouble.'

'OK, but how's Cape Town going to make any difference?

'It was where Frank met Mira for a start and there are things I need to look into.' Briefly, I explained what I'd discovered among Mira's possessions in Frank's house and how this shaped my view that there might be more to the situation than met the eye.

Ayesha finally saw the logic of what I was saying. 'You promise to be careful?'

'I'll tread lighter than a spider's feet, I said. 'Besides, nobody knows me in Cape Town.'

'Please stay safe, *mon ami*. You will ring me soon, won't you?'

'I will, Ayesha. I will.'

I expected a call from Bezuidenhout and wasn't disappointed. It came through as I was finishing the last of my meal. I let it go to voicemail and heard him say: *I'd be grateful if you could contact me urgently. There was an-er-incident earlier today involving a vehicle registered to you. Unfortunately, a fatality resulted and we're unable at present to verify . . . blah blah.*

In other words, could I be kind enough to check in with him so he didn't have to go on believing I might have checked out. Thinking about it though left me in something of a dilemma. Currently, he had two people listed as missing: the driver from the vehicle repairers and me. Obviously, I was under an obligation to contact SAPS to advise them I was safe and well so the driver's relatives could be officially informed of his loss. To do anything else would leave his family nursing the agony of not knowing what had happened. On the other hand, staying well clear of SAPS seemed like a very good idea.

I resolved the situation with the help of the waitress after paying the bill. 'Can I borrow your cell?' I asked her in Afrikaans.

Suspicion flooded her face, and she began to back away. 'You were using your own phone half an hour ago,' she said accusingly. 'Why do you need mine?'

'I was, but now it's died. The thing is I need to call PE urgently.' I fished a 200-buck note from my pocket. 'I'm happy to pay and it won't take long.'

She looked at me and she looked at the note, the equivalent of a day's pay. 'I've a break coming up soon. You want to use my phone, you'll have to wait.'

'That's fine,' I said with a big smile. 'In the meantime, can you bring me an espresso?'

I drank the coffee patiently. By that time, the place was mostly empty, and I had an unrestricted view out to sea over the harbour wall. Away down the coast I made out the shape of a PetroSA rig, its contours softened by the heat haze. I assumed it was laid up for some reason as the oil fields are located over 100 miles south of the Bay.

When the waitress returned, she sat down opposite me and produced a top of the range iPhone. 'My whole life's here,' she said apprehensively, taking the banknote I promised her. 'Now, who is it you want to call?'

I gave her Bezuidenhout's number, and she keyed in the digits. When the phone rang, she passed it to me and moved a few metres away along the empty bench.

'Captain, it's Sol Nemo,' I said when he picked up.

'Thank you for calling. I'm relieved to hear from you Mr. Nemo.'

'I only rang so you can let the boy's family know. I doubt he was more than 20.'

'He'd just turned 19,' said Bezuidenhout sombrely. 'This is a very bad business. Were you hurt?'

'No, not really. I'm fine.' The captain was asking about physical injury and so that was what I addressed with him.

'I'm glad to hear that. I'm going to need a witness statement but for now tell me what happened.' I filled Bezuidenhout in after which he said, 'One of your neighbours said your car was parked out front.'

'They're mistaken. The spaces there are reserved for visitors. This morning they were empty.'

'I see. How do you believe the bomb was triggered?'

'It could have been a motion sensor or maybe it was triggered by remote.' The sudden realization that someone might have been watching for when the Mustang emerged from the basement distracted me and sent a shiver down my spine.

But Bezuidenhout was talking again. 'They're working hypotheses,' he said. 'We've a team collecting the debris. It'll be sent to Bomb Disposal in Pretoria. You know them?'

'Heard of them, but never had any dealings.'

'They'll need help and Interpol's likely to be the first port of call.'

Me, I was wondering where all this was leading. It seemed Bezuidenhout was in an expansive mood and keen to get me on side.

I soon found out which dead horse he was flogging. 'Do you recall my warning you to be careful?'

'I do.'

'Naturally, what's happened reinforces my concern.'

'Forewarned is forearmed,' I said. 'I can take care of myself.'

'Nevertheless, SAPS can protect you.'

'Frankly, Captain, I doubt that,' I said incredulously. 'I haven't forgotten the sequence of events on the night I tried to rescue Mira. It seems any SAPS initiative soon becomes public knowledge.'

Bezuidenhout bristled. 'You're not suggesting what happened this morning had anything to do with us, are you?'

'Frankly, I don't know what to think.'

'Well, you might like to think about this,' retorted the captain. 'Up until six hours ago, I was unaware you had a new address. I warned you some time ago you might be at risk. What heed you took of my advice I don't know but it's a fact that car of yours was highly distinctive. There are very few like it here. So, anybody wanting to know where you were had only to keep an eye on your car. I doubt it was that difficult.'

What he told me made sense. 'That could be why it was a bomb,' I said, thinking out loud. 'The car's bullet-proof. And I never drive with open windows.'

'Witness Protection would now be your best option. On a temporary basis of course. Just until all this is sorted out.'

I contemplated this for about half a second. 'No thanks,' I said. 'I'm going to hang loose for a while. But will you do one thing?'

'Depends on what it is.'

'I went to see du Toit a couple of days ago. I talked to him about the basis on which Frank's business had been sold. We didn't see eye to eye, and he ended up threatening me. To be honest, I didn't take him seriously. Apart from anything else, he struck me as a worried man. Given what happened this morning, why don't you apply some pressure? -Maybe, he'll crack.'

'And what do you intend to do?'

'As explained, I'll be hanging loose. And incidentally don't waste time tracing this call. It's borrowed from a friend and I'm leaving here right now.'

Mossel Bay was half way to my destination which was why I'd stopped there for lunch. The balance of the journey took me four hours and, on my arrival, I took the spur leading to Cape Town International Airport.

I booked into a local hotel as it was too late to look for anywhere else. But this was a short-term initiative as the place was far too

169

public for my liking. I resolved to move somewhere quieter the next day. In the meantime, there was the night to contend with. Sleeping fitfully, the Tomcat with the safety off within reach, I awoke the following morning hung over from the effects of too much sedative.

It wasn't a great start to my Cape Town investigation.

CHAPTER THIRTY-TWO

I ate a large breakfast late, drank plenty of water and three cups of strong black coffee, and checked out when the maid arrived.

I drove the Fiesta into the city centre and took the road past Zonnebloem, its empty hectares witness still to the apartheid-era clearances which designated it a whites-only area. Beyond was the V&A Waterfront with its outlook over Table Bay. Bypassing Duncan Dock and the container terminal on my right, I continued west and parked on the outskirts of the Malay Quarter.

My familiarity with Cape Town was limited but I had pleasant memories of the Bo-kaap and after locking the car set off on foot. The exercise would clear my head while I sought out somewhere to stay.

Built on the slopes of Signal Hill, the Bo-kaap is an area of narrow streets and 19th century houses each painted in primary or secondary colours. As an alternative to the mind-numbing monotony of much seen elsewhere, the variegated yellows, blues, reds, greens and oranges of the individual dwellings are a tonic for the spirit. No wonder then the area is popular with tourists who stroll around and visit the museum or sample Cape Malay food.

But for me somewhere higher up the hillside was essential where I felt less hemmed in by the network of streets and cramped alley-ways. So, despite the heat of the day, I bent my footsteps uphill where a sign directed me onwards and upwards to a guesthouse called The Lookout, apparently located no more than 400 metres distant.

171

After I'd trudged twice that distance, the folly of not using the car struck me.

I finally reached my destination like a man completing a couple of back-to-back triathlons. Leaning against a gate post and gasping for breath, I was hailed from the front door by a party I assumed was the owner. He was in something more than his middle years and his barrel chest was barely contained by a checked, short-sleeved shirt. I did no more than raise an arm in acknowledgement and stagger slowly in his direction.

'You look like you could use a drink,' he called to me with what I thought penetrating insight.

'Fresh lungs . . . would be . . . better.'

He laughed at that. 'Don't you have a car?'

'Back there,' I said, pointing down the hill.

'Not many people walk up here.' He stepped forward and shook my hand. 'I'm Ryker.'

'Sol . . . I'm not surprised . . . The sign said half . . . half a kilo.'

Ryker looked embarrassed. 'I got someone to repaint it a while back, but his idea of distance was way off. I've been meaning to sort it out ever since.'

It wasn't the only thing that needed sorting out. The exterior of Ryker's rambling house appeared unpainted since Mandela and the others started doing time across the Bay on Robben Island. Then, when Ryker showed me to my room upstairs, I noticed threadbare carpet and that the armchair by the windows had a rip in its brown leather back.

But for all that, the place suited me perfectly. One of the windows faced down the hill I'd climbed which meant any vehicle approaching could be seen a long way off. The other looked out east towards the Waterfront and the port area. If I was around in the mornings, I'd be able to sit and let the sun bathe my face.

I took the room for a week and sealed the arrangement with Ryker over a can of Iron Brew.

After that, I retrieved the Fiesta and drove back up the road to my new roost. I dropped off my clothes and changed into long pants concealing an ankle holster housing the Tomcat. Opinion divides as to the merits of wearing these on the inside or outside of the leg. For me it's the outside so I strapped it to my right leg as it's my right hand that hefts a gun. Having the weapon available like that meant I was neither paranoid nor relaxed concerning my present circumstances. As is so often the case, I live with an ongoing feeling of general unease.

CHAPTER THIRTY-THREE

That afternoon I drove the few kms to Camps Bay. I went south via the road that turns back on itself and brings you out into the main drag. With the Lion's Head rising precipitously into the sky in front of me, I cruised the length of the esplanade but found nowhere to park. Turning round I retraced my route and was lucky to dart into a space vacated seconds before by a white Mercedes sport.

By chance, I found myself within metres of Bennie's located opposite the long sandy beach. The venue was sandwiched between a couple of fancy boutiques on one side selling must-have stuff to must-have-money people and on the other by a café with duck egg blue parasols called The Pantry. It looked like a nice place serving nice food and nice drinks to nice white people.

A staircase led from street level up to the first floor. After my morning's exercise, I crawled with aching limbs up the steps to a pair of glass doors. Above them I read the word Bennie's picked out in diminutive and unlit neon script.

So far so underwhelmed, but I was in for a surprise on pushing my way in. Beyond the doors, there was a wide foyer with cloak and rest room facilities on each side. In the middle a grand staircase with shallow treads beckoned and I climbed once again, my feet cosseted by a royal blue carpet.

At the top I picked my way through dining tables with damask cloths lit by huge glass-sided lanterns and crossed a parquet floor. Next to it stood a drum kit and black speakers set up on a semi-circular stage. In front of me was a long bar counter, the shelved bottles behind reflecting a preoccupation with Cape wines and brandies. A fan stood on the end of the counter, its oscillations rustling the edges of a pile of papers held together by a large, bull-dog clip. But for that, Bennie's was as silent as a redundant chapel. I parked myself on a bar stool and rested my weary bones.

Barely having begun to enjoy my inertia, a voice suddenly shouted, 'Where the bloody hell have you been?'

I turned my head and saw a large white guy striding towards me. 'You talking to me?' I asked.

'I don't see anybody else here.' His voice hadn't moderated despite the fact he'd covered most of the distance between us. 'What sort of time do you call this?' he ranted. 'You were overdue an hour back.'

'Not me,' I said looking at his heavy jowls and bald pate. 'You've got me confused with somebody else.'

That brought him to a shuddering halt. 'Aren't you the repair man?'

'Repair for what?'

'Bloody photocopier.'

I tried to be helpful, 'I saw a sign down the street advertising copy services,' I volunteered.

The guy looked at me as though I was a half-wit. 'I've been here seven years. Don't you think I know that?' he declared. 'What I need is high-quality, four-colour prints for tonight's menu. Down the street, producing sharp black and white stuff is a big ask. I'd have to be bloody desperate to use them.'

I shrugged sympathetically. 'I could use a drink. How's about I buy you one at the same time? It might calm you some.'

I guessed the guy was the manager from the cut of his lounge suit. He looked at me suspiciously. 'What do you want?'

'Information,' I said.

'About what?'

'Someone who used to work here.'

'And you are?'

'Sol Nemo, private investigator.' I stuck out my hand.

I believe he took it because he saw the light of good fortune turning its seductive beam upon his face. 'Can't really serve you a drink,' he said in a softer tone. 'We're closed this time of day.'

'But I'm not a customer,' I said with a grin. 'What we may have here is a little trade which would benefit from a spot of lubrication.'

The manager saw my point and for the first time smiled. 'Got your drift,' he said. 'What did you say your name was?'

'Sol.'

'OK, Sol. I'm Marty. Give me a couple of minutes. First, I need to chase those buggers at the copier company. I'll phone from the office.'

He strode away and it wasn't long before I heard his voice raised in indignation, a torrent of words pouring out of him like water cascading down the spillway of a dam.

'Mission accomplished?' I asked when he returned.

'They've said no more than 30 minutes.' Marty positioned himself behind the bar and looked at me. 'What can I get you?'

'Castle Lite. And what will you have?'

Marty didn't answer but instead reached up behind him to the topmost glass shelf and brought down a bottle of 20-year-old KWV brandy. 'Shall we call it a double?' he asked.

I smiled. 'Is there anything else?'

I watched him pour himself a drink, take an appreciative sip and open a Castle Lite for me. He pushed the bottle over. 'That's 270 bucks,' he said.

I knew Cape Town prices were high, but this was ridiculous. I said nothing though and gave him 300. 'Keep the change.'

'Thanks. I assume there's more where that came from if I can help you.'

Wordlessly, I fanned out some high denomination notes on the counter. 'It's about Mira Zarakolou,' I said.

'Mira Zara . . . Don't think I know the name.'

'She was a singer. She had a night spot here a few years' back.'

Marty's face, which had worn a puzzled frown, cleared. 'You mean Mira Mercouri,' he said. 'At least that was her stage name.'

'And you knew her?'

'Sure. She did a cabaret act for a while. Must have been for about a year all told.'

'What can you tell me about her?'

'Who's asking?'

I kept the story simple. 'Her husband,' I said. 'Mira became Mrs. Zarakolou when she married him. She was kidnapped and subsequently murdered in PE earlier this year. You might have heard about it.' Marty's eyebrows lifted in surprise, but not by much. 'Not me,' he said. 'I'm not interested in the news. It's all so depressing. If she's dead, what's the husband's interest?'

'It's about closure, Marty. I think he wants to try and understand why it happened. He didn't know a lot about her when they married. And she has no family. He's asked me to see what I can find out. Forgive me, but you don't seem overly concerned by what I've told you.'

Marty took a slug of brandy. 'I'm not,' he said flatly.

'Why?'

'Let's put it this way: she played fast and loose. And she didn't care much who she hurt along the way. Personally, I steered well clear.'

I nodded. 'Her husband had some concerns about her fidelity,' I said, recalling the pass she'd made at me. 'Where did she come from?'

'Bloemfontein so she said. I don't know whether she was born or brought up there, but it was the place she talked about sometimes.'

'How did she fetch up here?'

'She walked through the door one day. That's all. I used to call her the blow-in from Bloemfontein.'

I laughed. 'How did she become the resident chanteuse?'

'That's easy. We had a talent night. She was here with some guy and she got up on stage and did her stuff. She did a version of *I Will*

Survive. It was a good choice as she certainly knew how to look after number one. Anyway, it went down a storm and things took off from there. She and Reeva got on particularly well.'

'Reeva?'

'Yes, Reeva Naidoo. She was the manager at the time. I took over when she left.'

'But by then Mira had already gone?'

Marty nodded. 'About a year or so before.'

'So, when did Reeva leave?'

'Four years back or thereabouts.'

'Why did she go?'

'She had some personal problems,' said Marty vaguely. 'I didn't see it was any of my business to get involved. I've got enough stuff of my own.'

'Do you keep in touch?'

'I've called her now and again. But it's always been work-related.'

'When was the last time?'

Marty hesitated. 'Must be about six months ago,' he said slowly. 'She called me with some tax query. Apparently, SARS were chasing her for money. I copied some paperwork and sent it to her.'

'Where can I reach her?'

Marty looked meaningfully at the notes on the bar. 'What's it worth?'

'For all this, I reckon you'll have to offer more than a phone number,' I said. 'You think you've got more than that?'

Marty gave me a knowing look. 'There'll be an address in the office. Give me a minute and I'll check.' He looked at my almost empty glass. 'You like another beer?'

'You want money for it?'

Marty looked at the notes again and laughed. 'Hell no,' he said. He reached beneath the bar, lifted another Castle and levered off the top. As I poured the beer out, he lit out for his office.

He seemed to be gone a long time. So long, in fact, that the missing copier engineer was suddenly standing at my elbow. He was carrying a heavy black case and looked as though he'd been running from Lucifer himself.

'I'm so sorry to be late,' he said breathlessly before I could explain my presence. 'It's impossible to park out there. And I was held up on my last job.'

'The apology's fine with me,' I said, 'but you need to talk to the manager. You can find him round the back of the bar.'

'Right.' The guy looked embarrassed, picked up his case and walked in the direction my head was inclined.

If I expected ructions when manager and repair man met, I was to be disappointed. Attributing this to 20-year-old brandy spreading its warming cheer like a charity hand-out at Christmas seemed a logical deduction. Plus, of course, Marty's easy acquisition of my money.

When the manager did come back, he looked triumphant. He was carrying a single sheet of paper which he pushed across to me. 'What do you think?' he asked too quickly, draining the last of the KWV.

I read his neat handwriting and made out a cell phone number and three postal addresses, one of which was 'care of'. 'You tried the phone?' I asked.

'Just did. Thought I might get an instant hit for you. It says the voicemail's full.'

'No email?'

''Fraid not.'

'And the addresses?'

'The Bishopscourt one's the oldest. I used the 'care of' address in Mitchells Plain to send the stuff she wanted for SARS.'

'Did she say why she was using that address?'

'No, and I didn't ask. As I said, we weren't close.'

'But you put yourself out to help her.'

Marty shrugged. 'I guess,' he said. 'Thing was she didn't sound too good. She was coughing a lot and seemed to be struggling to get her breath.'

'I see. This last address is in Brooklyn. Where's that?'

'On the other side of Table Bay. Off the N1.'

'OK,' I said, indicating the money. 'It's yours. There's just one other thing. What does Reeva look like?'

In the act of putting the money in his pocket, Marty paused. 'Hell, I don't know,' he said before trying to concentrate. 'She's in her forties, not a bad looker, bit overweight, shoulder-length black hair. I can't think of anything else.'

'Sure?'

'If it helps, her colouring's about the same as yours.'

'Right.'

'Where can you be reached if there's anything else?'

'Is there likely to be?' I asked.

Marty shook his head.

'Then I guess that's it,' I said and walked out.

CHAPTER THIRTY-FOUR

I had one other appointment that day and that was to see Anton Trollip. Arranging the meeting had been surprisingly easy and had been accomplished before I'd driven to Bennie's.

The Trollips' business address was located at the far end of Adderley Street in the Central Business District and a short distance from the Adderley Hotel. I left the Fiesta a distance away which was wise as the thoroughfare outside their offices was a parking lot, the traffic jammed up in both directions. Shaking off the dust of the street and the impatient honking of horns, I entered a plush apartment block, answered the usual questions at reception and rode the elevator.

Apartment 511 lay at the end of a corridor whose picture window offered a spectacular view of Table Mountain. I admired it for all of three seconds before the door was opened by a young black girl. Her hair was arranged in a topknot and her silver hooped earrings were large enough to have been used as deck quoits.

'Sol Nemo,' I said. 'I rang earlier.'

'Anton's expecting you,' she said. 'Unfortunately, his schedule's changed so he won't be able to give you more than 15 minutes.'

I shrugged. 'Half of that will be ample.'

If she was taken aback by my response, she made no comment and led me into the living room. A workstation and next to it a long table, hosting a bank of stock-dealing screens, were the predominant features. At the far end, beyond floor-to-ceiling glass, was a spacious balcony where a man, around ten years my junior, sat in a cane chair. He was poring over a sheaf of papers that rested on his lap and using a yellow highlighter.

'You can go straight through,' said the girl. 'Do you want me to fix you a drink?' She indicated a water dispenser and coffee machine alongside a stuffed bookcase displaying a battered cricket bat and three trophies.

I declined, slid open the balcony door and stepped out. The noise disturbed Trollip who looked up before getting to his feet. 'Ach, Mr. Nemo. Thank you for coming,' he said, extending his hand and smiling.

I shook it, said it was no problem and was about to park myself in the spare chair when he spoke up again: 'Might be best if you closed the door.'

I did as he asked and sat down. Table Mountain was framed behind Trollip's broad shoulders, the air so clear it seemed you had only to reach out to touch the browns and greens of its craggy surfaces.

'What can I do for you?' he asked. He had pale blue eyes in an open face beneath blond hair cut short.

'It may be more about what I can do for you,' I retorted.

'OK, I'm listening.' Trollip's tone was cautious. 'You said on the phone you had certain facts to share with me about Zap-It.'

I nodded. 'You bought the business from Frank Zarakolu. I had a long personal association with Frank. In fact, I regarded him as the father I never had.'

'I see,' said the businessman. 'My brother and I were saddened by news of his unexpected death. And, of course, now you've explained who you are, may I offer you my condolences.'

'Thank you. I appreciate that.' Quickly, I collected my thoughts. 'Frank only agreed the sale as he needed to raise money to ransom his wife. She was kidnapped in PE back in January.'

From the expression on Trollip's face this was news, but he refrained from comment. He did stiffen though and suddenly I found his gaze intrusive.

'Eugene du Toit,' I went on, 'became Frank's accountant a year or two back and held his power of attorney. Du Toit took sole responsibility for all negotiations with the kidnappers whose demand was for 50 million bucks. There was one attempt at an exchange which I fronted but it went wrong. That cost Frank 10 million. The balance of the money which was to have been used for the ransom was paid to Frank by du Toit. It wasn't used because Mira was murdered by her abductors. I've seen a bank statement of Frank's which shows a single credit of 40 million.'

'And that's significant how?'

'You tell me,' I said evenly. 'What intrigued me when I investigated was that Frank had easily realisable assets running into millions. I used to work for SAPS and the playlist in kidnap cases was that usually the outrageous sum initially demanded is dramatically scaled back through negotiation. As far as I can see, du Toit made no move to negotiate anything with Mira's captors. He simply proceeded to sell Frank's business. And, as it turned out, it went to you and your brother.'

As I finished speaking Trollip's face tightened and its colour changed to that of puce. 'I trust you're not suggesting some impropriety,' he said sharply.

'I'm not suggesting anything at all. I only came here to present you with certain facts. I'm not a fool, Mr. Trollip, and I've already taken steps to check out the *bona fides* of you and your brother. While I've no background in commerce or finance, I've contacts that do. The feedback I received was positive, both as regards yours and your brother's integrity and competence.'

A gentle answer turns away wrath and the proverb proved itself here. Trollip relaxed and let his brain once again rule his emotions. 'What are these other facts?' he asked.

'OK,' I said. 'Frank had another accountant for years before he transferred his business to du Toit. This guy explained to me that net assets on the balance sheet I showed him were around 40 million. He thought a valuation of goodwill at no more than 10 million was too low. I then contacted a firm of accountants engaged in corporate finance work who gave me an indicative value of 120-150 million. Their view was that security's a hot sector and that Zap-It has plenty of potential.'

Trollip nodded his head at that but then his expression became quizzical. 'Just how familiar are you with Mr. Zarakolu's financial affairs?'

'Enough,' I said. 'Frank was a straight guy. He made a lot of money, and he paid a lot of taxes. The financial paperwork I found in his house confirmed what I've always known about his straight-forward approach. All his assets are in SA, and I found his tax affairs up-to-date and in order.'

'So, your best view is that if there had been other sale proceeds from Zap-It you would have found them?'

'That's a fair summary.'

'Are you by chance a beneficiary under his will?'

I smiled. 'I am to the extent he bequeathed me his house in PE. The rest of his estate, and I mean the rest, bar some small bequests, goes to his sister and her children. I've no financial axe to grind, if that's what you mean.'

Trollip gave me a long appraising look and glanced at his watch. Making a decision, he abruptly levered himself to his feet. 'I'm very grateful to you for taking the time and trouble to come and see me,' he said giving me a boyish grin. 'Rest assured, Mr. Nemo, I'll take things from here.'

'That would be my great pleasure,' I said.

CHAPTER THIRTY-FIVE

I stared through the rain-spattered windscreen and glanced again at the sheet of paper Marty had given me. The numbers tallied and I knew this was the right street because I'd passed a sign when I turned off the highway running between Brooklyn and the Ysterplaat Airbase.

I cursed the weather, so different from the day before, zipped up my light waterproof and stepped out of the Fiesta. Wind and rain squalls from the north-west alternately buffeted and drenched me as I hurried towards the entrance to a building in need of a paint job.

But, once inside, I saw a linoleum floor polished so you could see your face and breathed air tangy with the smell of citrus. High up on the wall facing me was a cross made from cedar of Lebanon and beneath it stood a lit candle holder. It was tall, made from brass, and secured to the floor by a stout chain.

Away to my left stood a reception desk to which I directed my steps. It seemed unoccupied until, looking over the counter, I saw a seated figure hunched over a laptop. I cleared my throat noisily and, when that produced no response, was about to say something when I felt a touch at my elbow.

'She can't hear you,' said a voice. 'I'm afraid she's rather deaf. Perhaps I can help?'

I turned and tried to make eye contact but had to lower my gaze. The voice belonged to an old lady who was no more than five feet tall and whose lined face was framed by a spotless wimple. But while her skin may have been flayed by a lifetime's cares, her eyes seemed to reflect the bright light of some out-of-world spirit.

'Perhaps you can,' I said. 'I assumed this was a residential address.'

'In a sense it is,' the nun said with a beatific smile that melted her advanced years. 'The Sisters of Mercy operate an outreach service. We provide interim shelter for those suffering hard times. Can I ask what brings you here?'

'I'm looking for someone.'

'There are many on that path, my son.' She spoke in a serious tone, but her eyes had a twinkle in them.

I smiled back. 'There may be a misunderstanding. My name's Nemo. Sol Nemo. I'm a private investigator out of Port Elizabeth. I'm looking for someone by the name of Reeva Naidoo. She may have stayed with you or perhaps used this address as a point of contact.'

'And what purpose has this search?'

'I need to talk to her.'

'What about?'

'It's complicated.'

'Men's affairs usually are,' she said. 'My name's Sister Philomena. Perhaps you'd like to explain everything to me. But first we'll have to sit down. Standing for too long makes me faint.'

With that she slowly turned and led me along a corridor to a side door, opened it and beckoned me to follow her inside.

The room wasn't much larger than a cupboard and the smell of citrus was overpowering. Evidently, Sister Philomena concurred because she opened a latched window and sat down on one of two chairs. I took the other and found myself staring at a small crucifix above her head. The figure of Jesus was carved from ivory and in that restricted space the room took on the guise of a confessional. Instinct told me that spinning some yarn wasn't going to garner me much.

'Where would you like to begin, Sol?' asked Sister Philomena clasping small hands together in her lap.

I took my time and told her everything regarding Mira's kidnap and murder and then about Frank's death from a heart attack. 'I need to understand why Mira was snatched,' I went on. 'Ostensibly, the only reason was money and no doubt that was the prime mover. But I think what happened goes beyond that. I found things of Mira's that connected her to Manenberg and so to the same place as some of the kidnappers. That makes me curious. Also, the way she was abused after she was abducted suggests there was something personal about what befell her.' I paused and smiled self-consciously. 'I have a policeman's suspicious mind. Maybe, I've got it all wrong and will find out the hard way. In the meantime, I'm pursuing such leads as I can. Talking to Reeva Naidoo may get me further forward. Ultimately, I owe it to Frank because Mira's murder killed him.'

Sister Philomena heard me out in silence. 'Do you believe Reeva Naidoo's that important?' she asked.

'I honestly don't know. Apparently, she was close to Mira and presumably knew something more about her background. Do you think you can help me?'

The nun ignored my question and substituted one of her own. 'What information were you given in Camps Bay?'

'Just a phone number and three addresses.'

'One of which was here?'

'That's right.'

'You've tried the phone number?'

'It was the first thing I did. It goes to voicemail and the box is full. Maybe I can check out any number you might have for her.'

Sister Philomena shook her head. 'There'd be no point. Even if it was a different number, I couldn't give it to you.'

'But you could perhaps ask her to call me?' I suggested.

'Again, there would be no purpose. I can tell you Reeva wouldn't instigate contact with you.'

'Can I ask why?'

She pursed wrinkled lips. 'Because all I could tell her would be that a private investigator was anxious to contact her.'

'But I've explained . . .'

'You have indeed, but whatever impression I may have formed, she would be likely to form another by reason of your occupation.

And I wouldn't seek to dissuade her from her view on a slight acquaintanceship such as ours.'

'You won't help me then?'

Again, the nun chose to ignore me. 'What are the two other addresses you were given?'

'One is in Bishopscourt and the other in Mitchells Plain.'

'The Bishopscourt one isn't relevant.'

'Thank you for that,' I said. 'That leaves me with the address in Mitchells Plain. As it's 'care of', perhaps Reeva only visits occasionally. Or maybe she doesn't use it at all.'

Sister Philomena looked at me directly. 'Then perhaps you should abandon your quest and return home. Would anybody think the worse of you if you did?'

'I'm sorry, Sister, but that's impossible. I left PE two days ago after my car was blown up. The bomb was intended for me but ended up killing somebody else. The attack may have something to do with the accountant who negotiated with the kidnappers. He threatened me when I approached him for information. So, as you see, this has become personal.'

The nun was silent for a moment. 'Now I understand the turmoil in your eyes,' she said. 'And that's the reason I assume,' she added pointedly, 'you carry a gun strapped to your leg. Can I ask whether you ever read the Bible?'

'It's been a long while,' I confessed.

Sister Philomena's expression became philosophical. 'It's Matthew who tells us not to worry about tomorrow for tomorrow will worry about itself. Maybe you should go to Mitchells Plain, my son. Go to the address you've been given and enquire. Perhaps your journey will be a fruitful one, perhaps not. Ultimately, all these things are in God's hands.'

CHAPTER THIRTY-SIX

The rain continued blowing in hard off the Atlantic taking the temperature down to around 12 degrees. I felt the force of it at the V&A Waterfront when parking the car and setting off in search of something to eat.

The restaurant I chose fed me well enough and would have given me more by way of a view of Table Mountain had it not been obscured by clouds and the heavy squalls.

In the afternoon, I brought two pay-as-you-go phones and drove south out of the city centre on the M3. A few kms short of the Silvermine Nature Reserve I took a track leading to one of the Constantia wine farms but instead of stopping there carried on a short distance.

The gun club was happy to provide access to non-members in return for 150 bucks. Over the next couple of hours, with some helpful advice from an instructor, I renewed my skills with the Tomcat and afterwards bought the guy a couple of beers. I promised to leave positive feedback on the club's website.

By the time I got back to the Bo-kaap it had stopped raining and a reluctant sun was playing peek-a-boo with the clouds. But as the weather improved, my mood deteriorated. I began to wonder what was to be achieved with nothing more than my own resources on which to rely. Perhaps I should have seriously considered Bezuidenhout's offer of Witness Protection and left SAPS to get on with it. Maybe, in the fullness of time, they'd get to the bottom of who'd kidnapped and murdered Mira. But maybe, in the fullness of time, they'd get precisely nowhere as conviction rates for murder in our Rainbow Nation don't stand a lot higher than a puff adder's belly.

I wanted to talk to Ayesha, a feeling that grew exponentially as time passed. Using one of the pay-as-you-go phones, I called but her number went to voicemail. I left no message, being unsure how to frame it.

That evening I ate little. Trying to read, I found myself unable to concentrate and it was the same with the TV. I opened a half bottle of whisky and took a slug. And because the liquor applied a balm to the rawness of my emotions, the one drink led to another and to another after that. I fell asleep in the armchair.

Waking with a start later, I wondered why the ceiling was lit up. Looking from the window revealed the cause. Headlights were approaching up the road leading to The Lookout. As they drew nearer, the roar of a powerful engine reached my ears. Only it wasn't one but two engines. The vehicles were in convoy travelling so close together they appeared to be one. Up that steep, narrow road their speed was suicidal.

I felt their threat. My heart began beating louder than a Zulu drum. I struggled to catch my breath because my throat had closed up, my mouth dried out. At least, I had the presence of mind to turn off the bedside lamp. Then, with a strength born of naked fear, I shoved the armchair across the room. With it wedged under the door handle, I achieved a measure of security.

Below me, the vehicles skidded to a halt in front of the house. I heard car doors open and slam shut and after that the pounding of feet. It was followed by a crash as the front door gave way. I seized the Tomcat and took the safety off. I huddled in one corner of the room facing the closed door. Aiming the gun, I watched and waited, taut as stretched piano wire.

I heard voices at the bottom of the stairs. They were loud, excited and suddenly, and inexplicably, punctuated by peals of laughter. Distinctly, I heard a girl shout. That was then drowned in a chorus of catcalls. Next, an older man's voice yelling above the racket: 'Shut the fuck up!' To my surprise I recognised Ryker. 'I've got guests here!' he bellowed. 'Don't you kids ever think about anybody else?'

With that the commotion died down. I heard feet walking towards the back of the house. A door opened and closed. Silence flooded into the void left behind.

I lowered the Tomcat. My hands were shaking so badly I struggled with the safety. Putting the weapon on the floor, I leaned back against the wall. Sweat poured from me, and my skin was on fire. I gulped down more whisky mixed with water and sat in the armchair with my back to the door. To calm myself, my breathing took centre stage, and my fingers measured the expansion and contraction of my diaphragm. Slowly, I attained a state of something resembling equilibrium.

I dozed off again in the armchair. Waking in the early hours, I transferred to my bed. But, unable to sleep, I took a sedative. After that, there was fitful slumber, periods of rest broken up by seeing flashbacks of the Mustang exploding, its bonnet clawing its way into the sunlit sky of a South African morning.

CHAPTER THIRTY-SEVEN

Any member of the National Assembly or the National Council of Provinces will tell you apartheid ended a generation ago. Indeed, some of these fine representatives of ours continue to trot out the mantra that South Africa is the Rainbow Nation, despite the overwhelming body of evidence to the contrary.

Me, I believe they should leave the hallowed ground of the legislature once in a while and visit townships like Guguletu or Nyanga or Manenberg or Mitchells Plain. Fact is none of these black and coloured settlements is that far away from the cloistered comforts of Parliament's august walls. Visiting would allow those whose moral compass might need a reset, the opportunity to bear witness to the high levels of poverty, deprivation, and crime by which these places are plagued. In short, they are as far removed from the gentility of places like Camps Bay as beggars' hungry looks are to gluttons stuffing their faces with cream cakes.

In Mitchells Plain though, I blended into the background as the patina of my skin made me invisible. But the Fiesta stood out because of its newness and because the roads were relatively free from traffic. I parked close to the Promenade Shopping Centre and walked through to the far side past shops selling furniture and clothing.

The address I sought turned out to be that of a *spaza*: a rundown general store selling an array of groceries, cosmetics and household necessities with extensive shelving devoted to alcohol. Cement walls, metal grilles and a sign advertising Coca-Cola peppered with what looked like buckshot comprised its frontage. Farther along the crumbling street, devoid of trees, lay a hairdresser, a games shop, and an internet café. On the far side two cars were parked behind a chain-link fence. They'd have been wowing the motoring press as regards technical innovation and stylistic flair around 30 years ago.

I ventured into the *spaza* through a narrow doorway. There was a counter at one side, and I made for it. At my approach, a thickset party in a black T shirt lifted himself out of a beaten-up chair and looked at me pointedly.

'Hi,' I said. It was about as much of a greeting as I could summon having woken up hung over and woozy from the effects of sedatives. To cap it all, I now had a blinding headache for which the sunshine had to take all the blame.

The shopkeeper said nothing but folded his arms across a massive chest. But it wasn't flab he was showing off. It was hard muscle achieved over years of pumping iron. I knew because there were guys like that in SAPS. I'd worked with some of them, and they were always useful to have around if anything kicked-off.

'There's a lady who uses this address for messages and post,' I began. 'Her name's Reeva Naidoo.'

'Not a face round here, are you?' interjected the shopkeeper.

'You're right,' I admitted. 'I've come from Port Elizabeth. You think you can help me?'

'You wanna buy something I can help with that.'

I changed tack. 'How's about aspirin and a bottle of water?'

'Second aisle for aspirin. Water's on the back wall.'

I found what was needed, returned to the counter and made a further attempt to connect. 'It was a tough night,' I said with a rueful grin indicating the aspirin.

'Uh-huh.'

'Didn't sleep much and now I've this bitch of a headache.'

The shopkeeper looked at me without interest and shoved my change towards me.

'Look, I'm trying to find a lady called Reeva Naidoo,' I went on impatiently. 'I've been referred by the Sisters of Mercy in Brooklyn. I was there yesterday. They advised me to come here.'

At the mention of the Sisters, the shopkeeper's demeanour altered. 'Who did you meet?' he asked.

'Sister Philomena.'

'What did you say your name was?'

'I didn't, but it's Sol Nemo. I'm a PI.'

The guy's eyes bored into my face unblinkingly. 'Well, Mr. Private Investigator, you're evidently one rich dude who likes living dangerously.'

I looked at him surprised and followed his gaze to my left wrist. In my befuddled state, I'd forgotten to remove both my Panerai Submersible and my white gold Cartier bracelet.

'That sort of superfly stuff gets you cut up round here,' he said. 'I guess maybe life's different in Port Elizabeth.'

I shook my head. 'Same problems, smaller scale.' I removed both watch and bracelet, before transferring them to my pants' pocket. 'You think you can help me?'

'First call is to the Sisters.'

'And then?'

'If that checks, I can make another call.'

'I'm grateful.'

'Can't promise you nothing.'

'I can make it worth Reeva's while.'

'What do you want?' he asked curiously.

'Information,' I said. 'Years back Reeva worked at a place called Bennie's in Camp's Bay. There was a singer there who was the wife of a good friend of mine. She was murdered earlier this year. I'm trying to find the person responsible.'

The shopkeeper made no comment. 'You're gonna have to wait,' was all he said.

I shrugged. 'They also serve who only stand and wait.'

I made to go, but the guy's voice swung me back. 'Go get yourself

194

a coffee, bro. And maybe something to eat. You look like shit. Try the café along the street. They'll see you right.'

The place to which he directed me was the internet café. It was set back from broken pavement behind a low cement wall. There was a board outside advertising copying, printing, scanning, and fax services in an italic script bleached by the sun. Below that, somebody had scrawled New Coffee Shop.

The description proved a misnomer as the so-called shop consisted of no more than a dispenser mounted on a bench against a wall. Adjacent to it were cans of Funky B, a selection of sandwiches in cling film and some fruit including kiwi and bananas. If you wanted to park yourself, you had to borrow a chair from those drawn up in front of cubicles housing ancient computer terminals. To one side was a photocopier churning out flyers supervised by a man whose features looked unexpectedly familiar.

'Hello,' I said as the guy turned towards me. 'Did I just meet your brother along the road?'

'Cousin Abdul,' he said with a grin. 'What can I do for you?' He was built the same way as his relative but lacked his commitment to physical fitness.

'I was told I could get a drink and a sandwich.'

Abdul's cousin told me to help myself and, after paying for everything, I took a chair and sat outside. I balanced it all on the low wall and settled down with my back to the sun.

First, I took aspirin with water before starting on a tuna sandwich and a mug of coffee. I ate ruminatively until something brushed against my legs. Looking down, I saw a small cat. Its haunches were so thin they were concave, and it had only one bright yellow eye. But, despite this handicap, its tail was lifted in a cheery greeting as I stroked its head. Thinking the animal must be hungry, I fed it small pieces of tuna from the palm of my hand feeling the roughness of its tongue as it hoovered up the morsels of fish. When the food was gone, the cat leapt onto the wall and hunkered down in a sphinx-like position facing me. Occasionally, it raised its head and gave me an inscrutable look out of that one bright yellow eye.

Much later Abdul called to me. By that time, the cat was long gone as was my headache. I got up, stretched and walked back to the *spaza*. At the rear was a storeroom with one heavily barred window and a steel door that was propped open giving a view of a sunlit yard. Between the shelves, piled boxes and closed crates, there was little space except in the middle of the floor where a solitary figure sat on a red plastic chair.

Marty at Bennie's had described a woman in her forties with black hair. He also said she was overweight and wasn't a bad looker. The woman in front of me bore no relation to this description, even allowing for the intervening years.

Reeva Naidoo was emaciated and her clothes, bought at a time when her circumstances were evidently much different, hung shapelessly on her frame. Her hair was streaked with grey, but it wasn't that which irresistibly drew my eyes. It was the livid burn marks down one side of her face and neck that were as physically disfiguring as I suspect they were psychologically damaging.

'I'm grateful for your agreeing to meet,' I said softly after she raised tired dark eyes to my face. 'My name's Sol Nemo. I've come here from Port Elizabeth.'

She nodded in acknowledgement and, taking this to be an invitation I sat down awkwardly on a packing case to one side of her.

'Sister Philomena said I should reach my own decision about whether to see you,' she explained in a flat voice. 'But she advised it should be on neutral ground and with a minder.'

'You're safe with me here Reeva,' said Abdul cutting in. To emphasise the point, he gave me what I thought was an unfriendly look and took up a position with arms akimbo.

But Reeva didn't seem to have heard him. 'I was staying with the Sisters until a few months ago,' she went on. 'They offer a home to those down on their luck. But it's temporary so, when they say, you must move on.'

'I'm sorry to hear all this.'

'I'm living with my aunt. It's not convenient as we're sharing a one-bedroom place with her two sons and ...' Her voice trailed away, her head sank towards her lap, and she started to sob.

Her circumstances weren't the reason for my visit, but I couldn't ignore her distress. 'Things must be very difficult,' I said. 'Please, will you tell me what happened to you?'

I'm a good listener which is why conveying her story took Reeva a while. She told me she had been married a long time but had no children. Her husband was a drunk and had abused her for years. Eventually, she'd had enough and quit the comfortable marital home in Bishopscourt. He paid her out, she claimed, by getting someone to throw acid in her face. Prior to the attack, the person who discovered where she was to be found was a private investigator. Hence her wariness about seeing me. The physical and mental trauma caused by the assault had meant her giving up her job at Bennie's and that led to a downward spiral. While the Sisters of Mercy provided a safety net, she remained unemployed and by her own admission both depressed and anxious. Though her husband was rich from an inheritance, he'd thwarted her attempts to secure a financial settlement by hiding behind lawyers.

I let her talk herself out and allowed the silence that followed to hang in the air for a moment or two. Eventually, and as Abdul disappeared to serve a customer, she lifted her eyes and said, 'Thank you for listening. It's much appreciated. Somehow, it's always easier talking to a stranger.'

'You're right.' I thought back to my time at the Steinberg Clinic and my sessions with their psychiatric team. 'But sometimes,' I went on, 'a friend with insight and empathy can be even better.' I changed the subject. 'I guess you spoke to Sister Philomena about me.'

'Abdul contacted her. Then she rang me, and we spoke at length. She explained everything about why you're here and what you're trying to do. But I'm not sure I can help.'

'We'll see,' I said. 'Marty seemed to think you had a close relationship with Mira. Was she the sort of friend we were just talking about?'

For the first time I saw Reeva smile though the expression gave her damaged face a freakish appearance. 'No,' she said firmly. 'That wasn't like Mira at all. She had little interest in other people. She was entirely self-centred.'

'But when I spoke to Marty, he told me the two of you were close.'

'We were close in the sense I liked her upbeat attitude to life. She sort of carried you along with her, if you were in the mood. She could be a real tonic if you felt like life was tearing your heart out.'

'Where did she come from?'

'Manenberg.'

'Is that so? -I heard she was from Bloemfontein.'

'From Marty I suppose?' I nodded and Reeva smiled again. 'That was typical of Mira. She made it up as she went along. Anything that gave her an air of mystery appealed to her. She would tell you she blew in from Bloemfontein as she put it in one breath and the next day she'd tell you she had connections with the Greek royal family. If you were in the right frame of mind, it was all rather amusing. And frankly Mira didn't care whether you believed her or not. It was enough that she was the centre of attention.'

'What did she do in Manenberg?'

'I think it was where she was brought up. Nothing more than that. She told me she'd spent time over the years in various places right across the country. Singing was her first love, of course, but if she couldn't get the work, she waited tables and served drinks.'

'Marty said she got the job at Bennie's by chance. She turned up on a talent night, did her stuff and it went down a storm.'

Reeva reflected. 'It was a bit more involved that that,' she said. 'We gave her a spot once a week for a while and gradually increased our commitment. It really took off after she and Bennie's got a write-up on one of the Cape Town entertainment sites. In it she was compared favourably with Edith Piaf or some such nonsense. But then she was sleeping with the journalist who wrote it. Mira conducted her relationships with men the same way she conducted every other part of her life. There was little continuity or stability and, if something didn't suit, she took steps to change it.'

'But she married Frank and left Cape Town,' I pointed out.

'She went with Frank to escape.'

'What was she escaping from?'

'Circumstances. She wasn't getting any younger and she kept telling me she didn't have much behind her. That sort of situation can eat away at you.'

The realisation of what she said made Reeva cry, tears which she brushed away with a hand whose nails were badly bitten.

'How did their relationship evolve?'

'Frank used to come across for long weekends. As I recall, that went on for quite a while. But it wasn't exclusive, not as far as Mira was concerned. When he went back to Port Elizabeth, she did whatever took her fancy. That meant she usually had somebody else in tow. Because I knew what was going on, I tried to avoid Frank. I didn't want to find myself answering awkward questions.'

These revelations were depressing as I recalled the way Frank always spoke about Mira. For him the relationship with her was his lodestar. He would never have done anything to jeopardise what he believed he had with her. Evidently, she didn't see things the same way.

But there was no point dwelling on the past. What concerned me now was that the conversation was going nowhere. There was nothing so far that gave me any better insight into why Mira might have been kidnapped following my hunch that more than money had been involved.

I changed tack. 'Did Mira keep in touch with anyone from Manenberg?' I asked. 'Somebody for instance she might have grown up with. Or somebody who was significant regarding her later life?'

Reeva shook her head. 'Not that she grew up with. But there was one person from her past. He was a guy who only ever came to Bennie's twice. On the first occasion, there was a huge row between him and Mira. It was really embarrassing because it was after one of her sets. A lot of the customers were very upset.'

'What was the row about?'

Reeva shrugged thin shoulders. 'I didn't hear it. What I got from my staff was that this man said she'd stolen from him. When I took it up with Mira, she brushed it aside and said it was all a misunderstanding. She told me she'd sorted everything out.'

'Would you happen to remember the guy's name?'

'It was Swartman. Gert Swartman.'

I was impressed. 'You've a good memory,' I said. 'This must have happened at least five years ago.'

'I remember,' said Reeva, 'because Swartman came back after Mira quit. It was very late one night. We were clearing up and out of the blue he strode in as though he owned the place. He spoke to one of the waiters who pointed me out to him. The next thing I knew Swartman was in my face.'

'What did he want?'

'He wanted Mira. He said he knew she'd left and he needed to know where he could find her. At that stage, Mira had been gone about a month. I told him I couldn't help.'

'How did he react?'

'He was obviously furious, but not in an aggressive way. He realised if he started anything my colleagues would have thrown him out. No, he was softly spoken and in a way that was more frightening because his tone was so menacing. He was a big man too, nearly two metres I reckon, with a bull neck and eyes full of demons. Shoulder-length white hair made him even more distinctive. He told me Mira had stolen things which were of value to him. They weren't items with monetary value, he said, but they were things that were irreplaceable and of great sentimental value. He wanted them back and to do that he needed to find her urgently.'

'What did you do?'

'Well, I knew where she'd been staying in Camps Bay. I gave him that address with a clear conscience. Mira told me she'd be gone from the place within a week of quitting Bennie's.'

'And did Swartman come back?'

'I've never seen him since. When he left that night, he gave me a business card. He told me I was to call him if Mira was in touch or if I had any other information.'

'I don't suppose you kept the card?' I asked.

Reeva shook her head. 'I didn't,' she said. 'In fact, I was so angry at the way he intimidated me that I tossed it in the garbage.'

'That's a pity.'

'I'm sorry. I guess it could have been helpful.'

'Maybe. Maybe not. We'll never know, will we?' I smiled at Reeva but I'm sure disappointment was written all over my face.

She saw my expression and said hesitantly, 'I don't remember any of the details, but I do recall the address related to a wine farm. Maybe that could help you.'

I made a non-committal reply and thanked her for seeing me. I expressed the hope that things would change for her and very soon. Sorrowfully, I watched her get to her feet and walk to the front of the shop. I hung back until she'd exchanged a few words with Abdul and left the premises.

'Nice lady with a very sad story,' I said, sauntering over to the till.

Abdul glanced up from a stock sheet he was checking. 'One of the best,' he said. 'The aunt she's staying with is my sister-in-law. With everything that's happened to Reeva, I'm left wondering some-times where God gets to.'

I took that under advisement. 'I bought lunch from your cousin and spent time talking to someone rooming with your sister-in-law. You all related round here?'

'We take care of our own, Sol. No other fucker's going to.'

I nodded sympathetically. 'What happened over the acid attack and her divorce?'

Abdul was dismissive. 'SAPS investigated and came up with zip. That was like a great surprise to nobody. Regarding her divorce, she needs one of those legal guys in the city to work a little magic. Problem is they want thousands of bucks up front before they open a case file.'

'Does her husband have assets?'

'House in Bishopscourt is worth upwards of 10 mill. I checked it out a while back.'

I absorbed this and then came to a decision. I reached into my pants' pocket, took out the Panerai watch and pressed it into the shopkeeper's hands. 'It's a limited edition,' I said. 'Do you know where to turn it into cash?'

Abdul's eyes widened as he looked down and then up at me. 'Are you serious, bro?'

'Yeah, I'm serious. Just make sure you find her a lawyer who's meaner than a cobra with a head cold.'

'When I tell Reeva, she'll say she saw God in you.'

I was embarrassed. 'If she does, you tell her it was nothing but a trick of the light.'

CHAPTER THIRTY-EIGHT

I knuckled tired eyes, yawned hugely, and crossed to the window in my room that looked over the Waterfront. Desk-based research was never my forte but, in this instance, I had no choice. The Cape Town telephone directory had yielded nothing, so I'd been forced to gain an on-line acquaintanceship with the winelands of the Western Cape. Thus far it had taken the whole morning and part of the afternoon on the day following my return from Mitchells Plain.

I started with as much knowledge of wineries as the average politician has of the real world. Sure, I was aware of Constantia and Stellenbosch and understood there was any number of separate commercial enterprises located in each place. What I failed to appreciate was that there were a lot more scattered throughout the Western Cape, from the Olifants River Valley to the Klein Karoo, and that trying to find a party by the name of Swartman in one of them could take a while. Maybe it would take a very long while.

I sought to be logical in my approach. As Swartman had visited Bennie's late at night, I assumed he was to be located within a reasonable distance of Camps Bay. On that basis, I worked outwards from there in concentric circles. But the fact was that these circles became ever wider with no tangible result. Where the internet had no information regarding directors and/or senior management of individual companies or cooperatives I put in calls.

I dished out the usual stuff appropriate to this sort of fishing: *'Yeah, hi there. My name's blah-de-blah and I'm calling from blah-de-blah. Could I speak to Mr. Swartman? Oh really? -You don't have anyone of that name? Can I ask did he move on? Right, you never had anyone of that name. I'm sorry to have bothered you . . . Yeah, you have yourself a great day too.'*

I pressed on for the rest of the afternoon but began to lose hope towards the end of it. After all, I was working with information which was years out of date. Swartman could have died or moved on or maybe Reeva's recollection was plain wrong. Memory sometimes plays strange tricks and can convince you that something's one thing when it turns out to be another.

I gave up in the early evening and took the Fiesta down into the heart of the Bo-kaap. I was ravenous and the prospect of enjoying some company led me into a little place off Bree Street that served a passable chicken curry and tasty samosas washed down with a couple of Castle Lites.

I took the opportunity between courses of trying to reach Ayesha again and this time came up trumps.

'I've been thinking of you,' she said. And it was the first thing she said.

'And I you.'

'Look, Sol, do you mind if we talk tomorrow night? I'll be back from Pretoria by then. Are you OK?'

'I'm fine,' I answered honestly, my mind still lingering on those first words of hers. 'Sounds like now's not a good time.'

'I'm sorry, but I'm dressing for a concert at the State Theatre. A car's coming for me in ten minutes.'

I was wondering who she might be going with and what the occasion was. And that reference she made to a car: whose car was she talking about? Or was she referring to nothing more than a taxi?

More than curious, I nevertheless buttoned it. 'OK Ayesha,' I said. 'It's no problem. I'll call you tomorrow night. I hope you enjoy the concert.'

'A bientot, mon cher ami.'

* * *

I got started again on the net some time after 9 p.m. My focus was now on the Robertson Wine Route running through the Breede River Valley. It was located almost two hours east of Cape Town and at the edge of the winelands region. As with all the Routes, there were dozens of estates and cooperatives. Wearily, I began the task of looking at each one individually.

By now, I knew this was a mechanical process often best dealt with by working my way through various tourist websites and compiling a tally of businesses which I cross-checked one with another to avoid missing individual locations.

I kept at it until midnight and covered about 70% of the possibilities. But this left me with a checklist of calls I would need to make the following day.

I was tired and my mind began to drift. I had a map of the Robertson Wine Route open on the screen, each estate or cooperative marked with the symbol of a wine glass. A key told me those coloured orange were open to the public, those marked green could be visited by appointment only, and those which weren't coloured were closed.

This last group piqued my curiosity. One thing I learned from my day's labours was how keen most places were to capture the tourist buck. In some places, this seemed to be the key objective to the extent that cultivating grapes and producing wine looked like something of a secondary consideration. Most establishments were enthusiastic about gawping visitors tramping around their properties enjoying guided tours, taking lunch, and sampling the local produce. Several estates went further by offering accommodation, hosting business events, and providing picturesque venues for weddings, anniversaries and other special occasions. One enterprising dude was even happy to offer tours in an open-topped Cadillac dating from the 1950s.

I looked at the map more closely. I couldn't see anywhere which was closed to the public so why that uncoloured symbol in the key? I enlarged the map and began scanning in earnest.

I found what I was looking for in the top corner near a place called Ashton, off Route 62. It lay in the shadow of a nature reserve and went by the name of the Namtraws Wine Estate. There was a telephone number, an email address, and the briefest of descriptions. I found no other information and no photographs. The place went to the top of my list of calls for the following day before I went to bed.

I had no expectation of unbroken sleep, and that night was no exception. But rather than waking up anxious, I woke because something was nagging at my brain. Switching on the bedside light, I picked up the notebook I'd been using and wrote the name Namtraws in block capitals: N-A-M-T-R-A-W-S. Then I slowly wrote it backwards: S-W-A-R-T-M-A-N.

CHAPTER THIRTY-NINE

I slept fitfully after that and got up early. Deciding there was nothing now to keep me in Cape Town, I gave up my room and collected my gear. I figured that, even if the Namtraws Wine Estate proved a dead end, I could locate myself elsewhere in the Western Cape and be closer to the regions not yet investigated. These included the Klein Karoo plus Agulhas and Elim down near the coast. I also factored in that my staying in one place for too long wasn't perhaps the healthiest option.

I left Cape Town after buying a small pair of binoculars and refuelling the Fiesta. After that, my heading was for the N1, later picking up the R60 at Worcester close to the KVW House of Brandy. Once off the main highway, the cut and thrust of lunging traffic was no more and I drove east at a steady 80-100kph. My route took me along a single-track road which ran along a wide and dusty valley floor. In the distance on either side, I saw black-capped mountains, sometimes their lower green slopes lit by the piercing rays of the sun. This is a rural South Africa with which I have no great affinity having spent most of my life in large towns and cities. Tourists though think differently as I was soon to discover.

Passing the southern edge of Robertson, I continued east. On the road to Ashton, traffic increased and occasionally I saw large artics carrying crates of grapes. When I left the main highway there were a few spots of rain forcing workers in blue overalls sitting on the curb to seek the shelter of an adjacent farm shop.

The Namtraws Wine Estate faced the road a few kms out of town and I pulled over close by. Keeping the engine running, I looked out through the intermittent sweep of the wipers. Steel gates topped with barbed wire were open but a sign in Afrikaans and English informed the world there was no admittance except on official business. Beyond the entrance lay a concrete yard stacked high with empty wood and plastic crates confirming the proximity of harvest time. Behind them stood a gaggle of single storey buildings, their defining characteristic a shabby drabness. Apart from a couple of guys smoking cigarettes in a lean-to next to a small office, the place was lifeless.

I backed the Fiesta up and retraced my route. I didn't drive far but rejoined the R62 and followed a coachload of tourists into a wine farm with B&B accommodation. As the rain stopped, I parked and attached myself to the tourists and walked towards a thatched building with white-washed walls. I guessed iron-bound wagon wheels propped by the entrance were supposed to give a suitably olde worlde feel to the place. Inside, I grabbed a brochure as one of the farm managers greeted us. He said his name was Alec Ferguson.

For the next hour, I listened to a history of the wine industry in SA; learnt about the science, production and study of grapes; and was shown everything from individual vines to bottles of their best Shiraz, merlot and cabernet sauvignon. After that, came the pairings of various wines with cheese, chocolates and cured meats. This put everyone in a good mood for a long lunch and the chance to pour more vino down their necks. I let the opportunity go as I wanted to talk to Alec.

'That was a fascinating talk,' I gushed, moving in on him.

He was a tall man with ascetic features, and he gazed at me short-sightedly through glasses whose lenses could have stopped bullets. 'Thank you,' he said. 'One tries one's best.'

'You did much more than that Alec,' I enthused. 'You really held my attention and I've listened to quite a few presentations I can tell you.'

'A regular, are you?'

'No, I'm working,' I said. 'I've been in the area a couple of days. I've been undertaking a reconnaissance.'

'Reconnaissance? -I'm not sure I understand.'

My smile was ingratiating. 'I'm the legs for a group of investors in Cape Town. They've tasked me with researching this wine route. And some others. They're looking to make two or three acquisitions.'

Irritation unexpectedly paid Alec's face a visit. 'I can assure you this estate isn't for sale,' he said.

'I didn't believe it was,' I said quickly. 'I read the family's been here for seven generations. Since 1873, isn't it?'

'Quite so. And may I say you'll not have much luck elsewhere round here.'

I shrugged. 'My only role is to report back on what I find during my visits. For instance, I came across one place earlier that looked as though it had potential.'

The manager was intrigued. 'And that was where?' he asked, despite himself.

'The Namtraws Wine Estate.'

Alec laughed. 'Your investors would need deep pockets if they wanted a return out of that place.'

I pretended to consider. 'I can see it lacks a tourist offer, but surely the harvest makes money.'

'Maybe, but most of what they produce goes for blending.' Alec's tone was contemptuous. 'I don't think the quality's that great. And there are certainly no top wines, either red or white.'

'Who owns it?'

'The last I heard it's a company. There's an old man who's lived there for ten years or more. He has a house at the back of the estate. Keeps himself to himself and flies in and out by helicopter.'

'Have you met him?'

Alec shook his head before glancing at his watch. 'You're going to have to excuse me,' he said. 'I'm talking to another group soon.'

'Of course. I'm very grateful to you for your time.'

Alec made to leave but then a thought struck him. 'If your investors need help in viticulture and oenology, I could be useful. I've post-grad qualifications from Stellenbosch plus 30 years' experience.'

'Rest assured, it'll be my pleasure to recommend you,' I said, grabbing his hand and pumping it. 'Do you perhaps have a business card?'

CHAPTER FORTY

I had some lunch and bought extra provisions by way of bread, meat and water for later. After that, I returned to the Namtraws Wine Estate but drove past the entrance and took a route which wound ever higher into the foothills. Soon road became track running between lush meadows watered by a stream that tumbled over moss-covered rocks.

I found what I sought a few minutes later. It was a narrower track that broke off decisively and followed the contour of a hill. I slowed to walking speed and, spotting a shallow gully, coasted into it and switched off. Stepping out of the Fiesta, I smelt the clean fresh scent of the *fynbos* growing all around me.

Taking the binoculars, I followed the track farther around the hill. Caution inhibited my progress because there was little cover except for a thin screen of bushes.

From the hillside, I could look straight out into the vault of a sky decorated with slow-moving fluffy clouds. But behind these were others etched in black that threatened further rain showers. Yet they didn't hold my attention for long once I spotted the huge house lying below me.

It was away to my right and, despite my viewing it almost end on, it was difficult not to be impressed by its scale. It had a wide front-age and comprised three storeys of concrete, steel and glass under a series of flat roofs. In the open-plan garden a swimming pool, done out in white Italian marble, was the central feature and beyond it, across an expansive lawn, stood an open-sided *braai* where feeding the 5000 would have been a breeze. On the far side was an ornamental pool with a chrome dolphin leaping in the air, its mouth jetting water.

My contemplation of this vista was interrupted by the sight of a man who emerged onto a flagged terrace above the pool. Crouched down and using the glasses, I saw a phone pressed to an ear with one hand, the other holding a large cigar. From the stabbing gestures he made with the double corona it seemed he was a tad exercised about something.

As my observation continued, he descended two flights of wide wooden steps and stood by the side of the pool. Dressed in a tailored, short-sleeved shirt and khaki culottes with matching deck shoes, he was a big man with a bull neck and, incongruously, a mane of white hair which reached to his shoulders. This attribute though didn't detract from his arrogant air of authority. From what Reeva had described to me, there was little doubt I was looking at Gert Swartman.

At that moment, Swartman turned his head and raised his eyes toward my vantage point. Fearing he might see the sun reflected on the lenses, I dropped them into my lap and shrank back into the undergrowth. Perhaps it was fancy, but I felt the intensity of his gaze as he slowly scanned the hillside where I was now lying flat on my stomach.

When I did venture to look up, Swartman had turned away and was climbing back up the stairs to the terrace. There he lingered a moment before retreating into the interior of the house.

With care, I picked up the glasses again and, making sure I wasn't facing into the sun, began a reconnaissance of the compound. In the distance there was a hangar, its purpose made clear by the hard standing out front painted with a capital H inside a white circle. It was reached from a short road that ran from a line of garages close to the house and shaded by a copse of acacia trees. To one side of these, a sports car was being washed by a black guy in red overalls. Behind him and partially obscured by a fold in the ground were a

212

few low buildings that were probably either staff quarters or storage areas.

On three sides the compound was surrounded by vines, the boundary marked by a tall wire fence. Gates set into this provided vehicular access to the vineyard and, I reckoned, beyond that to the public road where I'd stopped that morning.

As I shifted the binoculars to my left, I was surprised to see a man dressed in army drab stroll into my field of vision. He was carrying a rifle and had a holstered side-arm at his waist.

I persisted in my observation long enough to see him meet another party similarly attired who approached from the other direction. The two halted, exchanged a few words and crossed over to resume their respective beats.

This level of active security surprised me. Swartman wasn't one of those Afrikaaner farmers who for years past have had cause to fear for their safety. On the contrary, Swartman either had enemies against whom he needed to protect himself or he thought his wealth might of itself invite malign intentions.

Carefully, I retraced my steps to the car, and walking past it, followed animal tracks downhill. At this point, I was on the other side of the hill and heard the beat of engines. Intervening trees though prevented me from learning the source of the noise.

All was revealed when I was able to look out a moment or two later. Beyond a wide strip of uncultivated land, I saw a vast expanse of vines in serried rows, their grapes being gathered using machinery. It was a two-man job using a tall mechanical harvester and a tractor pulling a trailer into which the fruit spilled from an overhead conveyor. The size of the estate meant the task might take a week or two, but this sort of automation was one more contributing factor in the harsh reality of our Rainbow Nation's mass unemployment.

I climbed back up the hill, the walk in the late afternoon sun making me hot and thirsty. After taking a long drink, I reversed the Fiesta and headed back the way I'd come.

Driving back as far as Robertson had no purpose other than to occupy my time. I bought a small flashlight though and found a cafe where I browsed the pages of the Cape Times.

When once again I headed east, the last vestiges of daylight, marked by a series of pinkish streaks, were fleeing the sky.

CHAPTER FORTY-ONE

I pulled up an hour later in a spot about a kilometre from the entrance to the Wine Estate and at the end of a track by a stream. There was a flat area of beaten earth where cars parked during the day and from which I assumed their owners hiked or unloaded bikes. But, when I rolled into the far corner of it and switched off, the area was deserted and dark.

I'd given thought as to what to do next and decided that exploring the buildings near the road was my best option. Contemplating anything as risky as trying to gain entry to Swartman's house seemed dumb. Patrolling guards with rifles were a considerable deterrent on their own and who was to say what other security measures there might be.

I removed the contents of my pockets and stowed it all in the boot. Once locked, I placed the Fiesta's ignition key inside the exhaust tailpipe and left with nothing on me but the flashlight and the Tomcat.

The estate yard and buildings were mostly in darkness as a single overhead light was bent and out of alignment. This suited my purpose but didn't help as to how I was to gain access to the place. In the end, I worked my way along the fence a distance before finding a spot where animals had burrowed. With difficulty, I followed their example and emerged on the other side dusty and dishevelled.

From there, I picked my way back through an area used as a general dumping ground for piles of rubble, smashed packing crates and scrap metal. Beyond an ancient saloon car, with three of its wheels missing, the estate buildings loomed.

I tried all the doors, but they were fastened from the inside or padlocked. As an alternative, I sought a window and eventually found one that hadn't been closed properly. Using the grip of the flashlight as a lever, I forced it wide, inserted my hand and tugged the frame towards me.

After shining the torch into the interior, I climbed into a large storage shed. Half the space was empty, but the rest was filled with stacked crates of freshly picked grapes. I drew my gun and crossed to an internal door, the smell from the fruit rich and intense in that confined space.

On the other side was a garage with roller shutters. It housed the harvester and tractor I'd seen earlier and a long work bench with an array of tools. I passed the flashlight over these before my attention was drawn to another door in the far corner. This one was of stout construction, had frosted-glass panels and resisted my attempt to open it. Thwarted, I shone the light onto the shelves of an adjacent bookcase and identified a box filled with several unmarked mortise keys. I put the Tomcat down on one of the shelves and began the tedious process of working my way through them, flashlight in one hand, each key to be tested in the other. Finding the right one took too long.

There were a couple of rooms beyond, the first being a general office with an exit to the yard. From the numbers of shelved box files, and the paperwork scattered around a desktop PC, this was the accounts area. Idly, I riffled through a pile of unpaid invoices and correspondence covering everything from vehicle repairs to yeast starters and from toilet paper to light bulbs. But, despite the variety of this material, there was nothing to hold my attention.

Next, I turned my attention to the inner office. This was a smaller space that reeked of stale cigar smoke, despite the air-conditioning unit standing in one corner. It was dominated by an oak partner desk with a green leather inlay and executive chairs with high backs. A filing cabinet stood along one wall and there was a small safe on the floor. Everything was locked, including the desk drawers.

I returned to the garage and passed the beam of the flashlight over the bench. A heavy screwdriver suited my purpose best and I retraced my steps. Levering open the desk drawers to the accompaniment of splintering wood was the work of only a few seconds. Examining their contents though didn't take me any further forward.

The filing cabinet proved more of a challenge to the brute force provided by the screwdriver but, at last, its contents were exposed. It was just that the mysteries revealed were unworthy of the effort expended. It was no more than a depository for a mass of paperwork dating back as long as 20 years. Much of it seemed to be supplier stuff in the form of invoices, brochures and catalogues and was about as engaging as turning pages in a phone directory.

There were other files though in the bottom drawer. I began riffling through these, but it wasn't long before here too frustration set in. Set in until the torch beam fell on a manila file at the back. The tab identified it in italic script with the single word: *Alchemy*.

Intrigued, I took out the file and opened it. There were various invoices and documents inside but the key one was a bill of sale for a motor yacht by the name of *Alchemy*. Attached to it was a photograph. I brought the flashlight up close and played it over the picture. It was only then I gasped out loud and my heart started to hammer in my chest.

The photograph featured two men. One was Eugene du Toit, and the other was Gert Swartman. They were standing on the yacht's aft deck and toasting each other with champagne flutes. Du Toit had managed to crack his face open with one of his unpleasant smiles while Swartman, long white locks in abundant evidence, contented himself with a supercilious grin. The yacht was moored beneath a harbour wall which displayed a large sign spelling out the letters SANC.

I stared at the picture for a long moment and would have taken it but at that moment became aware of a noise. Quickly, I closed the file, dropped it back into the drawer and shut off the torch. I rose to my feet, turned round and faced the desk. As I did so, a light snapped on and a voice said quietly: 'Move and I'll drop you where you stand.'

CHAPTER FORTY-TWO

I couldn't move because I was rooted to the ground. My fear stemmed from the pistol pointing at my head from the other side of the desk. The pistol was held by a man with a bald head whose eyes were pitiless.

I glanced down to the desktop. The screwdriver was within reach in front of me. It might as well have been a million miles away. I couldn't have got to it fast enough. It wouldn't have made any difference had my gun been lying there.

Gun! Where the fuck was my gun!? Then I remembered. And I remembered too how I left it on the shelf when I was trying out the keys.

Baldie misread my expression as some precursor to action. 'You'll be dead before flexing a muscle.' Impatiently, he gestured with the pistol. 'Put the torch down. Put it down slowly and then put your hands on your head.'

I put the torch down slowly and put my hands on my head.

The next thing I was reeling. The blow came from nowhere. It was a left to right upward slashing motion, the barrel of Baldie's gun connecting with my cheek and opening it up like a fish being gutted. I felt hot blood start from my face as I fell backwards. Cannoning into the back wall, I cowered there, my hand over my bloodied cheek.

'Stand up!'

I stood up, slowly and reluctantly. The side of my face was on fire and swelling rapidly under the trauma of the impact.

Baldie angrily motioned for me to put my hands back on my head. 'Who the fuck are you?' he yelled.

I played it dumb. 'I-I meant no harm, sir. I-I was hungry. I was-was passing by. I knew there were grapes.'

'No grapes in here.'

'I-I was looking for cash,' I admitted. 'I've got nothing, sir. And my wife and . . .'

'Where you from?' he interrupted.

Thinking fast might be the only way to stay alive. 'Ashton,' I said. 'I-I mean the township at Ashton.'

'What's your name?'

'P-Pieter K-Khan.'

'You don't seem too sure.'

I made an effort. 'My name's Pieter Khan.'

'ID?'

'N-No sir.'

'Turn out your pockets.' I made to comply and started to lower my hands, but Baldie's voice brought me up short. 'Slowly!' he commanded. 'Do it very slowly.'

With infinite sluggishness, I lowered my hands and pulled my trouser pockets inside out. Then, at his bidding, I made a full turn so he could check there was nothing hidden behind my back.

It may have been wishful thinking but, at that moment, I thought to get away with it. After all, I'd taken nothing and was dirty and dishevelled enough, from my burrowing under the fence, to look as though I spent my days living in a shack. I reckoned he might think he'd taught me enough of a painful lesson to make an end of the matter and kick me out.

But, as soon as my hopes inflated, they were punctured. Disappointed, I watched him speed-dial on his phone.

'Yeah, that silent alarm's a real bonus,' he said to somebody. 'Caught this guy red-handed. Broke in he says looking for cash. Busted into that desk of yours. You want me to call SAPS?'

I waited, in pain and in fear. Frankly, his calling SAPS was more than acceptable. If he came to know what I knew, it was game over. Unhappily, whoever he was talking to wasn't making quick decisions about anything. What that person was doing was asking questions.

Baldie responded deferentially: '. . . Says he's from the township . . . Tall piece of piss . . . Whining about his wife . . . No ID . . . No, nothing I've checked him out.' There was a pause until he said, 'OK. I'll wait.'

My captor stared at me and grinned. 'Boss wants to have a chat with you,' he said. His eyes briefly shifted from my face to the smashed drawers of the desk. 'I think he's going to be upset about this,' he went on. 'It's an antique and like all that fancy stuff it'll cost plenty to fix. Still, seeing as you ain't got no bucks, he'll find some other way for you to pay up. He can be quite inventive like that.'

I stared at the floor and said nothing. The pain in my face was acute and my head throbbed. Blood leaking from the broken skin near my cheekbone tickled me as it dribbled down to the line of my jaw. I lowered one hand to brush it away, but an upward jerk of the gun barrel dissuaded me.

Baldie and I stood facing each other across the desk for what seemed like forever before I heard a vehicle pull up outside.

Seconds later a couple of burly guys burst into the room, grabbed me by the arms and bundled me outside into an SUV standing in the yard. They put me in the back of the cab between them while Baldie went up front and took the wheel. Sitting there, I was lean meat sandwiched between thick slices of bread.

We drove deep into the estate along a cinder track that twisted and turned through its middle. Under a clear sky, little was visible except endless lines of vines and one long, low building we passed at high speed. Situated close to it was a water tower with an iron ladder.

I guessed where we were heading before we arrived. I wasn't surprised then when the house I'd had under observation hove into view. Seen from ground level, it was even more imposing for it was exceptionally wide and rose into the sky through a series of interlocking terraces. Achieving this effect must have used vast quantities of concrete, steel and glass in order to create a mansion where sharp corners and straight lines were the predominant features. I believe it's what's called the minimalist style, but for me the place looked as soulless as a shopping mall.

We stopped near garages. I was manhandled out of the SUV and frog-marched across to the steps where I'd seen Swartman. Baldie took the lead at the top and made for a living room on the far side, the interior of which was visible through its floor-to-ceiling glass walls. I noted the door we passed through was bullet-proof and I'd have bet money the walls surrounding it were similarly protected.

The space beyond, almost large enough to house a jumbo jet, was all pastel colours as reflected in its floor coverings, furnishings and furniture. It was relieved only by a series of bronzes set on marble plinths at regular intervals along the three sides that were fashioned from glass. At the back was a huge home TV screen tuned to CNN. The sound was off but the images from a war zone someplace didn't need amplification.

Swartman stood with his back to us looking at the screen but at our approach he turned in our direction. Reeva Naidoo had described his eyes as being full of demons. I took that under advisement but there was something about the intensity of his stare that was unsettling, and which left you feeling alone and vulnerable.

I was marched to within a couple of metres of him while Baldie stood off to one side, a wolfish expression disfiguring his features.

'What happened Yash?' asked Swartman looking at the ugly weal that had been raised on my cheekbone and the blood that was still dribbling from it.

'Payback for what he did to your desk,' said the man I'd dubbed Baldie.

Swartman nodded his head approvingly and his mane of white hair trembled. 'And for breaking in,' he said. 'Let's not forget that.' He half turned back to the TV which was screening images of a town being shelled. 'Without law and order,' he went on pompously

222

indicating the TV, 'what have we got? -Fucking chaos, that's what we've got.'

It seemed to me it was about time I said something. 'I-I'm very sorry, sir. I-I was desperate. You see my w-wife's not . . .'

And that was the second time I missed a blow coming in my direction. Not that I could have done anything to prevent it as I was held as tight as a straitjacket. Swartman hit me in the solar plexus with all the weight of his heavy frame. The guys holding me let me drop and I collapsed on the floor in breathless agony. Not satisfied, Swartman waded in with his feet as I curled up in a foetal position to protect my head from repeated kicks.

Swartman was breathing hard by the time he stopped but I was struggling to breathe at all. I seemed to have pain centres all over my body as I fought to get air into my starved lungs. By the time I dared to lift my eyes from the marbled floor, my attacker was sitting in an upright chair while the three others looked on like students observing some bizarre master class.

Swartman reached over me and grabbed my hair tugging my head up toward him. His face came in close, and I smelt stale smoke on his sleeve and brandy on his breath.

'What's your name?' he said softly, searching my features with eyes dark as tar pools.

'P-P-Pieter K-Khan.'

'And where are you from Pieter?'

'Z-Zolani.'

'I know Zolani. How did you get here this evening?'

'I-I walked.'

'If you look up in Zolani, what can you see?'

I hadn't a clue what could be seen but I knew my only chance of getting clear of this was to stick to my story. 'I-I can see the sky, sir,' I said.

Swartman tugged my hair painfully. 'Don't trifle with me,' he snapped.

'Y-You're confusing me,' I whimpered. 'All I see is the s-sky when I look up.'

'What's your address in Zolani?'

'I-I can't tell you that, sir. I-I have m-memory problems.'

'Really?' Swartman's voice dripped disbelief while his hand gave my hair another tug.

'Y-Yes sir. I-I have epilepsy,' I replied, winging it. 'But I c-could take you there.'

Swartman abruptly changed the subject after looking down at my feet. 'For a dumb fuck with nothing to your name,' he said, 'you've expensive tastes in shoes.'

I was wearing a pair of loafers. They weren't new and they were scuffed but they were Gucci all the same. 'I-I was given them, sir,' I said.

'How so?'

'I-I was looking for gardening work in Ashton last year. I went to this house and the man there saw my old shoes. H-He gave me these because he didn't like the colour. He said his sister bought them.'

Swartman's eyes bored into me relentlessly and I knew what he was being told wasn't gaining much traction.

'You been to PE?' he asked abruptly.

I feigned ignorance. 'PE sir?'

'Port Elizabeth.'

'I-I never left the Western Cape.'

'How long you lived in Zolani?'

'Three, maybe four years. I-I don't remember too well.'

'Where did you live before?'

'M-Mitchells Plain.'

'Which part?'

'N-Near the P-Promenade Shopping Centre.'

It was at that point I felt my nerves could stand no more. I only had to give one demonstrably false answer and I'd be cashing in my chips. The time was up to rely on good fortune and Lady Luck.

'What do you . . .?' began Swartman.

He broke off as the back of my left hand tapped him across the mouth and then hit him again as my arm went into spasm. I followed that up by drumming my right leg on the floor before getting my left limb involved as well. Then, as Swartman had let go my hair, I allowed my head to flop over and hit the floor as my whole body shook in imitation of a major seizure.

By that time, Swartman had got up from his chair and stood alongside Yash and the two henchmen. For the moment, they were speechless as they watched me thrashing around uncontrollably on the floor.

I made the performance last a full minute. After that, I brought it to an end as fast as it had started and let my limbs relax. But my head stayed on the floor and my eyes were closed. I struggled to stay calm.

Somebody's hand reached down and felt for a pulse in my neck. When it found one, it delivered a slap to my face. I didn't move a muscle. Nor did I move when hit again.

'What do we do now?' It was Yash who spoke.

'Wait.' It was Swartman's voice. I heard somebody pacing up and down. Seconds later, I heard his voice once more. 'Fucking voice-mail again!'

'Who you after, Gert?'

'Du Toit. I tried yesterday. Same result as now.'

'Maybe he's not around for a reason.'

'Like what?'

'How should I know? -Is it important?' There was silence for a long moment, before I heard Yash's voice again. 'You want to talk to him about this guy, don't you?'

'Amongst other things, but he's now the priority.'

'You can't think he's somehow connected to PE, can you?' Yash sounded incredulous. 'That maybe this is Nemo?'

'Fit looked pretty genuine to me,' piped up a voice I'd not heard before. 'My sister-in-law's nephew . . .'

Swartman cut him off savagely: 'When I want your view, I'll fucking ask for it.'

'Don't you have a snitch in SAPS?' asked Yash.

'Not mine-du Toit's.'

'If this is Nemo, Gert, how did he find us? There's no traceable link with PE. Never has been.'

'This guy don't smell right.'

'OK, but that don't make him Nemo. Maybe his name really is Khan. Maybe he happened by and thought he'd get lucky.' Yash laughed mirthlessly. 'Maybe he knows different now.'

Swartman didn't join in the laughter. 'You live in a shit-hole like Zolani,' he said, 'you can't be too particular about anything. Look at his nails. Why aren't they broken? Look at the skin on his hands. Why's there no ingrained dirt? He doesn't add up and I want to know why.'

'So, what happens now?'

'Get him out of my sight,' snapped Swartman. With that he kicked me viciously again and it was all I could do not to cry out. 'Toss him in the winery for now,' he ordered. 'If I don't tell you otherwise, put some guys into Zolani early tomorrow morning with his picture. Let's find out if anybody knows this cunt.'

I heard Swartman step away and suddenly the room was filled with sound from the TV . . . *Jets continue to pound what the government says are rebel strongholds. Evidence on the ground though suggests this is no more than . . .*

I heard no more as Yash and the others lifted and then carried me out of the house.

I was put back in the SUV and the four of us drove in the same configuration as before. In my state of feigned unconsciousness, they sat in so close that we were like pages in a book.

Yash stopped at last in the shadow cast by a large building, the ground around it lit by what must have been a near full moon. I was manhandled out unceremoniously and bundled across the intervening ground to where Yash held open a door. With no thought of the consequences, I was flung through it. Petrified, I found myself falling into a black void.

226

CHAPTER FORTY-THREE

When I woke up, I was lying at the foot of a short cement staircase. Though the distance I fell was not much more than a metre it seemed my head and shoulder had connected with the floor first and I knocked myself out. Dazed, I stared about me and crawled towards the source of a weak light. There was a door that was slightly ajar and inserting myself between it and the jamb I levered it open.

Beyond, in a cavern of a room, was a line of tall steel tanks. The polished surfaces of these were dully lit by the moon which was visible through windows high up beneath a beamed roof. What I also observed was that each of those windows, even had I been able to reach them, was barred.

My head ached abominably; even more so when I turned it gingerly to face away from the tanks. I looked along a corridor to where wooden barrels were stacked on their sides until they disappeared in the darkness. A low brick wall, built out at right angles, divided the wine processing plant from the maturing liquor.

I crawled beyond the doorway and tried to stand but fell back nauseous. After that, I was physically sick and sank back down to the floor exhausted. I sat like that for a while drifting in and out of consciousness. When next I stirred, it seemed the light from the moon had shifted.

I must have been feeling better because it dawned on me time wasn't on my side and night wouldn't last forever. I made another effort to get up and managed to stay upright by propping myself against the wall. While my head still ached, it wasn't the only source of pain. I knew there must be a mass of bruising to my torso from the kicking but one area that was particularly tender suggested I might have cracked a rib. The side of my face where I'd been pistol-whipped felt like it had swollen into a massive contusion and the taste in my mouth was bitter as poison.

Searching for water, I shuffled slowly towards the barrels stopping at regular intervals because it was dark, and I felt unsteady. This part of the winery was older than the rest and its roof much lower. It was lit by a single window at chest height about half way along its length. So dirty that it admitted little light, each of its closely fitted bars was securely anchored in the brickwork. I knew because pulling at all of them left me close to despair.

Where the barrels gave out, an internal door set in a brick wall gave onto another corridor with rooms on each side. Here some light managed to intrude through a skylight, and I made for a steel door at the end which I was sure led outside. It was little surprise though to find it locked.

I turned my attention elsewhere and found a toilet with a washbasin. I splashed water on my face, rinsed out my mouth, and then drank my fill. It revived me somewhat and gave me the strength to explore elsewhere.

The room next door was a store filled with large plastic containers; packets and bags of various sizes arranged on shelves; plus a couple of ancient carboys packed with straw which stood on their own.

The space opposite contained a trolley, a heavy-duty jack, polypropylene rakes and shovels, quantities of tubing and large rolls of stretch wrap amongst other items I didn't recognise. In one corner was a stack of plastic crates filled with empty wine bottles and close by a large box holding cleaning paraphernalia.

The last room was an office, but it was very small and in almost complete darkness. I could make out a desk and chair and that was about it. I negotiated my way past the seat and rummaged sightlessly in the desk drawers. After a couple of minutes, I found an opened packet of cigarettes and an old plastic lighter. I flicked the wheel, and it sparked first time. I put it and the cigarettes in my pocket.

Making my way back to the wine tanks, I explored the area behind them. The windows were five metres above my head and there was no means of reaching them. Even with a set of steps, and there was none, I was confident the bars would have defeated me anyway.

In that instant, it hit me I wasn't going to get out of the place before they came back in the morning. What would happen after that I didn't like to contemplate. Particularly when they discovered nobody in Zolani knew a guy by the name of Pieter Khan.

With that revelation, I felt the blood begin to pound in my ears and my heart thud in my chest. I broke into a sweat and was all at once struggling to breathe. Terror suddenly overwhelmed me, and I felt dizzy. Shuffling to the wall opposite the tanks, slid down by them.

With my eyes closed, I began the process of calming myself by breathing in through my nose and out through my mouth. In through my nose and out and through my mouth. Over and over, I repeated the exercise trying to focus on nothing but the air passing into and out of my lungs.

Gradually, I restored some sense of equilibrium. I opened my eyes again and began to look around. Idly, I took the cigarettes out of my pocket, selected one and lit it. I gave up smoking more than ten years ago, apart from the occasional cigar, but still enjoy the aroma of burning tobacco. Idly, I blew on the glowing end and turned it strawberry red. From somewhere I recalled the temperature at the tip of a cigarette could be upwards of 900 degrees C.

I lifted my gaze to the wine tanks. There were eight of them in a row but only the two farthest from the stacked barrels were still reflecting moonlight. I'd thought the tanks were all the same but the one on the end was open to the air and marked Fermentation Tank Two.

Something slowly began to take shape in my mind. Despite my enthusiasm as regards his efforts, the talk given by Alec Ferguson at the wine farm had been no more entertaining than watching dust settle. Long-winded on the chemical interactions that occur during the wine production process, I did grasp that grape sugars during fermentation are converted into ethanol using yeast as a catalyst. The ethanol or alcohol which results is highly flammable and its vapour heavier than air. When pure, its flash point is less than average room temperature.

I got to my feet again and stubbed out the cigarette. I shambled back past the barrels with an uncertain gait. I still had a headache, my cheek throbbed without let up and my conviction as regards a cracked rib increased as the discomfort in my chest grew.

I looked in each of the rooms at the far end for petrol, paint thinner, turpentine, acetone or anything else that could be used as an accelerant. I spent longer than was wise, particularly as there was nothing to assist me. Thus, was rendered stillborn my hope of creating a Molotov cocktail using one of the wine bottles I saw earlier.

I cast around for alternatives. The need was for materials that would burn easily, and I chose toilet paper, torn-up rags from the cleaning box and some straw taken from the carboys. Introducing these items separately into three empty wine bottles was tedious through the narrow necks. But I discovered a screwdriver with a long thin blade, and this was useful in tamping down the various items. The object of the exercise was to fill each bottle leaving some space in the middle of the interior into which I could drop a lighted cigarette. Hopefully, this would continue to burn and ignite the stuff around it.

When I had the three bottles filled to my satisfaction, I transferred them to a spot between the fourth and fifth tanks in the winery. All I had to do now was to lob one of the bottles into the open tank at the end. I prayed it would shatter on contact and the lighted cigarette and burning materials would react with any ethanol vapour to trigger an explosion.

If this sounds like the plan of a suicidal madman, I must confess I was probably more than a little mad at that stage. I was mad with fear, mad with pain and mad with frustration at my impotence. It seemed to me that, if I didn't hazard this, I'd be left with nothing but the passive wait for my captors' return. The element of surprise might allow me to bludgeon one or two of them with whatever came to hand but the outcome against armed men was never going to be in any doubt. *Do not go gentle into that good night.* was advice well-matched to my current mood.

I lit a cigarette and drew on it repeatedly until a couple of centimetres were glowing bright red. I dropped it into the first wine bottle and standing clear of the tank lofted it into the air.

I reckoned though without the acute pain in my chest in raising my arm. Crying out was the only upshot of my spoiled throw. The bottle fell well short and shattered on the concrete floor. The only consolation was that the scattered contents were burning. I crossed over to them and bending down spotted the cigarette tip still glowing brightly. I stamped everything out with my left foot.

Now I tested the limits of my arm action. Either over arm or under arm there was a pain barrier that meant the strength of any throw from a remote position was in considerable doubt. It gave me another decision to make but I didn't hesitate. *Do not go gentle . . .*

I left one bottle behind me and took the other to the open tank and stood beneath it. The top was about a metre and a half above my head. I fished out another cigarette from the packet, put it into my mouth and lit it. Again, I drew on it vigorously before dropping it into the bottle. Then, as though shooting basketballs, I jumped up and lobbed it base first into the empty tank. I heard it clatter inside as I turned and threw myself in the other direction. Crouching down, I covered my head with my hands and waited.

The seconds stretched . . .

And stretched some more . . .

Nothing happened.

Nothing fucking happened.

I looked over to the last bottle and knew I'd have to use it. I started to stand but was all at once engulfed in elemental forces of light and sound. The first blinded me and the second smashed against my eardrums. Despite protection from the intervening tanks, I felt the shock wave lift me.

It was only when I looked out towards the rear wall that my heart leapt. Through the smoke of a growing fire, I saw a section had collapsed.

Collapsed, opening an escape route!

Collapsed, giving me freedom!

Beyond lay the moonlit night and the shadowed rows of vines.

I made for them at a shambling run. At that moment, I had no thought for the pain in either body or head. My focus was the liberating power of fresh air and physical freedom restored to me.

At the wall, I clambered over shattered brickwork and ran headlong into the vines.

My haste proved wise: behind me, part of the roof collapsed with a huge crash.

In no time, I reached the iron ladder at the side of the water tower. Winded, I began the long climb up its side, each step higher a painful ordeal made worse by vertigo. I didn't look down but kept my eyes riveted on my hands.

Finally, I reached the top. As I stepped over the retaining wall of the tower and onto a ladder on the other side, I looked down. Half the winery was now open to the sky and ravaged by fire. The other half looked likely to suffer the same fate.

And in this wholesale destruction I found elation and an affirmation of life. I'd *raged, raged against the dying of the light* and come through because, as I watched, hungry flames from the doomed winery leapt with increasing ferocity 25 metres into the dawn air.

CHAPTER FORTY-FOUR

But the joy was only momentary because I spotted approaching lights. They came from the direction of Swartman's house. I ducked down and began to descend the ladder inside the tower.

When my head was perhaps a couple of metres below the top of the retaining wall, I discovered there were no more rungs beneath my feet. To my left and below was a profusion of foliage. It wasn't clear whether it was rooted at ground level or had seeded itself in the wall. In the darkness of the interior, I couldn't safely go down and so waited for sun-up.

But, while I saw nothing hanging there on the ladder, I heard plenty. Even standing where I was, the roaring of the fire was menacing. So great was it that it almost drowned out the arrival of fire crews, but not the two further explosions that detonated like thunderclaps.

Eventually, dawn advanced sufficiently for me to see what my hideout looked like. The space in which I found myself was around five or six metres deep and about 10 metres across. It was empty, apart from an area of brackish water in one corner. From its state of repair, the tower appeared unused for decades. At one point a third of the way up, the concrete wall had fractured allowing buddleia to take hold in the crevices. It had grown profusely and hanging branches now grew out thickly to create not only an area of shade but also one of concealment.

The ladder didn't run down to the base of the reservoir but stopped nearly a metre short. I crouched as best I could on the lowest rung and jumped down to the ground. That way I hoped to avoid further pain to my torso but ended up jarring my legs. I didn't dwell on the discomfort though and quickly moved under the canopy of the buddleia. Arranging myself on my side, with the curvature of the wall at my back, I was well hidden. After the trauma of my captivity, I was mentally and physically exhausted.

It was the whop-whop-whop sound of a helicopter that woke me up. Frantic for a second or two, I imagined it had a bead on me. But when I turned my head and looked up there was nothing but sky. The machine was out of sight and relieved I heard it shear away soon after. Gradually, the sound of rotor blades disappeared into the distance. Its presence though had vindicated my decision to hide in the water tower. I knew vigorous searches for me would be instituted and staying so close to the winery would keep me safe.

I worried though about the Fiesta. It would occur to Swartman to have a search made for a parked car somewhere in the locality. I could only console myself with the thought my vehicle wouldn't stand out from those belonging to visitors. Or at least that would be the case during daylight hours when the parking area was occupied.

The day turned hot and in the empty reservoir there wasn't a breath of air. I became ravenous, but worse was thirst. More than once I contemplated the filthy water a few metres away. It was though no more than a large puddle and from its murky brown colour obviously contaminated. Yet the sight of it made me torture myself with the prospect of slaking my thirst in other ways. A bottle of Castle beer with condensation dripping down its sides would be a good start, as would a long drink of orange and lemonade with ice, or simplest of all would be plunging my face into the mountain stream close by my parked car.

I turned away from the puddle and faced the wall again lying on my side. There was nothing on which to rest my head except my arm and the bare concrete wasn't conducive to giving my battered body much respite.

234

In this fashion, the hours melted away as slowly as icebergs in the Southern Ocean. I measured their passage by the track of the sun as it arced across the sky. But I counted my blessings for I was left undisturbed. It's true somebody set my heart racing that morning by climbing the external ladder, but I believe it was only a fireman searching for another source of water. In any event, whoever it was quickly descended when a glance over the rim would have been enough to confirm the tower was empty.

I didn't move until well after nightfall. When I did it proved a painful and exhausting business. My inactivity during that long day had caused my muscles to stiffen and lack of food and water made me feel weak and light-headed.

The escape ladder was a distance above the bottom of the reservoir. The force of gravity had assisted my descent, but it did the opposite in my efforts to climb up. In my debilitated state I lacked strength in my arms and suffered acute pain in my chest trying to lift my legs high enough to get a purchase on the lowest rung. But avoiding pain and discomfort meant staying where I was indefinitely. So, through gritted teeth, I reached up high, grabbed a rung and hauled myself upwards in one rapid movement. For a moment, my feet scrabbled to anchor themselves but, when they did, I was able to relieve the weight on my arms. After that, I leant in against the ladder and waited for the torment the effort had cost me to subside. It took a while but soon my slow ascent was begun one rung at a time.

I didn't know what to expect when I reached the top and was cautious about putting my head above the parapet.

The scene that confronted me was a revelation. Simply put, the winery had ceased to exist. What was left was a mass of smashed and burnt timbers, twisted metal and piles of rubble. At the end of the building which had housed the storerooms and the small office nothing remained but fire-damaged walls open to the sky. At one point, the conflagration had spread beyond the boundary of the site leaving behind scorched vines and blackened earth.

I eventually climbed down the ladder. I was cautious on two counts: one because of my vertigo and the other because my legs now felt like rubber. Long before reaching the bottom, the smell of the fire filled my nostrils. It was pungent and bitter and penetrated to the back of my throat making me cough.

Without looking back, I skirted the ruins and headed along one of the rows between the vines. Reaching a wire fence a few minutes later, I found a break almost at once and passed through.

On the other side, there was undergrowth interspersed with a few beech and yellowwood trees. I negotiated the area with difficulty, falling over twice in making my way out.

At a road, it wasn't clear in which direction I should go. I decided left but after 200 metres knew that downhill was my best option. It had taken me a while to fathom this which I put down to exhaustion.

I made no such mistake when close to my car. I didn't approach it directly but cut across a field and came in from one side. This tactic delivered the crucial benefit of allowing me to drink my fill at an intersecting stream. At no time, before or since, has water tasted as sweet. With hands cupped, I gulped down my fill before bathing my battered face.

After that, I made for the Fiesta but kept it under observation for several minutes before venturing too close. It was parked as I had left it and stood alone in deep shadow.

Satisfied at last that no harm would befall me, I crossed to it and retrieved my keys from the exhaust pipe. A moment later, I slowly drove away using only side lights. It was only at the main road that I put the headlights up and my foot down. It stayed that way for 30 kms at which point I felt free at last of the Namtraws Wine Estate.

CHAPTER FORTY-FIVE

I pulled over soon enough after that. My preoccupying thought was food having eaten nothing since the afternoon of the previous day. I remembered what I bought and was soon wolfing down what was left.

Afterwards, I gave thought to my next move. Or rather the move after that as the next one needed to be a visit to a doctor or hospital. I had significant pain in my chest and the contusion on my right cheek persistently throbbed. It occurred to me the wound had become infected.

I journeyed east and stopping at the first large town, searched out the hospital. It was a 24/7 facility and I had them look me over after showing my medical access card.

Fortunately, there were no broken or cracked ribs but there was very extensive bruising. They gave me analgesics that they said would help make breathing less painful and then turned their attention to my face.

This proved the bigger problem. After they cleaned it up, they didn't believe the wound was infected but they suspected a fracture of the zygomatic bone. The degree of swelling though made establishing the exact situation difficult, even with the assistance of X-ray. They gave me antibiotics as a precautionary measure and told me I needed to consult a trauma specialist elsewhere and that I should do that soon.

After that, I changed my clothes in a communal rest room and trailed back to the car. By then it was well past midnight, so I curled up in the passenger seat and slept. A combination of painkillers, antibiotics and the ongoing regime of sedatives knocked me out until well after sun-up. In fact, I was awoken by an ambulance siren as it tore up the incline past the Fiesta to the main hospital entrance.

Before falling asleep, I determined that an approach SAPS in the Western Cape was my best move. But how this was to be achieved wasn't an issue I'd thought through. Pitching up at the nearest police outpost and telling my story didn't strike me as a sensible way of getting anything done any time soon. I was also concerned about my personal safety. If I had issues with SAPS in the Eastern Cape, I had to be equally wary of their counterparts headquartered in Cape Town. Unfortunately, SAPS is a flawed organization with both corruption and incompetence featuring prominently on the charge sheet. Fact is that over a thousand serving officers across the country have convictions for serious criminal offences, including rape. Stuff like that doesn't do a whole lot for trust.

I mulled this over at breakfast taken in the centre of town. It was at a café in a Victorian building whose iron columns with fancy scrollwork supported a verandah above. I could have eaten outside but chose to remain indoors where my damaged face only offended the back wall.

It was while drinking my third cup of strong black coffee that the identity of who I would approach at SAPS was resolved. That left me with the more difficult question of where a rendezvous might take place. With a view to resolving this conundrum, I bought maps of both the Western and Northern Capes. An hour later, I returned to the Fiesta and set off once again.

CHAPTER FORTY-SIX

I crossed the N1 and headed into what long ago was named the Karoo or the land of great thirst. Semi-arid and sparsely populated, its vast plains were carved up into sheep ranches in the 19th century because that was about all the landscape would support. As it lay within striking distance of Cape Town, I made for Sutherland, its claim to fame resting on the presence of SALT, the South African Large Telescope, which attracts significant numbers of tourists. But, on the day I passed through, the town was only as lively as a dead cricket.

I drove on until I joined a dusty track that passed through a dun-coloured landscape stretching limitlessly under a big sky. It was broken up by low hills and it was towards these I navigated, dust billowing from my wheels and liberally coating the scrub on either side.

I found what I was looking for a couple of kms farther on. It was a *kopje* rising perhaps 30 metres above the surrounding terrain. More than that there was a gully at its base where a couple of quiver trees grew. They looked like heads of broccoli and cast some shade when I tucked the car in close between them.

Taking the binoculars, I climbed the rock-strewn hillside disturbing a basking lizard on my way up. Like him, I was pleased to feel the heat of the sun on my back and on my face as I turned it towards its soothing rays.

On top of the hill and standing amongst low bushes and small boulders, I slowly scanned the landscape in all directions. In the still clear air, I was able to see huge distances in every direction without obstruction. Satisfied this was the right spot, I made my way back to the Fiesta and retraced my route to the highway.

I drove 100kms to Fraserburg and sought out the town's police station. Located in a side street close to the main drag, I parked where the front entrance was in view.

My chosen contact inside SAPS Western Cape was Brigadier Joubert. We'd met when I drove across from Port Alfred to identify Mira's body in the safari park. On brief acquaintance, he struck me as a fair-minded guy who knew what he was about. That didn't answer the question though as to whether he could be trusted or, for that matter, whether our respective interests coalesced. Hence my need for caution.

To be specific, I was aware cell phones can be tracked because getting one in the first place requires ID plus proof of address. I had no way of knowing whether SAPS might already be targeting my comms as there were people on the inside who had corrupt interests to protect. Ergo, in circumstances like mine, the best advice was to make any calls from a busy area; use a handset with no history; dump the phone once used; and then get the hell out of it.

I knew contacting Joubert might require making several calls. Even if I thought he might get back to me, as to when he might do that was out of my control and I needed to retain the initiative. Changing locations and phones each time would be a real pain in the arse.

As a result, I tried an experiment. I walked 200 metres past the SAPS station to where there was a bench beneath a rangy palm. I rang SAPS HQ in Cape Town, got the expected runaround, said I'd call again in an hour, and rang off.

I slipped the phone onto the dusty ground behind the bench, got up and walked back to the Fiesta. Through the windscreen, there was a clear view along the length of the street.

My thinking was that if the phone was being tracked some eager party would emerge from the station to investigate and locate it.

Even in this remote area, triangulation would position the phone within a radius of perhaps 100 metres.

I waited for something to happen and in time it did. It wasn't what I expected though. It manifested in the shape of an elderly and overweight woman who collapsed onto the bench with her miniature Schnauzer. After she got her breath back, she fed the animal tidbits and didn't move off, the dog in her arms, until she was well rested. Throughout, my mobile remained undisturbed in the dust.

Half an hour later, a SAPS *bakkie* pulled out of the police station car park and headed in my direction. I felt my heart rate leap momentarily and a tightness squeeze my chest. But I needn't have worried as its driver, yawning hugely, passed me doing no more than 20 kph.

And that was it for a while, apart from a couple of plain-clothes staff who came out, lit up briefly and afterwards walked back into the building.

When the hour was up, I returned to the phone and called Cape Town again. I didn't reach Joubert but was told he was aware I was trying to reach him. Apparently, he was in a meeting and couldn't be disturbed. I said he should expect a call back after a further hour.

I left the phone as before and spent more time dozing behind the wheel. Over that period, there were various comings and goings from the SAPS station but nothing that caused me any qualms.

At that point, it was safe to conclude that the phone, bought several days before, wasn't being tracked. That could be because nobody had thought to do so or because there were administrative delays before data regarding an individual phone purchase could be processed.

I finally got hold of Joubert when the angle of the sun had stretched the shadow cast by my car to its maximum extent.

'What do you want?' he asked cautiously, after I told him my name.

'Cooperation,' I said. 'We met after Mira Zarakolu's body was discovered.'

'I remember.'

'I've further information for you. Information which may change the whole view of it.'

'I see.' From his tone it was evident that Joubert didn't share my conviction. 'What is this information?'

'Do you know the name Gert Swartman?'

Now I detected an intake of breath. 'It's a name I've not heard in a while,' Joubert conceded quietly. 'What do you know about him?'

'A good deal, but I don't think this is the appropriate occasion.'

'You'd prefer to meet?'

'That would be sensible.'

'Perhaps you can come into HQ here in Cape Town.'

'Negative that. I wouldn't feel safe. Any meeting will have to be on neutral ground and in a place of my choosing.'

The Brigadier hesitated before responding. 'Let me indulge you for a moment: what have you in mind?'

'I want you to contact the Air Wing and organise a chopper. This is urgent so doing something for tomorrow would be best.'

Joubert must have been taken aback as there was silence. When he did speak, the sarcasm was palpable: 'And once I've dragooned the Air Wing, what's to happen then?'

'You and the pilot will fly a route I'll give you later. Somewhere along the flight path I'll signal from the ground. We can talk after you've landed.'

'I'm really not sure I can do that,' said Joubert firmly. He paused. 'Actually, I don't think I even want to.'

'Yeah,' I said. 'I guess, Brigadier, this is all a bit of an impertinence. But, you see, it comes down to the value you place on my life against that which I place on it myself. I had a brush with Swartman and only my good fortune means I can talk to you now. That sort of experience makes you kinda careful.'

'And where did this brush take place?'

'Near Ashton in the Western Cape. Do you know Swartman has a place there?'

242

'I can assure you that SAPS has known for a long time where Gert Swartman is to be found.'

'And?'

'And what?'

'I detect frustration in your voice,' I said. 'It's as though his whereabouts aren't really of any significance.'

'You're right,' admitted Joubert heavily. 'Let's leave it that Swartman's been a person of interest for many years. Would you like to tell me what happened to you?'

'I was held against my will and beaten up.'

'How did that come about?'

'I broke into his place and got caught.'

'And your actions had something to do with Mrs. Zarakolu's murder?'

'Very much so.'

'I see,' said Joubert thoughtfully. 'Would you be willing to make a statement to that effect? -Even though you'll likely incriminate yourself?'

'The stakes are much higher than that,' I snapped. 'You'll get a statement if it helps matters.'

'It would help considerably. I've a boss wedded to the notion that all our actions must have legitimacy, if later queried. A witness statement meets that criterion. Can I ask why you've not taken this to our SAPS colleagues in the Eastern Cape?'

'Firstly, Swartman lives on your territory and secondly I don't trust them. There's an informant within their command structure. My car was recently blown up in PE. Perhaps you heard about it?'

'I heard,' said Joubert, 'and appreciate how you might feel. But if you don't trust Eastern Cape, your attitude now suggest you don't trust us either.'

'You can take that view if you want. All I'm doing is looking after my interests. That means avoiding unnecessary risks.'

Joubert sighed. 'All right,' he said philosophically, 'I suggest you call me again in a couple of hours. Hopefully, I'll have some news by then.'

I drove into the centre of town, principally in search of food. I would have preferred to have sat down to eat something, but Fraserburg seemed short of options. In the end, the local supermarket sold me bread, mozzarella cheese and polony.

At the same time, I took the opportunity of filling up the Fiesta and buying a can of petrol. Appropriate material to start a fire eluded me until I spotted a small tyre fitting business. From a pile of covers at the side of the premises, I rescued two worn-out scooter tyres and transferred them to the boot.

When I rang Joubert again, his attitude had changed markedly. He appeared much more motivated, though I wasn't sure to what that could be ascribed. I was too much of a cynic to believe it had much to do with any better understanding of my position.

'I can be airborne by 9.30 tomorrow morning,' he announced.

'OK. What are you flying?'

'A Robertson R44.'

'That has four seats, doesn't it?'

'It does. It's the smallest machine the Air Wing operates.'

'Fine,' I said, 'but this trip is you and the pilot only. If I see anybody else, I'm gone and gone for good. Likewise, if I see anybody on the ground the outcome's the same. Do we understand each other?'

I didn't get a response except a request for the flight plan.

I summed up. 'First, stay low and cruise at minimum speed so we don't miss each other. Do you have a pen?'

The Brigadier said he had a pen.

'I want you to fly east to Robertson and circle the town for a couple of minutes. After that go north-west to Worcester and do the same thing. When that's done head for Laingsburg, then Sutherland and finally Ceres. In each case the pilot should go point to point. Is that clear?'

'It's clear. How will you signal from the ground?'

'Black smoke. But give me your number and make sure you keep your phone switched on.' Joubert gave me the number of his cell.

'Thanks for that,' I said. 'Lastly, I suggest you talk with SAPS in the Eastern Cape and get an update.'

'Rest assured, Mr. Nemo, that's already in hand.'

Two minutes later, I pitched the phone I'd been using out of the car window as I gathered speed away from Fraserburg. Paranoia had found expression in my discarding one phone and buying another.

CHAPTER FORTY-SEVEN

I made it back to Sutherland in around an hour and a half along a road almost devoid of human habitation. The sky was cloudless and filled with stars, stars with a particular luminosity because of the absence of ambient light. But I could have been making a journey across the surface of the moon so inhospitable was the terrain picked out in the headlights. And in all that time on the road, I passed only two vehicles.

I found a place for the night in a B&B on the outskirts of town. It was a single storey dwelling with an ornately rounded gable in the Cape Dutch style.

It was cold when I stepped out of the car onto waste ground at the side of the place. I donned a light pullover and crossed to the front door.

'Hi,' I said to the seated party who opened up for me. 'Would you have a room for the night?'

'I guess.' From a wheelchair, a man smiled at me disarmingly and pushed heavy glasses up the bridge of his nose.

As he wheeled back, I stepped inside the door and saw his gaze focus on the side of my face.

'Mugged,' I said in the hope of forestalling questions.

'You had it looked at?'

'A day or so ago. But I need to see a specialist so I'm heading back to Cape Town.'

'Is that where it happened?'

I smiled at him. 'Ironically it is,' I said. 'I had somebody to see up here today, so it's had to wait.'

'Haven't been to Cape Town in 20 years,' said my host conversationally. 'And if I never see it again, that'll be too soon. You want a hand with your luggage? My son's out the back and I can fetch him.'

'I'm fine,' I said. 'I don't suppose you have any spirits, do you?'

'Drown your sorrows?'

I tried to grin. 'And help anaesthetise the pain.'

'Of course. You get your stuff and I'll see what I can find. You want something to eat?'

I declined, fetched my holdall from the car and walked inside. I was surprised to find a bottle of Klipdrift thrust into my empty hand along with a key. 'You're in the room at the end of the corridor. It's a double so you'll have more space.'

'That's much appreciated. What do you want for the bottle?'

'Ach, man, take it. There's not much more in there than fumes.'

I looked at the bottle which was nearly half full. 'A bit of an understatement,' I said smiling.

'You're welcome. It's been sitting around forever. I'm not allowed to drink, and my son hates the stuff.'

I made my way along the corridor to the room. It was spacious enough with an en-suite bathroom and double bed pushed against a rough stone wall painted mustard yellow. On the bed sat two small teddy bears dressed in pink and blue sweaters.

I dumped my bag, went into the bathroom and found a glass. I unscrewed the top of the Klipdrift, poured a generous measure and drained it in one gulp. It blazed a trail down into my stomach where it spread its warmth and peace, before telling me I was desperately tired. Kicking off my shoes, I lay back on the bed.

I don't know how long I slept. At one point, I looked out of the window, and it was as black as a witch's hat. Later, my chest began to hurt, and my cheek thought it would be pally and join in. I took painkillers mixed with the rest of the brandy and that did the trick.

When I awoke again there were fingers of light spreading across the sky.

But I didn't surface feeling calm. I came to with a great churning in my guts. It wasn't the usual anxiety but a response to a possible airborne threat with which I had a rendezvous later that morning.

CHAPTER FORTY-EIGHT

No question, I was a trespasser at the summit of the *kopje*. and the little guy didn't like it. But he wasn't able to do anything about it, so he regarded me with a cold eye for a few seconds, blinked and headed for cover. I watched him vanish fast as light over the edge of a rock. Shifting my cramped leg made a shallow furrow in the sand. I doubted such a violation of his habitat would see the lizard's return any time soon.

Above me, the kind old sun roused my spirits as it cast ascendant rays on my wounded face and battered torso. With my back against a boulder, I sat dressed in long khaki pants and a beige T shirt. It was my best shot at camouflage. In the gully at the base of the hill, the Fiesta stood under the quiver trees. A thick layer of dust over the bodywork made it almost indistinguishable from the landscape.

Once again, I boxed the compass through the binoculars but saw no more than groups of sheep too far away for their bleating to be audible. I settled back and took a swig of water from the bottle I brought with me. Lugging it plus the can of fuel and the scooter tyres to the top of the hill had taken it out of me. But it shouldn't have left me feeling as knackered as an 85-year-old.

The route from Sutherland to Ceres, a distance of about 160 kms, lay in a broadly south-westerly direction and it was in that quadrant that I'd looked for the vantage point I now occupied. It meant that after the chopper reached Sutherland and finished circling it should pass more or less overhead.

When the machine did appear, it was earlier than expected. I'd calculated how long it ought to take but was a half hour adrift. Helicopters though are noisy, and I heard this one when it was still approaching Sutherland from Laingsburg. It gave me ample time to pour half the petrol onto the tyres and apply a match. After a small whoosh as the fuel caught light, the fire took hold and began to stream acrid black smoke straight up into the still air.

I didn't hang around. Grabbing the water and the binoculars, I descended and came out close to my parked car. Moving off a distance to the left, I found a cluster of thorn bushes and knelt beside them. I wasn't invisible but you had to look real hard to see me.

It was soon apparent the smoke had been spotted. What had been a steady clatter from distant rotor blades increased exponentially as the chopper wheeled and made for the blaze.

Overhead, it hovered directly above the fire for a few seconds and then stood off, the downdraught whipping up a swirling storm of sand and dust. I turned my face away but too late to avoid a grit storm. That set off a coughing fit that made my chest ache. A moment later and still hacking, I took out the phone and sent Joubert a text: *Move 500m north from fire. Set down. Switch off.*

Nothing happened until I observed the chopper's white fuselage, its side lettered in blue with the word POLICE, cease to hover. Cockpit pointed down, it descended gradually before searching for a spot to land. It took a minute or so as the ground was strewn with rocks and patches of scrub.

When it finally came to rest at an angle to me, I focused the glasses on the cockpit. I could make out two figures, one of whom had to be the pilot but the other, sitting on the far side, was too far away to be identified. I kept looking until the machine's engine died. Slowly, the two main blades came to rest and hung drooping from the rotor mast.

I sent a further text: *Step out unarmed. Walk towards fire.*

Almost at once, one of the cockpit doors opened and a figure clambered out. He was dressed in a light blue, short-sleeved shirt with navy epaulettes mounted with the hexagon and three gold stars of a SAPS Brigadier. I've a good memory for faces and the one I was looking at was that of the avuncular Joubert, his shirt stretched across his belly tight as a filled spinnaker.

He began walking towards the *kopje*. and the spiralling smoke. In one hand he carried a phone and appeared unarmed for there was no gun at his waist and I saw no tell-tale bulges in the pockets of his pants.

I shifted the binoculars back to the chopper and saw the pilot sitting at the controls. It seemed he was completing a log which rested in his lap and required frequent reference to the instrument panel in front of him.

Just when I judged it was safe to show myself, I heard an engine. It came from somewhere behind and was approaching fast. Very fast. I swivelled my head and saw a large Jeep. But it didn't make for me. Instead, it tore towards the chopper. Next, its driver spotted Joubert and targeted him.

The SUV stopped in a cloud of dust by the Brigadier's side. I raised the glasses to my eyes. An elderly guy in a check shirt was leaning out of the cab and Joubert started to talk. The conversation lasted only a minute before the Jeep made a slow turn and headed back the way it had come. Calmly, Joubert resumed his walk in my direction.

When he was within 100 metres, I stood up and raised a hand in greeting which was reciprocated. By that time, the pilot had climbed out of the chopper and moved a short distance away. I observed him light a cigarette, the smoke lazily drifting away in the still air. I found this relaxed action of his disproportionately reassuring.

'Before you ask, Mr. Nemo,' said Joubert without preamble when we were a few metres apart, 'that was the farmer.' He gave me a fixed smile.

'What did he want?'

'Wanted to know why there was a police helicopter on his land disturbing his sheep. And why some damn fool had lit a fire.'

'What did you tell him?'

'I told him the truth.'

'And what's that?'

'Simply, that I'm conducting police business. The rendezvous is here because of its distance from Cape Town. I said you were jumpy, so the location wasn't agreed in advance for security reasons. The fire was to guide me in.'

'And he bought it?'

Joubert shrugged heavy shoulders. 'Who cares? -The main thing is I got rid of him. I did say though that the fire would be put out.' For the first time, the Brigadier took note of my face. 'Swartman's handiwork?'

I shook my head. 'One of his henchmen.'

'Have you had it looked at?'

'Yes, but it needs further investigation.'

'The best place for that will be Cape Town.'

'I know, but as of now there's a greater priority.'

'I agree.'

'Swartman and du Toit know each other,' I said flatly. 'It's been that way for years. I found a photo of the two of them together.'

The Brigadier raised bushy eyebrows in surprise. 'How very interesting,' he said thoughtfully. 'How did you get on to him?'

Patiently, I explained how my days in Cape Town had been spent and gave him an account of my time in Swartman's hands.

'He's lived there a long time,' said Joubert. 'SAPS have followed his career in narcotics for 20 years or more.'

'And never had enough to nail him?'

'That's about the sum of it. We put him under surveillance for several months a while back but that went nowhere. In the end the operation was abandoned on the grounds of cost.'

'What's his background?'

'He was born and raised in Manenberg. It's our belief he controls much of the drugs trade there. His is a carrot and stick approach. It clearly works as it's kept him from ever being charged with anything.

If one of his people is picked up, they say nothing. If they're jailed their families are looked after and we understand a big cash bonus is paid when they're released. On the other hand, cross him and this benevolence turns into a homicidal hatred. The last person who went up against him was found in scattered pieces. Each body part had the word TRAITOR burned into the flesh.'

I blanched and inwardly shivered despite the heat of the day. It made me realize, if any reminder was required, how lucky I'd been to escape from the winery.

The renewed sound of Joubert's voice though dispelled these unpleasant musings. 'Now, I've something to share with you,' he announced.

'OK.'

'Du Toit's been arrested. It was at a farm near Uitenage.'

'On what charge?' I asked, unable to keep the surprise from my voice.

'For the moment, it's money-laundering, but others will follow. He's been the target of a Hawks' undercover operation for some time.'

I whistled. The Hawks, or to give them their proper name The Directorate for Priority Crime Investigation, is tasked with tackling organised crime and corruption. Often used as a tool of the political elite, its impartiality has been called into question more than once. 'How much is involved?' I asked.

'I don't have figures but it's substantial involving several large businesses in Port Elizabeth.'

'I assume all this came from Captain Bezuidenhout.'

Joubert nodded. 'I talked to him last night.'

'And when did he first become aware of the Hawks' investigation?'

'Only recently.'

'I bet he wasn't happy. How long's it been going on?'

'It seems they've been working a case for several months. He told me he was furious when told by the Provincial Commissioner a few days ago. Apparently, the PC was the only person in the Eastern Cape who knew about the Hawks' involvement.'

'They must have been particularly circumspect and adopted a need-to-know policy.'

Joubert shrugged. 'I can't comment. Fortunately, I've had little involvement with the Hawks. My view is they have their own agenda and as a policeman that worries me. In this instance, it could be their interest is as much about the fact du Toit's white as it is about any crimes he's committed.'

I said nothing. The ongoing conflict between black and white in our Rainbow Nation leaves me distressed. Fact is the colour of my skin leaves me stranded in the middle between the two groups and, as often as not, despised by both.

'Once Bezuidenhout was informed,' Joubert went on, 'he had the foresight to insist the Hawks locked the farm down and imposed a news black-out. He realized du Toit must be fronting for somebody else and that there was a conspiracy. Further evidence for him, he said, was that business with your car. Organising a bomb needed specialist contacts, probably overseas. Du Toit may have wanted you taken care of, but it wasn't something he could do himself.'

All this made sense, but I was still puzzled about one thing. 'I'm surprised the Hawks couldn't track the money,' I said. 'If I'm right in thinking it comes from Swartman, that would be in Cape Town.'

The Brigadier nodded. 'Bezuidenhout told me the Hawks have spent their time on forensic accounting work. They've been gathering information to build a watertight case. It's not helped that du Toit himself hasn't offered any co-operation. In fact, he's not said a word. For the moment he's being kept incommunicado. Callers are being told that he's travelling overseas and can't be reached.'

I'd been mulling over everything while Joubert had been speaking. What he told me cast rather a different light on Bezuidenhout. I'd been inclined to the view that he might be corrupt but now it seemed my suspicions were misplaced. 'I had my doubts about Bezuidenhout,' I said. 'Looks like they were wrong.'

Joubert gave me a small smile. 'He told me relations between you were somewhat strained. He said you were holding him at arm's length even though he offered you protection.'

'It wasn't personal,' I said. 'SAPS in the Eastern Cape is prone to leaks and I was concerned about my safety.'

Joubert sympathised and changed the subject. 'Bezuidenhout told me they found messages on du Toit's phone from someone called Trollip. They weren't specific, but they were certainly angry. Would you happen to know anything about them?'

'They'd have been from Anton Trollip,' I began, before explaining their significance as regards the sale of Frank's business. 'I'm certain du Toit defrauded them. As he held Frank's power of attorney, he'd have received the purchase price from the Trollips and then been responsible for remitting the proceeds to Frank. I believe du Toit's records will show a substantial difference between money coming in and money going out.'

'That'll be something else for the Hawks to look at.' The Brigadier looked at me quizzically, 'I have to say I'm still not entirely clear about your ongoing interest in all this.'

'What did Bezuidenhout tell you?'

'Just that you became involved after Mrs. Zarakolu was kidnapped. And that Frank Zarakolu was a good friend of yours.'

'It went a long way beyond that,' I said. 'I knew Frank more than 20 years. Originally, he got me out of a very bad place. After that, he became like a father to me. I believe Mira's murder killed him.'

Joubert looked at me keenly and wordlessly clapped a hand on my shoulder in a gesture of support.

I gave him a smile though it hurt my face. 'So, Brigadier, what happens next?'

'We need to go. I'll give you a ride back to Cape Town. You can make a statement at HQ providing the pretext for a raid on Swartman's estate. At the same time, I'll get clearance and put together a task force.'

I mulled this, but not for long. 'Thanks for the offer of a ride,' I said, 'but I'm going to take my car. All my stuff's in it.'

Joubert was about to say something but, seeing the resolve in my face, changed his mind. 'In that case, I'll arrange an escort.'

'That isn't necessary. I'm perfectly capable of finding my way to Cape Town.'

'I disagree,' said Joubert. 'You don't look at all fit to me. I'd hate you to have an accident on the way. Besides, I need to protect my assets.'

I couldn't argue with that and in his place would have done the same thing. 'OK,' I said. 'What do you want to do?'

'I'll make a call for the escort.' The Brigadier lifted his eyes to the top of the *kopje*. where smoke was still streaming into the air. 'Do you think you could deal with that? I don't want some spat because the farmer complained. And jurisdictionally, this isn't my stamping ground.'

A couple of minutes later, we shook hands and parted company. I watched him walk towards the chopper and I trudged back up the hill. It nearly killed me, but I killed the fire.

I saw no sign of the little guy and could hardly be surprised. What with my invasion of his territory followed by the tyre burning and the noise and dust from the helicopter I felt sure the lizard had had enough and relocated in disgust.

CHAPTER FORTY-NINE

I don't know what Joubert told his opposite number in SAPS Northern Cape and it's possible that whatever was conveyed got lost in translation. Frankly, what he said wasn't important. It was the way I was treated which was the only thing that mattered.

The guys who turned up from the Sutherland police station couldn't have been more solicitous. They arrived with a flask of coffee on the off-chance I might want some, I did, and with some sandwiches, which I didn't. They asked which my preferred car was and whether I wanted to ride up front or in the back.

I stuck with the Fiesta and rode up front with the driver. But if he thought I was going to give him the inside track into what had happened he was mistaken. Fact was I couldn't tell him anything and any way I fell asleep within a few short minutes.

They took me to a hospital in Cape Town and stayed with me while I underwent a CT scan of my cheek. This revealed a hairline fracture that would need to be dealt with. But, given the swelling to my face, I was advised to report back as an out-patient a week or so hence. Alternatively, I could access help elsewhere as they could transfer my records. Once they checked my meds, they let me go.

After that, I was taken to SAPS HQ. It was an ugly red-brick building located on the corner of two streets, its windows covered with close-meshed metal grilles painted white. The appearance of the place was softened though by magnificent trees that created pools of deep shade on the pavements outside.

257

I was escorted into the building and passed over to Detective Services. The Fiesta's keys were returned to me, and it was arranged for someone to take a witness statement. This process proved to be as tedious as that which I'd endured in Bethelsdorp earlier in the year. After an hour though, I was interrupted by Joubert who burst into the room we were using.

'I'm sorry,' he said as we both looked up startled, 'but your statement will have to wait. There've been developments and we need your help.'

Mystified, I followed the Brigadier out of the room, along a corridor and into a lift. We ascended a floor, walked the length of a featureless passageway and into another room.

Though he didn't say so, this was clearly Joubert's office as a brigadier's uniform jacket was hanging on an old-fashioned hat stand. Beyond it, a floor-mounted SAPS flag was displayed adjacent to a desk loaded with files and several framed photos. But it was to the far end of the room I was taken where a tall man leant over a table studying a map. At our approach he turned and replaced the worried look on his face with an attempt at a smile.

'Bruce, this is Mr. Nemo,' said Joubert. 'Mr. Nemo, may I introduce Colonel Kornfeld. He's heading up the task force we've assembled.'

I shook Kornfeld's hand or rather he grasped mine in a powerful grip that would have crushed my fingers had he exerted more pressure. 'Pleased to meet you,' I managed to say.

'Likewise,' said Kornfeld. 'Look, Mr. Nemo, we don't have a lot of time so let me come straight to the point.' He lifted a photocopy of a plan off the table and passed it to me. 'Does this resemble the house you were taken to?'

I took the document from him and studied it briefly. It was dated 1977 and showed a two-storey dwelling of modest proportions. 'No, it's not,' I said. 'Or at least if this was the original house it's since been massively altered.'

Kornfeld turned to Joubert. 'You know what this means, don't

258

you Luc? -If I put a team in using this we're asking for trouble. We'll be blind from the off and likely to be on the back foot thereafter.'

'Aerial photographs would help,' ventured Joubert.

Kornfeld looked at his watch. 'But is there time? We've only got about three hours of daylight.'

'If I get on with it straightaway,' said Joubert. 'Ashton's the closest town to the estate and that's about 150 kms from here as the crow flies.'

'OK, Luc. I'd be grateful if you could arrange it.'

Wordlessly, Joubert left the table and walked across to his desk where he lifted a phone.

'When's this planned for?' I asked Kornfeld.

'Tomorrow. Half an hour before sun-up.'

'Why so soon?'

'Luc's concerned about how long the lid can be held down on the PE end. He thinks Swartman could find out and disappear.'

I considered this. 'Am I right in thinking that Swartman and the Brigadier have some personal history?' I asked.

Kornfeld gave me a bleak smile. 'Luc ran a surveillance operation on Swartman some years back,' he said. 'It was authorised 24/7 for three months and came up empty. It was sanctioned after a SAPS undercover cop disappeared. Several of his body parts turned up subsequently. He'd been brutally tortured. Luc thinks Swartman was responsible. The cop was the husband of one of his cousins.'

'I see,' I said soberly. 'How can I best help, Colonel?'

'By taking me through everything you remember about the estate.'

I started talking and Joubert joined us at the point where I was explaining that the glass of the living room where I'd met Swartman was bullet-proof.

'Are you sure?' asked the Colonel.

I nodded. 'I noticed because the door had multiple hinges on account of the weight. And the glass wall into which it was set was extraordinarily thick.'

Kornfeld looked over to Joubert and was about to say something before changing his mind. Instead, it was the Brigadier who spoke. 'It's done,' he said to the two of us. 'The chopper will make a single pass over the house and immediately return to base. The footage should be here in the early evening.'

After that, I spent more time with them as they quizzed me about the layout of the estate, its various outbuildings, the physical barriers that would have to be overcome and the deployment of Swartman's henchmen around the place. They were kind enough to say I'd helped, but I doubted it. Too often, they asked questions to which honesty meant I had to confess ignorance.

When they let me go, I was passed back to Detective Services to resume work on my statement. That took another hour including a paragraph to the effect that others were possibly being held on the estate against their will. Of course, there were no grounds for this assertion, but it served a purpose in reinforcing the pretext for the raid. When we were done, I was free to leave. Joubert said that if he wanted anything further, he'd call me but when he hadn't done so by 6 p.m. I took off. My request to be allowed to accompany one of the task force teams was predictably turned down.

Minutes later, I retrieved the Fiesta from the car park and headed out into the evening traffic. Even though I had no expectations otherwise, the way things had turned out was an anti-climax leaving me feeling about as useful as a gun without a trigger.

CHAPTER FIFTY

Distracted, I headed off in the wrong direction towards the district of Gardens but didn't realise until about a kilometre too far south. Turning round proved difficult because of a road closure and afterwards I took the shortest route to the V&A Waterfront as I needed somewhere to stay.

I chose a hotel within a short distance of Helen Suzman Boulevard and checked in. I believe they thought the livid blue and yellow bruising to my face lowered the tone and for two pins would have liked to refuse me entry. My physiognomy was also an uncomfortable reminder to others that the world beyond the cosseting gentility of the Waterfront could be nasty, brutish and short.

I showered and made myself presentable. Afterwards, I chose a pair of blue chinos and matched them to a cream shirt, though putting it on reminded me of the tender state of my ribs.

In the restaurant, I'd have sat out on the deck under an umbrella but the breeze off the water had an edge to it. They fixed me a table inside and organised matters such that the damaged side of my face wasn't visible to those of a sensitive disposition.

As I lingered over my meal and the evening advanced, it struck me I was at the end of the road. Swartman was in the frame with du Toit and I'd had a hand in sticking it to them both. And given what had emerged from the Hawks' investigation, it didn't take much deduction to conclude that the money du Toit was laundering probably came from Swartman and the drugs trade. I speculated about how all those bucks might be transferred but my instincts told me it was by light aircraft. The reality was a small plane could accomplish the journey across the sparsely populated terrain in less than three hours. Indeed, it was the means by which du Toit had taken himself off to Cape Town after his first meeting with me.

Had I still been employed by SAPS, this sort of outcome would have been hailed as a major coup which would later turn into a celebration once Swartman had been arrested and charged. But I no longer worked for SAPS, so my interest was personal relating to Mira's murder and my curiosity regarding her relationship with Swartman all those years before.

As regards this, there seemed to be no answers and I wondered whether the truth would ever emerge. What had happened to Mira was one crime amongst a great many that SAPS would investigate as far as Swartman was concerned. But would I get any of the answers or would Mira's murder become lost amongst multiple charge sheets and case dockets?

What was clear was that I wasn't going to get any satisfaction sat on my arse in the restaurant of one of Cape Town's best hotels. With that deduction made and with the number of diners around me diminishing rapidly I came to a decision. I wasn't prepared to stand clear and forego the opportunity of trying to find out of what was happening on the ground. I might not be part of the action, but I could attempt to witness it.

The ormolu clock in a gilt case which hung above the reception desk in the hotel's grand foyer struck 10 o'clock as I passed by on the way to my room. My plan was to grab some sleep before driving to the Namtraws Wine Estate in the early hours.

CHAPTER FIFTY-ONE

I left Cape Town on the N1 passing little at that time of night except large artics making their way north-eastwards, perhaps as far as Jo'burg. Once I left the main highway though the road was quiet, and I made good time across the darkened landscape.

I drove a little way beyond Ashton rather than turning off by the road entrance to the wine estate. I guessed there would be some sort of SAPS lock-down in the local area and I didn't want to be questioned or find the Fiesta stuck behind a security screen. I thought myself better off on foot, particularly as there was a good deal of natural cover.

Parking off the road where the car couldn't be seen, I retrieved the binoculars from the boot. Then, because there was a chill in the air, I slipped on a light windbreaker and zipped it up before heading off.

The moon had waned somewhat since the time of my escape from the winery, but it still offered sufficient illumination to light my way. This was a mixed blessing as it made progress easier but also made me easier to spot.

I struck out cross-country with the objective of intersecting the road that climbed up into the hills and which I'd driven days before. It was farther than I thought but, when finally stepping out onto the tarmac, the sound of a radio from somewhere downhill reached my ears.

Hugging the verge where there were bushes, I crept slowly towards the source of the noise. Fifty metres farther on and around a corner, I spied a *bakkie* with its sidelights on. The bursts of static between radio transmissions made it likely it was a SAPS unit. The glow of a cigarette confirmed there was one person on board, but it was too dark to tell if there was anybody else.

Retracing my steps uphill revealed the track I'd followed in the Fiesta. Beyond the gully where I'd parked, I pushed on round the shoulder of the hill and was soon able to crouch down in the *fynbos*.

Swartman's house lay below beneath grey streaks that were beginning to lighten the eastern sky. As they grew, the moon was slowly bleached and began to fade away. There were no lights in the house itself but plenty of ornamental illumination outside. These too though began to lose their lustre as they competed against the advancing dawn.

I ran the glasses over the place, but nothing stirred. Of the guards patrolling the boundary there was no sign. Likewise, I detected no one else up and about as the light thickened. In fact, the only activity was at the circular pond where the fountain continued to jet water from the dolphin's mouth.

I sat back and watched the sky turn from grey to a grey-blue and a few high clouds begin to assume shape and form. It wouldn't be long before the sun began to haul itself into the sky again. Already there was a glow in the east that was strengthening with every passing minute.

Kornfeld had said zero-hour for the operation was half an hour before sun-up. It looked like they were going to miss that by a margin. I began to wonder whether they'd called it off or postponed for some reason.

The noise that came to my ears a few minutes later was faint and far away. It was like someone using a fret saw. But I saw nothing and assumed it came from the far side of the hill. For a while it got no louder and was no more than an accompaniment to the spectacle of the rising sun.

Quickly though, that sound ceased to register because it was over-lain by the roar of powerful diesels. They were approaching fast and the noise they made rose to a crescendo as they got closer. But, even as they did, they faced competition from the whop-whop-whop of an approaching helicopter. In seconds, it pulverized the racket from the diesels with its own deafening tumult. Jerking my eyes skywards, I saw an Air Wing chopper climb over the top of the hill. Slowly, it positioned itself directly above the house, the undergrowth all around flattened by the down draught.

Transfixed, I gaped as four helmeted guys abseiled from the belly of the machine. They descended onto the uppermost terrace of the house. Each of them was dressed in combat fatigues and held an MP5 close to black body armour. As I watched, one man stepped forward and directed a burst of fire at a side door. When the lock shattered and it swung back, another of the group lobbed a stun grenade inside. I didn't hear it detonate above the crushing din from the chopper. I knew though what the effect would be of the 170-deci-bel bang and intense light flash as the grenade exploded: anyone inside would be temporarily blinded and disorientated.

One after the other, the guys went through the door their subma-chine guns levelled. Once inside, I knew they'd split up and work their way down and through every room in the house. Anyone offer-ing resistance would be dealt with and anyone pointing a gun would be taken out.

I shifted my eyes and looked down into the compound. I was in time to see two Nyalas, armoured personnel carriers, storm through the compound gates. Once inside, they divided and made long sweeps to right and left dropping off men at intervals. These manoeu-vres invited a response as I saw figures emerge from outbuildings with guns blazing. But they were ill-matched against trained men armed to the teeth who were supported by heavy machine guns mounted on the carriers.

It was over in seconds. Or so I believed until instinct drew my gaze back to the house. From a terrace on the far side, I observed

Yash, the man who'd pistol-whipped me. Incongruously, he was dressed in only red boxer shorts. Incongruous, because he was carrying a shoulder-launcher armed with a rocket-propelled grenade. Seemingly in slow motion, I watched him take aim at the chopper through the optical sight and fire. His target was no more than 200 metres above him. Even a blind man in his cups would have struggled to miss.

The warhead blasted into the machine and blew up the fuel tank. For a second, the chopper seemed to hang paralysed in the air. In the next it disappeared in a fireball. Then it was plunging to the ground. Skimming the swimming pool, debris falling into the water, it cart-wheeled into the open-sided braai. Horrified, I saw a part of it bury itself under the rafters. Secondary explosions blew out a section of the roof which collapsed onto the burning wreckage.

I was left numb but only until I looked back at Yash. He'd reloaded and was aiming at one of the unsuspecting Nyalas. Though it was useless, I shouted a warning. It was drowned by the sound of the weapon being fired. Following its trajectory from my vantage point, I watched as it passed closely over the top of the carrier.

That was the end of the killing spree. The launching flash and whitish, blue-gray smoke betrayed the RPG's location. The Nyalas responded with fire from their heavy guns ripping into masonry and roof tiles near the spot where the RPG had been fired. As they did so, several armed men sprinted towards the house. Of Yash there was no sign.

Nor was there any sign of Swartman. My assumption was he must be in the house. I wondered whether he'd been captured or killed in a shoot-out.

The minutes dragged and all that happened was that the men emerged from the house and descended the wooden steps above the pool. They had no prisoners.

I took up the glasses again for a closer look over the compound. The two Nyalas had come to rest at opposite ends of the house. There were a number of bodies scattered on the ground but from their dress none was police or task force. A medic was tending one man shot in the stomach. Another who was wounded in the leg was patiently awaiting his turn.

Idly, I lifted the binoculars a fraction and pointed them in the direction of the helicopter hanger. It appeared locked up and deserted. One of the Nyalas had initially dropped a couple of men close by but even now they were walking back towards the house. Clearly, there was nothing for them to do.

Something though caught my eye on the far side of the men. The ground dipped at that point and I observed a slowly rising cloud of dust. I watched as it lazily billowed into the early morning air. I shifted my line of sight and saw a small car picking its way along a rough track. It was travelling at no more than walking speed and appeared to make no noise. Perhaps I was too far away to hear its engine but the guys walking from the hanger surely must have heard yet they kept coming and didn't turn round.

I watched the car's progress and wondered whence it had come and who was driving. Refocusing the glasses, I made an effort to concentrate. From a long way off, I targeted the driver's window and saw it was open. I discerned the outline of a man behind the wheel, but he was in shadow. What were not were his long white locks.

I had found Gert Swartman.

The image slipped out of focus within seconds as the car's direction of travel altered. For a moment, I thought my imagination was working overtime but knew my eyes hadn't deceived me.

With that realisation came a better idea of what everybody was up against. The car Swartman was in had emerged from a remote corner of the compound. Maybe there was a small dwelling situated there that the gangster used as his sleeping quarters.

Thinking about that, it made perfect sense from Swartman's point of view. Anybody who wished him harm would automatically approach the house. It was the seat of his power; it was the place which proclaimed his great wealth; and it was the place where all his creature comforts were to be had. But short of turning it into a real fortress, it was also the place where he could find himself captured or killed. In those circumstances, laying your head down somewhere else, particularly during the hours when an attack was most likely to come, had much to commend it.

What was I to do now? -Making my way down from the hillside to the compound would take several minutes as I had no line of communication with the task force. And, once down, I'd have a lot of explaining to do which would waste further time.

I tried to route a call via SAPS in Cape Town but found there was no signal.

My frustration grew because I was stymied. Swartman could have headed off in any one of several different directions. Finding him would be a matter of luck.

I looked down from the hillside to the compound. Some effort was being made to extinguish the helicopter fire but with limited success. The wreckage was still burning fiercely and was now unrecognizable. There was no sign of the two wounded men seen earlier. Looking over it seemed everybody was now waiting for the crime scenes units to appear after which everybody else would be given the order to pull out.

I decided to do the same. There was no more to be gained by hanging around, so I got up and retraced my steps.

The walking allowed me to ponder. If Swartman was clever enough to sleep away from his house at night, it was logical to assume he had some back-up plan if he ever needed to make himself scarce.

I'd reached the edge of the road before it came to me. I wondered why my brain hadn't worked faster. With new purpose, I stepped out the distance to my car.

I made one small detour on the way and that was to the parked *bakkie*. It hadn't moved and the radio was still intermittently squawking. The cab though was deserted and when I looked in there was a SAPS bunny jacket on the passenger seat. Beneath it I found a Vektor pistol. Such carelessness with weapons isn't that uncommon in SAPS: in one province a while back thousands of guns went missing in a single year. Viewed in that light, my taking one pistol might be judged as inconsequential. Or that was the way I chose to salve my conscience. Besides I was only borrowing it in the absence of my own weapons.

Twenty minutes later, I was behind the wheel of the Fiesta and heading south towards the coast.

CHAPTER FIFTY-TWO

The symbol of an anchor emblazoned on the hillside and marked with the letters GB is often thought to refer to Gordon's Bay which it overlooks. In fact, its origin lies with General Botha after whom the original naval station, built in the north-east corner of False Bay, was named. Today, the site serves as the South African Naval College. It was this reality that enabled me to deduce the geographic location of Swartman's yacht as the photo I found of Swartman and du Toit showed a SANC sign in the background.

From the photo, the vessel had a beam of around five metres with a large aft deck and stairs leading up to the cockpit. Identifying her in the marina located adjacent to the College proved easy from my observation point on the hillside. The name *Alchemy* was picked out on her side, and she was the largest craft moored there by several metres and the most expensive by several million bucks. First impressions suggested she was fast, well-appointed and capable of navigating seas far from the sight of land.

Scanning her through the glasses, I concluded how well her name described Swartman's criminal empire. His business was about turning narcotics into dirty money which was then cleaned through the process of laundering. Or put another way it was the alchemy by which a mountain of human misery was transformed into a mountain of hard cash.

On the far side of the yacht's teak aft deck, walls of smoked glass hid the interior from view. She was berthed at the end of a double H configuration of pontoons and her bow was pointed towards the open sea beyond the narrow harbour mouth. At any moment, she looked as though she might slip her moorings and vanish into the heat haze.

I watched her for two hours and saw nothing which gave any indication that anybody was aboard, let alone Swartman. But, through the binoculars I observed a Nissan Leaf in the car park. It's one of the few electric vehicles sold in SA and almost as rare as the sight of leopards strolling in Cape Road. I liked to think it was Swartman's and would explain why he'd been able to steal away silently from his estate.

A delivery to the yacht took place later in the morning. It was of boxed groceries brought by a guy who drove up in a small van and walked out to the end of the pontoon. It was evident he didn't expect to see anyone as he dumped the stuff on the deck and departed without a backward glance. That rather suggested the yacht could be planning to leave, perhaps under cover of darkness.

Later, when I saw blue smoke drift upwards from an open hatch at *Alchemy's* bow, it became time to investigate. I fancied it might be cigar smoke. Whatever it was, it confirmed that somebody was aboard and that I wasn't going to learn any more sitting in my car. Starting up, I drove down the hill.

I turned into the car park at the side of the Harbour Lights Restaurant, found a space and switched off. I got out and the smell of cooking reminded me of a missed breakfast. Donning the SAPS bunny jacket took seconds and adding an old baseball cap I unearthed in the boot seconds more. Pulling the peak down low over my eyes, I picked up the Vektor and checked the clip. After that, I thrust the gun into the waistband of my pants before doing up the zipper.

I strode towards the moorings looking to neither right nor left. A few people clocked me but only for the reason it was a hot day for a jacket. I kept it on because it was my passport if challenged.

Half way along the pontoon at which *Alchemy* was berthed, that challenge came. An elderly man with a small paint brush in his hand stepped off his boat and blocked my way. 'Can I help you?' he asked pointedly.

'Boat at the end-Do you know who's aboard?'

'Who's asking?'

I pointed to the SAPS badge on my jacket. 'SANEB,' I said. 'Out of Cape Town.'

'San what?'

'Narcotics Enforcement. Who's aboard?'

'I-I don't know. The man who owns it comes and goes. He may be there. I thought I heard something early this morning. What's all this about drugs?'

I ignored his question. 'What does he look like?'

'Big frame and thick neck. White hair which he wears long. Sometimes has it in a ponytail. Looks ridiculous at his age.'

'Do you know his name?'

'Eckhart . . . Eckmann . . . something like that.'

'OK,' I said. 'I want you to stay on your boat. If you see or hear anything that worries you, call 10111. You clear?'

The elderly man nodded. 'What are you going to do?'

'Take a look.'

With that, I negotiated my way past him and kept going. Drawing closer, I undid the bunny jacket. Transferring the Vektor to my right hand, I took the safety off. A short gangplank took me to the aft deck. The groceries were where they'd been delivered. I stopped by them and listened. I heard nothing, but caught a distinct whiff of cigar smoke.

I crouched and moved towards the salon door. The handle was chrome-plated and slid effortlessly on its steel tracks. I passed through and closed it behind me. A subdued hum from air-conditioning was the only noise.

I looked about me. It wasn't a huge space, but it was opulently appointed. A thick white carpet complemented bay windows with polished chrome surrounds and walls of cherry wood. A flat screen TV was encased in the same material and looked out on a couple of love seats and a built-in, blue leather sofa. Eyeball lights in the ceiling cast a soft glow over everything. At the far end, a panelled door stood ajar giving a view beyond of an antique dining table and chairs.

For a moment, I stood irresolute. Then I heard someone moving about. The sound came from the far side of the dining room. I thought it was from the galley as someone was noisily rummaging in a drawer.

As suddenly as it started, it stopped. But now the someone was moving towards me. I heard a muttered oath and a heavy tread on the dining room's wooden floor. Next a figure appeared in the doorway.

It was Swartman.

He had a cigar in his mouth and in one hand he carried a bottle of wine. He was well over the threshold before he clocked me. When he did, his reaction was immediate and violent. He threw the bottle underarm and lunged at me. I deflected the wine with my left arm and used my right to ward him off.

But that was the hand that had the pistol.

It wasn't my intention to fire, but the Vektor must have had a hair trigger.

There was a loud report and Swartman staggered backwards. He immediately clapped a hand to his upper arm. Blood was already staining his pale blue shirt. He sat down painfully on the sofa opposite me and spat out the cigar. Through pain-filled eyes he regarded me truculently.

I hurt from where the bottle had struck my forearm, but I kept the gun trained. 'We're going to have a conversation,' I began. 'Or rather I'm going to ask questions and you're going to answer them.'

'Fuck you, Nemo.'

'Ach, so now you know who I am.'

'After we found the piece you left behind,' spat Swartman, 'it wasn't that difficult. All that crap you gave me and the performance you put on were so much bullshit. I should have gone with my gut and wasted you.'

273

'Bit late now for regrets,' I said. 'In fact, it's a bit late for anything. You're finished and hopefully so's the outfit you run. By the way, in case you didn't know, du Toit's been arrested. Happened several days ago. He's been charged with money laundering but that's just for starters.'

What I said rocked Swartman. He said nothing but what came into his eyes from a very dark place, was comprehension; an understanding as to why he'd been unable to reach the crooked accountant.

'It was the Hawks,' I went on, 'and when they were done, they locked everything down. SAPS weren't involved. Tell me, who's your snitch in the Eastern Cape?'

'Go screw yourself.'

I shrugged. Blood was slowly welling from Swartman's arm over his fingers and down the sleeve of his shirt. 'That bullet could have hit an artery,' I said conversationally. 'My guess is you need medical attention. Else you might bleed to death.' I paused and allowed my words to sink in. 'Shall we wait and see what happens? -Don't know about you, but I've got all afternoon. Come to think of it, I've got all evening as well.'

Swartman glanced down at his arm and that was followed by a look of pure hatred. 'You can't withhold medical attention,' he said.

'Why not?'

'You're undercover SAPS. There are regulations.'

I shook my head. 'Don't know where you got that from. I don't work for anybody. Used to, but now I'm free as air.'

'I don't believe you.'

'Believe what you like. That's your prerogative but it's not me whose blood's making a mess of the sofa.' The sleeve of Swartman's shirt was now soaked and drops of blood had begun to fall onto the seat leather.

It was at that point the gangster began to understand. 'What do you want?' he asked through gritted teeth.

'Who's your snitch in SAPS?'

Swartman shook his head. 'Du Toit recruited people who were useful to him. Usually, clients with money problems. Whoever it was in SAPS would have met that spec, but I didn't know them.'

This sounded like something equating to the truth. 'What happened if du Toit wanted something taken care of?'

'Like what?'

'How about blowing up cars? Stuff like that.'

Swartman didn't bat an eyelid but what should I have expected from a sociopath? 'Oh that,' he said in a matter-of-fact tone. 'It was a party from Nigeria. Ordnance expert. Ex Army. Mercenary experience. Fucked up, didn't he?'

'Killed a young guy instead of me,' I said.

'Not my concern.'

'Fortunes of war and all that I guess.'

But my sarcasm was wasted as Swartman wasn't listening. He was looking at his arm and increasing the pressure of his hand over the site of the wound.

'Let's talk about Mira,' I said, changing tack.

'That cow.'

'So, you knew her?'

'Right, I knew her.'

'And?'

'We were together.'

'But not till death us do part together?'

'No.'

'How long?'

'Six, maybe seven years.'

'What did she do to piss you off?'

'She stole from me.'

I was incredulous. 'She stole from you!' I exclaimed. 'You've been stealing everything from everybody all your life, you miserable fuck.'

'What she did was different,' said Swartman with as much vehemence as he could muster. I noticed now his face had turned pale and he looked to have aged ten years. 'She took things that were personal. Things that couldn't be replaced.'

'What things?'

'Photos and other items. One of them was a watch.'

'How were they significant?'

'None of your fucking business.'

I motioned my displeasure with the aid of the gun. 'Keep talking,' I said.

Swartman shot me a vitriolic look and with a painful effort sat forward. 'They were my mother's,' he hissed, before leaning back and closing his eyes.

That came as a surprise. It was made more poignant by the uninvited recollection of my own mother. I had no photographs of her, and the memories were those of a six-year-old boy. I blocked them with an effort. 'What happened to them?' I asked.

'She told me she burnt the photos and pawned the other stuff.'

I guess that was the moment at which I came closest to feeling any measure of sympathy for Swartman. But it was a single moment and no more than that. 'I don't think that's right,' I said. 'I found some items in her house in PE. One of them was a watch with the initials DGS on the back.'

Despite his pain, Swartman did a double take. He made to say something but at once changed his mind. 'The watch belonged to my father,' he said with an effort.

'Why did she take the stuff?' I asked.

'Because she was a bitch and she thought she could.'

'And that was why you were trying to find her at the nightclub?'

'You heard about that, did you?'

'It was ultimately how I located you.'

Swartman made no comment. With every minute that passed he weakened and the colour continued to ebb from his face. He was still bleeding and there was a widening stain of blood on the leather of the sofa. It was very wet and had started to drip onto the white carpet.

'I got word months after I threw her out,' Swartman went on feebly 'that she was singing at some club in Camps Bay. By then I noticed my mother's stuff was missing. I went to see her. She was the only person who knew about it. But she screwed me around and I got angry. There were a lot of people about, so I left. Next, she sent a message saying she'd taken care of everything. Taken care of fucking what? -I didn't know what she was talking about. I went back to see her but by that time she'd left the club. Nobody knew where she was. Later, she said she'd disposed of everything and not to look for her.'

'I found her birth certificate,' I interjected. 'It showed she was born in Manenberg. Same place as you I heard.'

'We were brought up there. Our paths crossed over the years before we got together.'

'And much later they crossed again, didn't they?'

Swartman was very tired but took it into his head to get up. I motioned with the gun that wasn't a good idea. 'Du Toit recognised her one time in PE,' he said, his voice thin and strained. 'He'd seen her previously two or three times with me. We spoke about it. I decided to grab her using my people. It was all fine until you got pulled in.'

'But why kidnap her?'

'It'd teach the cow a lesson if she got slapped around for a while and it'd generate a lot of dough. The guy she was with was loaded according to du Toit and he said the dumb fuck would give anything to get her back.'

'You're right there,' I said tightly, barely keeping my anger under control. 'He would have given anything for her release. In the end, he did give everything. Her kidnap led to his first heart attack. He had the second after she was murdered. That one killed him.'

'Y-You talk like he was family,' said the gangster in a shaky voice. 'W-What was he to you?'

'I'm not going to explain myself to a piece of shit like you.'

My words hung in the space between us as heavy as the hand of death. Swartman looked at me out of pained and exhausted eyes in a white face. He gave me no further word and, as the minutes ticked away, I noticed the hand that had been attempting to staunch the blood slipped away and lay limp at his side.

Even at that point I could perhaps have saved him. But what purpose would be served? In due course there'd be an arraignment and a trial which would drag on forever. With what was recorded on any charge sheet, he'd draw a non-parole sentence. That meant a prison like Pollsmoor or more likely the living tomb of the C-Max at Kokstad. He'd rot there until he died. The whole process would take a lot of time, cost a lot of bucks and achieve what precisely? My way was clean and efficient and, because I'd be happy for SAPS to claim the credit, a lesson about the long arm of the law would be taught at the same time.

I watched him die. I knew it was a lot more peaceful than it would have been for his many victims. He slipped away without fuss or fanfare with only the discreet hum of the air-conditioning to mark his passage to whatever hell was surely awaiting him.

Eventually, I got up and crossed over to the sofa. Who would have thought the old man to have so much blood in him I thought as the smell of his gore filled my nostrils? I felt for a pulse in his neck but there was none. Taking off the bunny jacket and tossing it onto one of the love seats, I followed up with the Vektor. Then all that remained for me to do was to step out into the soothing balm of the sunshine on the aft deck.

CHAPTER FIFTY-THREE

Head down, I began walking back along the pontoon towards the car park.

'Freeze!' shouted a voice.

I froze.

'Hands on your head!'

I put my hands on my head and lifted my eyes. Two SAPS uniforms were moving towards me in an exaggerated crouch. It was as though they expected me to take a dive off the pontoon or execute some Houdini-like trick. One levelled a pistol and the other an assault rifle.

They halted a few a metres away and ordered me to kneel and then lie flat on the deck. Once I was down, the guy with the pistol holstered his weapon and approached me. Ordered to put my hands behind my back, he handcuffed me while his colleague covered the scene with his rifle.

'What's your name?' he asked, straightening up.

'Nemo.'

'Nemo what?'

'Nemo's my surname. My first name's Sol.'

'So, you're Sol Nemo?'

I confirmed I was Sol Nemo.

'You got any ID?'

'Front left pocket.'

He crouched down and pushed me none too gently onto my side so he could explore. Meanwhile, his colleague moved past us and made for Swartman's yacht.

An age passed before the guy with me had worked his way through my wallet. 'Says here you're from Port Elizabeth,' he said eventually.

'Yes.'

'You're a long way from home.'

'You're right.'

'What's your reason for . . .?' He broke off when his colleague's shouts distracted him. 'Wait,' he ordered me unnecessarily as he made for the yacht.

I was left staring back toward the car park where a small group of people had gathered. Trussed up, I felt vulnerable and humiliated.

The minutes ticked by until I heard the heavy boots of the SAPS officers as they returned along the pontoon. The one who put the cuffs on knelt by my side. 'Who's the stiff?' he asked.

'His name's Gert Swartman.'

'Did you shoot him?'

'Yes,' I said. 'Swartman was the target of a task force raid near Ashton early this morning. Unfortunately, he escaped. You need to contact a Brigadier Joubert in Cape Town. He knows about me, and he knows about Swartman.'

'You saying you're SAPS?'

'No, I'm not but . . .'

'So, what's with the pistol and jacket we found?' the policeman interrupted. 'The guy reporting a gunshot told us about some dude he spoke to in a SAPS jacket. He was wearing a baseball cap like you. Where did you get the jacket and the piece?'

'As I said I was in Ashton this morning.'

The policeman straightened up. 'I gotta tell you, bro, impersonating a police officer is serious. And then there's all the other stuff you're gonna have to explain.'

They called it in as I knew they would and while we waited for Detective Services I was lifted to my feet and transferred to a SAPS unit. One of the guys stayed with me in the vehicle while the other blocked access to the pontoon. I cadged a drink of water and tried to make conversation, but my captor was more interested in scanning his phone and texting.

Detective Services rocked up after half an hour in a dusty, unmarked saloon with its hub caps missing. Beyond a cursory glance in my direction, the two detectives who emerged from it ignored me and set off for the marina. Handcuffed to a door handle, I made the best of it as the minutes ticked by. Given the circumstance of a corpse found on a boat and a perp in custody, I guessed a sense of urgency wasn't necessary. It wasn't logic I could argue with.

It was a while before the two detectives got back to me. They sorted out the immediate jurisdictional issue by transferring me to the back of their saloon. For me, it made no difference as I was still handcuffed, this time to a grab handle.

'Boat's registered to a guy called Echtmann,' said one of the detectives turning to me from the front passenger seat. 'Walter Johannes Echtmann to be precise. Registration paperwork's all in order as far as I can see. By the way Echtmann has an address in Durban. You care to comment, Mr. Nemo?'

'It's crap,' I said irritably. Acute pangs of hunger made me keen for this rigmarole to come to an end as soon as possible. 'The guy's name is Gert Swartman. He was the subject of a raid near Ashton first thing this morning. He escaped and I followed him here.'

'Where you shot him?'

'Accidentally.'

'How so?'

'Swartman threw a bottle of wine and . . .'

An unexpected gale of laughter drowned out what I was about to say. 'Remind me, Rolf,' cried one detective turning to his colleague, 'never to lob you a bottle of beer again. Fuck, I don't want to get my arse shot off!'

I waited until their mirth had subsided and said soberly: 'I insist you contact Brigadier Joubert in Cape Town. It's imperative he knows what's been happening here.'

With that I lapsed into silence and despite their best endeavours to quiz me, I refused to say another word.

The stand-off lasted a quarter of an hour after which they conceded defeat.

In the scheme of things, this 15-minute interlude didn't amount to much as it was another two hours before Joubert arrived. But the exercise of his authority in the way in which I was handled preceded him. First, I was released from the handcuffs and, second, they gave me something to eat and drink. With what I thought marked reluctance, the detective called Rolf strolled across the way to the restaurant and bought a couple of bacon and cheese sandwiches. I washed them down with a large bottle of still water and looked out at the unfolding scene from the open car window.

SAPS blockaded the entrance to the car park and provided access to authorised vehicles only. Apart from several marked and unmarked police cars, there were scenes of crime, bomb squad and diving unit vehicles, the last of which appeared hauling a trailer with a large RIB. Its immediate purpose wasn't clear, and neither was that of the dog unit which somebody in their wisdom had also decided to summon. With the vehicles came a lot of people who often seemed to be milling around to little purpose.

The Brigadier's arrival coincided with that of a Forensic Pathology Service van which pulled up close to the water's edge. I saw Joubert climb out of his car and exchange a few words before he was approached by what I assumed was the SAPS CSM. They became engrossed in a conversation which continued as they walked towards the pontoons giving access to Swartman's yacht.

I must then have dozed off because I awoke with a start when somebody banged on the car's roof. I looked up and saw Joubert. 'Let's walk,' he said in a tone that brooked no dissent.

Stiffly, I climbed out and stretched before massaging the wrist of my right hand, still sore from the steel bracelet. I listened as the Brigadier curtly told the detectives babysitting me that we didn't need company.

'You certain that's Swartman?' he asked abruptly when we were out of earshot. He inclined his head in the direction of *Alchemy*.

'I'm certain. Remember I was up close and personal at the house that night. I'm not likely to forget his face for quite a while.'

'Paperwork on the boat says otherwise.'

'I know, but that doesn't change the facts,' I said, wondering why Joubert was labouring the point. In fact, I also wondered why the Brigadier's usually avuncular expression had been replaced by a frazzled look, his eyes pouchy and jowls heavy.

'How was it that you fetched up here anyway?' Joubert snapped, abruptly changing tack. 'And once you got here, why didn't you think it necessary to call it in? Maybe we could have got the bastard alive.'

'I thought he might disappear before you arrived.'

'Disappear where? -What did you think he was going to do? -Head for Antarctica? He could only have gone along the coast, and we'd have picked him up somewhere with little problem. That boat of his is hardly inconspicuous.'

I shrugged. 'I played the cards I was dealt. Have you come down from Ashton?'

Joubert nodded. 'I'd say the operation was a partial success,' he volunteered dismally. 'We recovered drugs and cash from a store-room, and we found direct links to du Toit. That's all very positive. Against that, we lost a helicopter. It was shot down by an RPG.'

'I know,' I said seriously.

'You know!' The Brigadier looked at me sharply. 'How the hell do *you* know?'

'I was there. I was on the hillside above the estate. I watched Swartman drive away and on a hunch came to Gordon's Bay. The clue was the Naval College sign in the photo of du Toit and Swartman I found. I told you about the picture when we met at Sutherland.'

'But you didn't say anything about the Naval College.'

'At the time, it wasn't relevant. The task force was supposed to grab Swartman at the estate. Or am I missing something?'

Joubert was breathing hard as he passed a hand across his tired face. 'It's been quite a day,' he opined wearily. 'I don't think the task force has ever lost personnel on an operation before. Today it lost two: the helicopter pilot and Colonel Kornfeld who you met at my office. We knew each other 25 years. Our daughters are friends for God's sake.' The Brigadier broke off to compose himself. 'We recovered three unused RPGs at the house,' he went on. 'They're from a batch stolen from the Infantry School at Oudtshoorn. SAPS appear to have done little to investigate, despite being advised by the Army that civilians had stolen them. As you can imagine, anyone who might be considered to have had responsibility for any of this is now trying to cover their tracks.'

'I don't see you doing that, Brigadier.'

For the first time, Joubert tried to smile. 'Some of us don't have that luxury,' he said. 'But what I do have is an opportunity to manage the situation here to best advantage.'

'I'm not sure I follow.'

'Let's get some coffee and I'll explain your position to you.'

The uniform of a SAPS Brigadier quickly forestalled questions that might have arisen as we passed through police lines on our way to the Harbour Lights.

Whether on account of the time of day or the massive police presence, the place was almost deserted. We settled down by tall picture windows overlooking the water and the boats. The sun was still out but there was some cloud beating up from the south-east promising rain later.

'So, what's on your mind?' I asked sipping an Americano.

Joubert leaned back in his chair, interleaved the fingers of his hands before resting them on his protuberant stomach. 'What I've pieced together thus far is as follows,' he began. 'On observing Swartman fleeing his estate and though knowing him to be the subject of a major police/task force operation, you failed by your own admission to report the matter to the proper authorities. This act frustrated Swartman's potential apprehension. Thereafter, you stole items of SAPS equipment, namely a jacket and a Vektor pistol, from an unattended police vehicle. On arrival in Gordon's Bay, you masqueraded as a police officer informing at least one member of the public that you were attached to SANEB. Later, you shot Swartman who was unarmed and resultantly sustained what proved to be a life-threatening injury from which he later died.' Joubert flung me an accusatory look for good measure before lifting his coffee cup and drinking deeply.

Finding myself suddenly on the back foot, I stared at him for a few seconds while my brain processed what he'd told me. 'Might be an idea if you got to the point,' I said at last.

'The point is this,' replied Joubert decisively. 'SAPS wants this whole business tidied away without a lot of questions left unanswered. In a few days time, it's envisaged there'll be a major press conference jointly hosted by the Provincial Commissioners of the Western and Eastern Capes' police departments. It'll be a good news story about effective cooperation in the destruction of major drugs and money laundering operations in both Cape Town and Port Elizabeth. We hope it will send a clear message to those who engage in serious crime and/or corrupt practices that they will be caught and held to account.'

'I understand,' I said, 'but there . . .'

Joubert held up a restraining paw and went on: 'SAPS will gratefully, but privately, acknowledge your contribution to its investigations undertaken at no small risk. But your role isn't something SAPS will recognise publicly in any shape or form. It's true we may have to concede that we used an undercover operative should probing questions be asked. That undercover operative is, of course, you but your identity will never be revealed. Do you understand what I am saying?'

'I get it,' I said. 'In return for keeping my mouth shut, you'll drop charges you might otherwise feel duty bound to pursue.'

The Brigadier smiled thinly. 'I think you've summed matters up very succinctly.' He drained the rest of his coffee and gazed out of the window. The bulky outline of *Alchemy* was clearly visible at the end of the moorings. 'By the way,' he asked, 'did you establish from Swartman before he died *why* he kidnapped Mrs. Zarakolu?'

I nodded and explained to him what I'd been told on the yacht. 'For Swartman,' I concluded, 'it was principally about reprisal and for du Toit it was about greed. All in all, it reminded me of one of those 17th century revenge dramas.'

Joubert looked askance. 'The pathologist's preliminary view on Swartman is the bullet hit the brachial artery,' he said. 'Prompt medical attention might have saved his life. How long were you with him?'

I cast my mind back. 'Clocking the time wasn't a priority. What I wanted was information.'

'Then what would you have done?'

'Had he been unharmed?'

Joubert nodded.

'From an emotional standpoint, I'd have shot him. From a legal one, I'd have handed him over to you. It was fortunate perhaps that there was no need to plump for one or the other because I can't tell you which way it would have played out.'

'All I can say,' added the Brigadier after a moment's thought, 'is that I'm glad we don't have to waste time and money in convicting and putting him behind bars. Pity the same can't be said for du Toit.'

We didn't talk for much longer and when we finished Joubert accompanied me back to my car. As I drove away, my rearview mirror revealed him watching my departure. But, after a few seconds, he turned on his heel and began walking back towards the water and the boats. Of course, I'd hear from him again; or rather from his HQ in Cape Town. The paper pushers and desk jockeys would make sure of that as they tidied everything away and made sure their arses were well covered from any possible blowback. But, for the moment, I was out of sight and out of mind.

CHAPTER FIFTY-FOUR

It was 700kms back to PE, but I decided to make the journey without an overnight stop. I'd wanted to get home as soon as possible but, once on the other side of the Storms River, began to question what was meant by the idea of home.

The fact was I didn't wish to return to my place at Seaview because of its isolation; Frank's house on Lovemore Heights was now no more than an empty shell filled with memories; and the apartment I was renting where the Mustang had blown up seemed like a dumb idea full stop.

I took the easy way out and booked into the Boardwalk Hotel in Summerstrand.

Next day was wild and wet with heavy rain battering the Boardwalk's faux Victorian architecture. Outside, the palms were shaking so much that the grass was soon covered in broken fronds. My mind was elsewhere though as I had only one objective and that was to get hold of Captain Bezuidenhout. It took a while to track him down but, as he was passing through Summerstrand later, we got together briefly in the hotel's cavernous reception area with its high ceilings and crystal chandeliers.

Our meeting was my chance to apologise for my mistrust of him and to explain the reasons for my change of heart. It was also an opportunity to exchange confidences and to agree to stay in touch. We parted company on the best terms we'd enjoyed since we first met on the night Mira was snatched back by her kidnappers.

Arnie and I had had no contact, let alone seen one another, for weeks so I put in a call and, when that went to voicemail, sent a text. I had to send another before there was a response and we arranged to meet two days' hence. I told him of my stay at the Boardwalk, so Barney's was convenient as the hotel overlooked it.

I killed the intervening time by updating on everything since my departure for Cape Town. I made a point of contacting the psychiatrist recommended me by the Steinberg Clinic. We'd met only once, and I wanted to renew the relationship as we'd established a rapport. When we did get together, I told him my anxiety wasn't under control despite medication and that I was again experiencing flashbacks. These could be acute during the small hours and left me terrorised.

He explained, as he'd done before, that my choice of occupation didn't assist my mental wellbeing and that there was a need to review my options. After all, he told me, my money gave me many avenues I might explore.

I responded by saying my downward spiral in mood wasn't helped at all by my loss of Ayesha.

Since returning to PE, I'd made several attempts to reach her but found her phone disconnected. It was the same with email, because my messages bounced back. That left me with one option and that was to drive to East London. It was a measure of my desperation that I thought this a sensible journey to make.

When I did make the trip, the house was as silent as a crypt. After knocking a couple of times, I looked through the wrought iron gate at the side. It gave me a view of the area where we'd shared breakfast, but I saw the table and chairs had been fitted with rain covers. As I turned away, a capful of wind lifted a few dead leaves and blew them across the decking. I saw in them a leitmotif for our relationship.

Lost in thought, I turned back to the car but came face to face with an old man. I recognised him from a house across the street as he was often sitting out reading a newspaper or book. His determined expression told me he had something to impart.

'Hi,' I said.

'Ayesha told me you might come by,' he said in a fatherly tone. 'She asked me to pass on a message.'

'I'm listening.'

'For the time being she's away and the house has been locked up.'

I expected him to say more but, when he didn't, I asked impatiently, 'Is that it? -Surely, she said something more.'

'Just that she wanted time out. Could be quite a lot of time though. She'll contact you in due course after she knows from me you came by.'

'You've a number for her?'

'I've no number. She said she'd call me.'

'How does that work?'

The old man looked at me sympathetically. 'You're the guy from PE, aren't you?'

I nodded dumbly.

'She told me she needed to know whether you had enough commitment to make a speculative but fruitless journey. I'll be able to tell her you did.'

That was as far as I could take it. What was to be understood from her behaviour was anybody's guess. Maybe, she was paying me back for not having contacted her from Cape Town. But frankly, that explanation seemed petty. Ultimately, I had to side with the wise man who said women were meant to be loved, not understood.

CHAPTER FIFTY-FIVE

On the day after my return from East London, I was a minute or two behind Arnie in entering Barney's. This wasn't by accident as I'd been watching for him from the grassed area adjacent to the car park. It was a while since we'd seen each other, and I was curious as to how he might look. His appearance though gave me no insight into his changed perspectives. Of course, I could have worked this out for myself in advance had I not allowed a perverse curiosity to get the better of me.

I got a drink at the bar and walked with it onto the deck which was half-full. Arnie was sitting head down and scrolling with his back to the ocean. I stood opposite him with a view of the grass where I'd been standing moments before. In the distance, people were strolling in the sunshine on Shark Rock Pier.

'I see you made out,' I said.

Arnie looked up startled. 'Hullo Sol.' Then he saw the glass in my hand and laughed. 'Man, are you so stressed you had to take a belt before we ordered?' I made no reply but took a large gulp of brandy. Then what I'd said registered. 'Made out?' he asked. 'What do you mean?'

'Didn't I see you arrive in a new Tiguan?'

Arnie smiled tightly. 'Ach that,' he said trying to sound casual. 'One of Esme's folks gave us a loan and I took some finance. You know how it is. I need reliable transport and the old car wasn't up to it.' He looked me over critically and for the first time noticed the state of my face. 'What the hell happened to you? You had someone look at it?'

291

I ignored his questions and sat down heavily. 'Don't know why it took me so long to work it out,' I began slowly. 'I should have got to it sooner. Must have something to do with all the crap I take every day to keep me on something approaching an even keel. It kinda dulls the senses. Come to think of it if I'd been sharper, maybe I wouldn't have got whacked so hard in the face.'

Arnie sat back on the bench as though I was infectious. He moistened lips that had become dry. 'You're not making sense, Sol. I really don't know what you're talking about.'

'Really. Well then, let me take you through it. For a start there was the night when I rescued Mira. Only I didn't because she was snatched back by a couple of guys I assumed were there to help. That was after calling you to get back-up.'

Arnie was incredulous. 'That's bullshit, Sol. I took a call which was passed on. It would have gone through several hands before anybody was sent. Come on, you know how this works.'

'I do indeed know how it works. And that was why things went no further. Because there was no conclusive proof. Later, there were two SAPS guys gunned down in Korsten. I'm sure you remember that, don't you? Their side arms were about to be checked. When they were, one of them came up a match with the shots fired at me. By that time, there was a short list of possible finks, but I was told your name wasn't on it.'

Arnie's face was now registering a chaotic mix of emotions and the tic beneath his left eye was starting to jump like a lighted firecracker.

On the grassed area, beyond Arnie's left shoulder, I saw a man who was familiar even though he had his back to me. Dressed in dark pants and a white shirt, his head was wreathed in cigarette smoke. As I fixed my eyes on Arnie again, the man turned to face me.

'I wanted to believe you weren't involved, Arnie, so went along with the official line. But now I think the intell was wrong. In other words, you knew exactly the threat posed by those two if they talked. And I think you made sure they never had the opportunity.'

292

'Man, are you fucked-up!' hissed Arnie. 'Whatever you're doing to sort out your head isn't working. You're getting paranoid in your old age.' Abruptly, he started to stand up.

'Sit down!' I shouted.

Shocked heads all around swivelled in our direction. Half-sitting, half-standing, Arnie was embarrassed so he sank down once more, much to my surprise. After a moment, he shook his head sadly. 'What's happening to you, bro? You got sunstroke?'

'The clincher,' I went on relentlessly, 'was the text message I sent you after my rental started in St. George's Park.'

'Text message! What fucking text message?'

'The one stored in my phone. It's marked as read. It was sent to you and makes compelling evidence. You were the only person who knew I'd moved. I'd been there no more than a few days. Yet the bomber found my car. That was down to information you supplied.'

Maybe if Arnie had gone on arguing it was all a mistake, I'd have believed him. We'd been friends a long time and, in the certainty that real friends are few and far between, the wise don't squander such relationships.

But Arnie didn't continue to argue it was all a mistake. Instead, he leapt to his feet. In the next instant, he dashed past me and headed for the entrance to the bar. But he didn't get that far because three plainclothes guys sitting at an adjacent table jumped up and wrestled him to the ground. I watched as they searched him for weapons and lifted him to his feet. In the next moment, they put cuffs on and hustled him away.

With tears pricking my eyes, I turned back towards the ocean and circled the air listlessly with my arm. From the grass below, Captain Bezuidenhout waved to acknowledge me and strode off towards the car park.

Endings have always been the soundtrack to my life.

AFTERWORD AND ACKNOWLEDGEMENTS

Firstly, thank you very much for finishing my book. I hope you enjoyed it as much as I enjoyed writing it. Most authors seek readers for their work and most, I believe, welcome feedback on what they have written. In that vein, and perhaps presuming on your generous spirit, may I kindly ask you to review my book and leave a comment. It doesn't have to be more than a line or two and I know from my own experience how helpful it is to others to see what people think of something they have read. **You can leave your comment at** https://john-constable-author.com/. Rest assured, I will read your review and take note of what you have to say.

Writing is a solitary occupation. A novel stems from a single idea which over time develops into a setting, a cast of characters and a plot. Draft succeeds draft and slowly the whole work comes together into what hopefully turns out to be a cogent and engaging story. During my journey along this road, I have asked for feedback at various points and would therefore like to acknowledge with grateful thanks the inputs of the following: Sue Brown, Vivienne Beeston, Isla Duncan, John Beavis and my peerless sister Gill Constable. Last, but not least, I would like to record my appreciation in respect of the efforts of my editor, Debi Alper, of Jericho Writers, the UK's leading literary consultancy. Debi's experience and insight has hugely enhanced the work of countless writers over the years and I am fortunate indeed to have benefitted from her commitment and sure touch as regards my own work.

What's next? I plan a series of Sol Nemo mysteries of which the book you've just read is the first. The second is entitled, *The Truth about Anton van Zyl* and I hope to publish it in the first half of next year.

If you would like to keep in touch in regard to progress with the new work, why not join the Sol Nemo Readers' Club? **It's easy to sign up at** https://john-constable-author.com **and in return I will send you a free, stand-alone, Sol Nemo short story**. Lastly, if you do sign up, I promise to contact you only occasionally, I will never pass your details on to anyone else and, if at some point, you decide to unsubscribe you can do so easily.

I hope to hear from you soon.

John Constable
Addlestone
Surrey
United Kingdom